THE SWEET TASTE
OF THE BILGE

BY M.T. HARBER

Mainsail Breeze
Maryland

www.mainsailbreeze.com

Mainsail Breeze Edition, January 2011

Mainsail Breeze
ISBN: 978-0615460727

Revised August 2012

Cover Design by Paul Rose

www.mainsailbreeze.com

Sail/Dive novel

Other Books by M. T. Harber

- The Eye of the Abyss

About M.T. Harber

Michael T. Harber is a writer and explorer. He has written a number of books, mostly to bide his time between destinations. He doesn't claim to be an intellectual, having dropped out of high school to travel, but as one who wanders the land where palm trees grow he has learned to tell a good story. His world is unlike many who wander this world. He has no fixed address, but prefers to lean on the compassion of friends and family who take him in when his wallet runs dry.

He met up with Paul Rose while Paul was doing some research in Key West, Florida. They had some rum, found an instant kinship, and have stayed in touch. They plan to get together in the Caymans sometime soon. M.T. has been known to work as a deck hand to make his passage from place to place. He has, therefore, boarded million dollar yachts as a cook, mechanic, captain's mate, and bartender – all without any previous experience or knowledge.

For my girlfriend

ACKNOWLEDGEMENTS

To my girl I call Trixie…
She doesn't have hair like a pixie.
 But she marks up my page,
 like an editor sage,
And she still looks damn sexy.

My friend Bill, he once said,
 'Think with the big not little head.'
 And he made many edits,
 to get put in the credits,
 But I chose not to instead.

I have a brother named Jim,
Who often goes out on a limb.
With changes he strives,
to bring the story alive,
and yes – I look up to him.

Oh Carol, I must give you credit,
you certainly know how to edit.
With many a mark,
you make the page dark,
and make me want to forget it!

Yes Alison marked up my book,
With all that I overlooked.
I thought I was done,
but she had so much fun,
with the Bilge being way undercooked.

And yes there are others,
Friends, sisters and brothers,
Who made the pages red,
As if the story bled,
Between the two covers.

1

The phone buzzed. This was no mystery or surprise. The phone always buzzed. As soon as George disconnected the line from his last call, the next one came. His greeting was usually followed by a tirade of expletives for having been put on hold for so long, and then an explanation of what was damaged or destroyed as a result of the motor. George looked at the number of callers queued up and waiting for service: thirty-five. He knew from experience that meant any given customer was listening to *The Girl from Ipanema* or some other mind numbing bit of Muzak for about five minutes. The music did nothing to soothe the tempers of those trying to get a piece of the money pie that the Watsitumi Corporation doled out in drips and drabs to silence the masses complaining about some design flaw or bad o-ring.

The rows of cubicles chirped with incoming calls and someone, perhaps George or another complaint department employee, would answer the phone, listen and wait until the irate customer stopped their rant to take a breath and take that opportunity to quickly inject the lines, "I am sorry for your inconvenience and would like to help reconcile...."

George's cubicle was typical of those around him. Beyond the bland blandness that surrounded him, a few decorations represented his attempt to bring life to the venus fly-trap that had been his life for the last six years. Facing him was a tropical calendar. He never looked ahead at the months to come. He didn't want to know whether June displayed a sailboat, or big palm tree surrounded by the watery Caribbean blues and greens. On the first of the month, he would slowly lift the calendar page to display the next photo. It was the most exhilaration he would receive while at work. But it was a mixed moment because after the great revealing, he would have to wait another month until he could unveil the next piece of paradise. He didn't use the calendar portion at all. His calendar was all managed electronically for him on his office computer. Whenever he was scheduled to attend a meeting or activity, a window on his computer screen would pop up with a blinking button and notify him. He had no control over the events on his calendar. From some other office, from some "higher up," he would be summoned to meetings. This occurred through the magic of the ever-populating electronic calendar. In fact, an entire team had been formed for the purpose of scheduling lunch and pottie breaks. These, too, found their way through the electronic ether and beckoned him, letting him know that he might want to take some time to relieve himself.

The desk itself was attached to the cubicle walls, so there was no hope of re-orienting his workspace within the confined space. Scattered about the desk were pen holders, notepads, and the sundry necessities of office life. In the far corner of his desk were a few pictures of his family. Most of the pictures were five or more years old. His son, Daniel, was off to college. Yet, in the picture on his desk, a much younger Daniel was forever posing in his baseball uniform, clean and pressed from some early spring many moons ago. Next to this was a picture of his wife, Alicia. She was dressed for some event long forgotten. George no longer knew where he stored the camera. He hadn't needed it. The only other artifact decorating the "desert sand" colored walls of this cubicle was a large picture of a sailboat thumb-tacked in such a way that most passersby would not see it.

He wondered if the sailboat picture would spark controversy should someone in management spot it hanging off to one side of his desk. It was his way to rebel. He had picked it up some years ago when he and his wife Alicia spent a weekend at a sailboat show. They dreamed about sailing one day, or perhaps living aboard one of those pristine showpieces that lined the dock. Hidden behind that picture of the Tartan 4100 was a napkin. It seemed an inconsequential thing, but he knew it was there. The napkin was the list. George and Alicia, one glorious Saturday so many years ago, sat down at an overcrowded restaurant and playfully wrote down what they needed to do to live on one of those million dollar boats. They talked about winning the lottery, selling the house, buying a boat, finding a slip and all of the other accoutrements they would need to live "the simple life." Ironically, the simple life always began by winning the lottery.

On his poster, the Tartan 4100 was cutting its way through white water. The captain had one outstretched arm with his hand pointing forward, his white hair streaming behind him. Younger people, all dressed in matching yacht attire, surrounded this sage at the helm. The dark blue hull sat in stark contrast to the white froth that blurred the edges of water and craft. A single line of large letters across the bottom of the poster read, "Be the dream." George had never won the lottery, nor had he accomplished one item on that list, but he quietly held on to the dream. He still had the poster and the napkin was safely tucked behind the glossy image of his dream world.

Rachael, a younger woman who once sat in the cubicle next to him, had adorned her space with pictures of Jimmy Buffett. No space was left uncovered. When it was her turn to bring in a birthday cake or throw some semblance of an office party, she was the first to speak up about the theme. She had tiki stands, grass skirts, parrots, and all the adornments of a plastic tropical world at her command. Human resources had another opinion about such an outburst of personality and contrived some rule about damaging the cubicle walls with thumbtacks forcing Rachel to remove her icon from the Watsitumi walls. She obliged – sort of. She removed the Jimmy Buffett pictures from the walls, but then taped them to all of her office folders. The printouts of her log files were neatly stashed in the folder with Mr. Buffet exiting his plane with a hand casually offering a greeting. Her quarterly reports, organized in a yellow folder, showed Jimmy playing a live concert on a beach somewhere. Needless to say, the Watsitumi resource personnel couldn't tolerate such insubordination, but they had not yet concocted a rule they could enforce against her. Like any large corporate force, they micro-managed her for months, building their case. At her quarterly review, she was dismissed on a series of trumped up charges. George could feel the crushing of the human spirit throughout the building as she was led out of the facilities by a security guard. Because the folders were part of the Watsitumi office supplies, all of the Jimmys artfully crafted into the office thrum, sat abandoned in the cubicle.

Though his own poster was a much milder attempt at bucking the system, he rarely looked at that sparkling Tartan sailboat anymore. It hurt too much. It was like a broken promise. His focus was on the call log, the callers on hold, and a status which, in real-time, rated him against all of the other "phone technicians." He had to work hard to maintain a yellow-green status, which on Fridays, would often slip into the orange status. He was struggling to be average.

Click.

Buzz.

Click.

"Hello, this is Watsitumi Corporation, my name is George Forder. How may I help you today?" The tirade ensued. Expletives were fired off like Fourth of July fireworks. George heard the words but they melded with the day-long song of the other frustrated masses.

George learned to mentally disassociate himself from the work, while still engaging in the mechanics of the tasks at hand. Over time he had become invisible. He had become an automaton whose career goal didn't extend beyond the next paycheck. He used to wake in the morning looking forward to going to work. There was a golden era in his career when he felt he was making a difference. He received pats on the back from the owners in the early days of the company. But this inhuman world of nondescript cubicles was a far cry from his career origin.

He hadn't always worked for Watsitumi, but he also had never really changed jobs. Years ago, he started out as a sales representative for *Run-Rite Motors. Run-Rite* started as a garage business with a few buddies - Jim Dalburth and Craig Lang - who dabbled with their hot-rods' motors. They tweaked and honed engines, often fabricating parts when none were available, to get just the right compression ratios. They were the envy of the town and the bane of the police. But their weekend hobby taught them how to reverse engineer a production line motor and make it special. In those early years they made their money selling upgrade kits for Oldsmobile and Chevy engines. Because of these two entrepreneurs, the decibel level of Main Street on a Friday night jumped considerably louder. It became matter of local pride to have a *Run-Rite* kit installed. With each new request from some hot-rod or jalopy, the boys churned out new headers, exhaust systems, or manifolds which pushed the engines to new heights of chrome and metal. They could take an average engine and make it sing.

The garage hobby turned into a business as friends and family wanted their cars fixed or some upgrade performed. Though starting with the racing crowd, it extended to family cars and mainline vehicles, forcing the young men along new avenues of production line parts. Not satisfied, they started designing their own engine. The two owners were proud of their work and were interested in creating a motor that would last. When they hired George, Craig and Jim had wanted a person to assist with assembling the motors. As their popularity increased the three upgraded from a garage to a small warehouse. George was not an engineer, but he had enough "good ol' boy" in him that the two owners brought him in and taught him what made *Run-Rite Motors* "the best motor company there ever was." They showed him how they upgraded from rubber to high grade plastic bushings because they could withstand the heat better. They opened their blueprints, letting him see the tolerance levels for the piston shafts.

George believed in the solid, American-made, products. With the continued growth in the company, George moved from the manufacturing floor to marketing. He marketed *Run-Rite* from the heart and his enthusiasm was infectious. The popularity of *Run-Rite* made George's job easy. Initially, the company started with car motors, but the market was limited to those willing to trade out their existing motor for a new one. The kits sold well, but few were willing to go through such a dramatic transplant. So, the small company turned its sights on other motors that could use some sprucing up. The burgeoning company made motors for everything from home air-conditioners to hand held tillers. Manufacturers of these products took notice and requested that these motors be installed on their base product, ever increasing the output and reputation of *Run-Rite.*

George was rewarded for his hard work. Every year they gave George a week off with pay. As the company grew, the two owners purchased a beautiful three bedroom cabin nestled near a lake. George could take his family to the cabin – gratis. He was surprised after one vacation getaway when, upon his return, he was introduced to three more people they hired. They were all brought on board to help expand the *Run-Rite* marketing umbrella. George thought he might be in charge of the crew, but the owners kept a tight rein, and he was now one of four promoting and proselytizing the benefits of the *Run-Rite* family.

With the advent of the expanded team, the company grew at an alarming rate and went international. *Run-Rite* was now making engines for cars and boats. They created generators which were used in hospitals and high-tech industries. George moved from department to department as the company morphed into a giant beast. Marketing was now left to a third-party company of young entrepreneurs who could take advantage of the electronic world. The electronic web was a foreign concept to George, but these young people in pastel polo shirts heralded *Run-Rite* into the electronic age. The original owners, now multi-millionaires, had left the company. They could be found in the business rags with a drink in one hand toasting their success on some paradise complete with palm trees and a tiki bar. If you took out the fat, balding men with their raised glass, the picture didn't look that different from the May picture of the tropical wonderland on George's calendar. They had made it. They were living the dream.

Eventually the company was bought by the Watsitumi Corporation and folded into one of the international pillars of global gluttony. Watsitumi now made motors. They also made condoms, dry wall, ketchup, and cell phones. The management that had been in place after the original two left was summarily dismissed as Watsitumi applied their philosophy of "promote from within" (after brainwashing), assimilating *Run-Rite* into a grand machine of faceless bureaucracy. This leadership exodus left George with a great deal of company history under his belt, but his failure to rise in the ranks left him an unknown relic in the Watsitumi Corporation. He was considered too old and too overpaid for the skills he could offer. He had never been particularly adept at computers and he didn't understand the "personal advancement before business" mentality that drove this company. George moved from the accounting department to quality assurance. He was then moved to shipping. Not making a splash there, he was transferred to the complaint department. At each step he was met by a boss who was at least ten years his junior. None knew anything about motors. They couldn't tell you the difference between a drive shaft and a dipstick.

By the time he was assigned to the complaint department, he had given up on the stroll up the corporate ladder. He realized he could listen to the calls coming in, collect his salary, and make sure his pension was secure. But when he made that paradigm shift, it made its way into his home life, pervading and dampening his drive to do much of anything. Routine had once been convenient, but had now become necessary. Television became the balm that ate his life one hour at a time. The dinner table was unused, in favor of the TV tray tables. Thursday was spaghetti night. The passion left and so did the sex. Work had castrated his life.

Click.

Buzz.

Click.

"Hello, this is Watsitumi Corporation, my name is George Forder. How may I help you today?"

As George spoke these words he looked over, catching movement and noticed the shoes, first. He had seen the shoes only on very rare occasions. It had become his habit to look down, so shoes became the first thing that he noticed when his cubicle space was invaded. These shoes were unlike any other shoes on the planet. The last time he saw these shoes was at a corporate pep rally. Of course he doubted these were the exact same shoes. How could they be? No shoes could remain looking as pristine as these. George's shoes had the distinct marks of a man who bends his toes in the process of walking. Occasionally George scuffed his shoes so his shoes looked normal. But these had absolutely no scuff marks. There was no "bend" in the shoes indicating that anyone had walked in them. They had a black sheen so bright that you could brush your teeth and fix your hair in their reflection. They were the shoes of none other than the Headquarter's CEO, Mr. Ishiri.

This was an unexpected visit. Mr. Ishiri was way too important to visit George. Should he stand and shake his hand? Should he bow? There was a cultural crisis in the making and George was unprepared. George just sat there well aware of the presence of this important man dressed in the perfect black suit and red tie.

"Yes, sir. I understand that the investigation of the fire indicated that the source was the engine. We need to determine if you have a record of its maintenance. In order to fill out a claim and find fault we need to prove that you properly maintained the engine according to the specifications in the manual."

The expletives flew, as they always did. What followed was the string of words that he had heard a thousand times from a thousand disgruntled customers. Sue.., bring you down.., destroyed my..., fucking idiots...., morons..., piece of shit engine..., could have killed.... George looked up and tried to smile toward the door. He hoped none of the words he was hearing in his earpiece would pollute the otherwise perfect Mr. Ishiri. While the earpiece blasted with the "chorus of love," George's head started spinning with the idea that his day had come. His seniority, good work, and diligence would pay off. Mr. Ishiri was here to recognize someone who had been there nearly from the start.

The key phrase came. George was hoping to get this one, because it meant the end of the conversation was at hand.

"Call my lawyer and he'll...."

"Sir," started George, picking up the response he had learned from the training manual. "Since you have indicated that you will be using a lawyer, it is my responsibility to inform you that he needs to contact us here at Watsitumi. We should have no further discussion because of the legal ramifications of your actions against the company. Note that calls are recorded and can be used in a court of law. Thank you for choosing Watsitumi. Good day."

Click.

Buzz. Buzz. Buzz.

George stood up. He decided to try a modified cultural synthesis by offering his hand and performing a short bow. This way he had his international code of conduct bases covered. But Mr. Ishiri neither responded with the outstretched hand nor returned the awkward bow. George left his hand out way too long and the plump fingers jutting out in Ishiri's direction turned from a greeting of friendship to an overweight intrusion. The space between them seemed to have suddenly grown cold. What had started as butterflies of excitement in George's stomach turned to lead weights of dread.

"Mr. Forder," started Mr. Ishiri. The words seemed long and drawn out. At least Mr. Ishiri had gotten his name right.

"Yes sir, it is a pleasure to see you today, sir," replied George as he slowly lowered his hand, like a flag on a pole when the wind had suddenly died. George glanced back and saw that his real-time effectiveness screen had gone from green to yellow.

Buzz. Buzz.

"Mr. Forder," said Mr. Ishiri again, slowly. He said it as though that was a complete statement. He said it as though nothing more needed to be said. George wanted more, but Mr. Ishiri seemed content simply to repeat the name. George sat back down. This seemed to be the catalyst to get Mr. Ishiri out of the name repetition mode.

Mr. Ishiri refused to enter the cubicle but stood just outside the invisible line that divided the hallway and George's personal space. The CEO didn't lean up against the partition. Of course he wouldn't. George doubted that Mr. Ishiri ever leaned, slouched, or crossed his legs. This would cause creases in his suit, and maybe cause him to bend his shoes in some way that resembled a normal human being.

"We have been reviewing our records and found that you have been doing an adequate job here at Watsitumi."

For a second, George paused. First he wondered who "we" were. There was only Mr. Ishiri, yet he was

11

talking in the plural, as though he was a man of such importance that he occupied more than one space in the physical realm. But these seemed like words of encouragement and George dare not interrupt.

"But we strive for *excellence*. Do you agree?"

"Oh, yes, I agr..."

Mr. Ishiri continued as though George had not even attempted a reply.

"Therefore, we need to make sure that our company works at a level which exceeds the ordinary. You have been with the company for some time, yes?"

George opened his mouth to reply, but paused, wondering if that had actually been a question. His hunch was correct. Mr. Ishiri continued his prepared speech without a hint of recognition that George was even present in the cubicle.

"And your records demonstrate that you have been average. Yet you're paid a good salary, well beyond that of your peers. We feel that we cannot reward average work with above average compensation. In these economic times, we need to present ourselves as a lean and mean entity, worthy of our world stature."

George could feel what was coming. His mind was scrambling at the avalanche that was falling in his world. As Mr. Ishiri went on with his diatribe, George was trying to quickly assemble a case for his continued employment.

"... years we have established high marks... better than our competition... grown when other companies have..."

George didn't comprehend anything anymore. He was too busy panicking. The words finally came at the end of a speech put together with the finesse of a Chopin piano concerto.

"...we are going to have to let you go."

Buzz. Buzz. Buzz.

George's electronic performance rating was now a deep orange. His face was much redder than the orange tint of the performance indicator which was beginning to blink. He thought of standing up but wondered if his knees had magically been replaced by jiggling jellyfish. If he could stand, George was taller than Mr. Ishiri and would present an imposing figure. But that might be considered a threat and George was not a violent man. In fact, he wondered how much of a man was left in him.

"I have put in a great deal of service here at *Run-Rite*..." George quickly caught himself. "... er Watsitumi and have been..."

Mr. Ishiri put up his hand and cocked his head as though these words were blocked by some invisible force-field. George decided to take the offensive.

"What about Arnold?" asked George, pointing to a cubicle three rows back. He opted to pick Arnold because he was a social butterfly who spent much of his time going from cubicle to cubicle talking to the other employees – mostly women. Arnold would relay the Monday sports statistics with the passion of a reverend and the accuracy of a Wall Street banker to anyone with whom he had made eye contact. George knew Arnold cheated on the lunch breaks and took an extra five to ten minutes each day. "My work is as good, if not better, than his."

"He is black."

The words were as offensive as they were unexpected. The nature of the response was so foreign to George that he couldn't muster a reply. George spent time trying to calculate a response. He wondered how to argue with this odd little man with the perfect suit and perfect shoes. Why had Mr. Ishiri personally come to let him go? Why not bring out the floor manager to do the job? There was the hint of a smirk in the face of this

13

otherwise stolid figure. Somewhere, deep in his heart, was the evil pleasure of destroying someone else's life.

"But I have been faithful..."

As if summoned from some unseen directive, a security guard appeared.

"You must leave immediately. You will be escorted out. Please remove any personal belongings..."

George looked at the cubicle and tried to assess what was his. It was all his. This was his world. For six years, this was all his - all of it. He gathered his family photos. He went to take down the calendar.

"That is company property. It came from the store," said the guard. "Do you have a receipt for it?" The palm tree seemed to hang lower in dismay over the green and blue water. Of course George didn't have a receipt. The images for June, July and August would remain unrevealed.

George took down the poster of the Tartan 4100 sailboat. The security guard snorted. George left the thumbtacks on the desk. Only then did he notice that Mr. Ishiri had vaporized shortly after the appearance of the security guard. Of course Mr. Ishiri didn't *walk* away. How could he? He would have bent his shoes.

As George took his cardboard box with the few remnants of his corporate life and walked down the aisle toward the exit, he felt the perspiration around his head and neck grow cold. There was a moment when his vision had narrowed as if he was looking through a toilet roll. He was hyperventilating and there was a single musical note in his brain, growing in intensity, and causing his vision to go blue. A few heads popped out from behind the cubicle, like dogs in the pound poking their snouts through the cage to get a better glimpse of the outside world, each one never breaking dialogue with the person on the other line.

14

"Hello, this is Watsitumi Corporation, my name is…"

As George opened the door leading to the parking lot, a hot shaft of sun broke through the ever widening crease between inside and outside. Unknown to George, back at his cubicle, his real-time personal effectiveness monitor had gone from orange to deep red.

2

Dread. Dread seeped through George's blood as he put his box representing the entirety of his corporate life into the trunk of his car. The anxiety didn't diminish as the security guard, with his arms folded across his chest, kept a silent watch from the entrance. The guard didn't want George to "key" anyone's car, or worse, come back with a revolver. With cold indifference the guard stood unmoving, like a Roman statue, waiting until George peacefully pulled away. The dread seeped through George's blood like some cold medical concoction sent through an IV bag. At certain points, the dread kicked off the "oh my God" syndrome.

His first "oh my God" thought was, "Oh my God, how am I going to tell Alicia?"

This was soon followed by, "Oh my God, we are going to lose our house."

Almost simultaneously came, "Oh my God, Daniel won't be able to continue his college education."

The "oh my God" trickled to more mundane issues like:

"Oh my God, I need to turn off the sprinkler system."

"Oh my God, I just bought $200 worth of groceries."

"Oh my God, there are three loads of dirty laundry."

The cycle of the "oh my God" phrase replayed itself with increasing rapidity and volume inside George's head, mixed with the slushy-stirry sound of the blood that was now pumping between his ears at four times the pressure than one hour earlier. George had arrived at that point of panic and dread where he suddenly felt he was no longer himself and had been replaced by a mannequin or robot that he was now trying to control. George started the car and even this simple operation took an incredible effort of will as he mentally calculated each step. It was as if this was some new activity he had never performed. He wondered, for the briefest moment, if this was the kind of feeling stroke patients had when their brains were rewired and the mental instruction to "lift your left foot" resulted in a "left elbow jab." The good news was that George had not gotten to the point of asking God to forgive him his sins and he had not started reciting the Lord's Prayer like some Buddhist mantra.

As he sat immobile, bemoaning his current state, the car was getting hot to the point where small dogs would have been slobbering and gasping for their last breath. He knew he had to leave the property, but where would he go? His first thought was to go home. No one was there.

Alicia wouldn't return for a few hours. When Daniel was in elementary school, she volunteered to help assist the teachers. After he graduated to junior high, Alicia chose to stay at the elementary school. The school offered her a low paying part-time position. She liked little kids. They listened (mostly). They liked and respected grown-ups (mostly). And, they seemed to have some creative spark that junior high and high school tends to extinguish. She would fill the dinner table with stories about these little kids doing some incredible ninety-degree kind of thinking. He tried to lose himself in last night's conversation. It was an effort of will to try and focus on some pleasant thought trying to suppress the monster that seemed to be taking over his body.

"...so Justin told me that he had to use the bathroom. Of course when we hear that request, we don't hesitate, especially with someone like Justin. Otherwise, we would be sending him home wrapped in a bath towel. So I send him down the hall, to make sure he gets to the restroom okay. And then, from the bathroom, I hear this screaming. I had no idea what was going on. I run down the hall thinking the worst." Alicia put her hands on her ears in a mock sign of distress.

"Well, it *is* the boy's room and there are strict rules about a female entering the boy's room. But the screaming seems to be getting even louder. I wondered if someone had snuck in there. Luckily, Mr. Thompson, the fourth grade teacher who was teaching across the hall, had heard it too. He came running down the hall, and opens the door."

Alicia paused for dramatic effect.

"And there is little Justin, standing on the booster box, washing his hands, screaming the alphabet at the top of his lungs."

"'What are you doing?' asked Mr. Thompson. The teacher had the door opened wide enough so I could sneak a peek and see what Justin was doing. The kid had soap and water everywhere. There were hand prints all over his shirt. He had repeatedly washed in the sink and dried his hands by wiping them on his clothes."

That beautiful little smirk only Alicia could give curled on the ends of her mouth. She paused for a second and then continued mimicking the sound of a small child perfectly.

"So Justin says 'Mama told me to wash my hands after I pee. She said that I had to say the alphabet real loud because my hands aren't clean until I do the whole alphabet. She wanted me to say it real loud so she could hear me because that is how long it takes to get them clean, but I could only get up to 'S' and I forgot where I was so I had to start over. Three times."

George remembered laughing, though his current predicament prevented anything close to mirth from rising to the surface. But the memory was locked in place and he wanted to replay this scene with as much clarity as his brain would allow. The escapist technique was working and he tried to hold on to that precious moment.

"'Mr. Thompson helped Justin down from the booster box, turned the little guy's hands over a couple of times and said, 'Yep, you got all the germs this time. I don't see any there. Good job.' He turned to me and winked. I thought I was going to die laughing!"

The fragment of memory died much too quickly for George and he failed to conjure any other pleasant recollection. The moment faded. At least for a small period of time he had been on autopilot. He didn't remember driving and obeying the string of stop lights that led to his home. He wondered if, in his altered state of consciousness, he had run through the intersections. As he turned the corner and saw his house down the street his stomach took the express elevator to his balls. The "oh my God" audio remix started replaying down the street and up the driveway.

He loved Alicia very much. Otherwise what came next would not hurt so badly. If he didn't care for his family, the loss of his job would be a glitch in an otherwise banal life. But he cared for them. He loved his son. Family was important. In this mental turmoil, he reflected over the last few years. He wondered if he hurt them through neglect. He assumed that because nothing happened, everything was okay. But the "status quo" might have been the slow death in their relationship. He couldn't remember the last time he and Alicia had made love. He couldn't recollect the last time he heard her express any romantic words for him. Neither had he started or ended his day with a simple "I love you." There was an implied devotion for one another. But the silent fog of complacency eroded away what was once a healthy marriage. "Keeping an even keel" meant doing nothing at all. No vacation. No surprises. No romance. Nothing.

He sat in the kitchen and waited. This was the communal hub of the house. Bills were paid here. Decisions were made here. It is here where they broke bread; they never ate in the dining room. The kitchen was the heart of home. So there he sat. Time had become totally meaningless to George. It would be hours before Alicia came home, but that was immaterial. The sunshine came through the sheers onto the kitchen table moving like a cat as it stalked its unwary prey. He would just sit. George was experiencing the opposite of exercise. When one exercised, the mind becomes still as the body goes through its exertion. George, however, was training for the Olympic angst trials. Sitting there, he spun out a cascade of worst case scenarios. At one point he cried, though he didn't know when he started crying, or when he stopped. He reached a guilt ridden transcendental state which included red and puffy eyeballs.

He thought about Alicia. She was still quite beautiful. She had cut her brunette hair short. It was grey around the temples. She had not attempted to cover up the indicators of her age and he was happy for that. The spots where the hair had lightened resembled angel wings. He told her that and she simply responded, "Well they need to be a little bigger to get this fat ass off the ground." Yes, she had gained weight, but she was nowhere near being fat. It was a product of a "good life." They had become sedentary, entering into their routine almost unconsciously, being slowly roasted by comforts and always easing into the path of least resistance.

Now, with the loss of his job at *Watsitumi*, their routine would be broken. George felt he had been stripped of his manhood. George tried to live the life of a typical American man. He went to work on time. He came home after a hard day of work. He ate bacon. He watched reruns. He had put in years with a company as a good and loyal servant. And, until now, he had covered himself with the warm and cozy blanket of triviality.

For a moment he pondered the social difference between men and women. He leaned toward the fifties style "Honeymooners role" of "supporter of the family," "the bread winner" and the "man of the house." Society, over the last forty years, changed some of the roles, but much of the social difference between men and women persisted. George didn't sew, nor had he ever beaten egg whites. Alicia had never taken out the garbage or changed the oil in a car. At parties, George noticed that men and women differed in their greeting. Introductions to strangers differed for men and women. Women, after sharing names, would ask "how many children do you have?" Men, however, immediately targeted, "So what do you do for a living?"

George had always answered, "I am a sales-rep for Run-Rite Motors." He said this with pride. His chest stuck out a little more because this was an American company. His answer was like raising the American flag, or opening his shirt to reveal the "S" emblazoned on his blue superman suit. When *Run-Rite* was bought out by Watsitumi, his entire demeanor changed. He tried to avoid the question altogether.

Yet, when the unavoidable question was raised, he hung his head and answered, "Oh, I just work for a multi-national company that makes engines."

He refused to say the name - *Watsitumi*. If the odd moment came when he did have to utter the name of the company, he tried to do it in a quick and subdued manner hoping the response would be ignored if not heard. However, if the inquirer pressed him for clarification, George knew he would have to repeat his answer, complete with the Watsitumi name carefully pronounced. What followed would always be some stupid retort.

"Watsitumi? Hah – I dunno What's it to you?!"

"Are you kidding me? Watsitumi? That's hilarious! *Wazzz – it tumi*" the respondent would chime in the worst possible oriental accent. The drunken ones made a ninja pose while reminding George he worked for foreign interests.

So George tried to leave it as, "an international engine manufacturer" or some other vague reference. Nonetheless, he could state, with pride, that he had been there for years. The job defined his position in society. It defined him as a hard worker. It defined him as a contributing member of society. It defined him as a responsible supporter of his family. It defined him as a success to his father and his father's name.

But that was stripped from him - without honor. He was now unemployed. He was a threat to society. He was a deadbeat. He was...

The door opened while these thoughts tumbled through his brain like a rocky slope in the middle of an avalanche. Alicia was home.

"Hey!" she said with a curious enthusiasm. "What are you doing home so early?"

She entered the kitchen and threw her car keys on the round oak kitchen table. They skidded across the surface like a plastic puck on an air hockey game.

Having spent most of her life with George, Alicia immediately sensed something was terribly wrong. The message came across at the speed of light. Her mood changed to dead serious. It was her way. She could snap from a happy-go-lucky, rather carefree person, to an intense analytical giant in a split second.

"What is it? What is the matter? Are you okay?" She placed her hand on George's forearm and sat down within his fight or flight zone facing him, eye-to-eye.

It was the contact. It was the moment of seemingly insignificant bonding that was the catalyst to cause George's floodgates to open. Unfortunately, it also rendered him mute. His shoulders started to spasm as his breath came in short pants. She spoke again. "Tell me. Are you okay?"

George could only nod affirmatively. He took control of his breathing for the few seconds it took to regain his power of speech. Finally he uttered in a half voice, "I was fired."

Startled, Alicia's eyes went wide.

"What?!"

It was as if his message carried a torpedo that sent her back in her chair. "What happened?"

Having recovered slightly, George started recounting Mr. Ishiri's ambush and the day's events that followed.

"They didn't give you any paperwork? They didn't give you cause for being fired?"

George had not contemplated the thought that he had been wrongly fired. He was so rattled by his world coming apart that he hadn't thought about the litigious aspects of his termination.

"No. At the time, it was such a shock, and the security guard was there..."

"What about human resources? Did you go through an exit interview?"

This was her way, George thought. She was so practical, and he was such a dreamer. When backed into

23

a corner, she would become Perry Mason, or some other version of a high price lawyer, ever probing the details, looking for a loophole. She picked apart how to leverage the events in his favor. He never contemplated these things. Not even in a rational state of mind, would he have pondered the notion of an exit interview, meeting with human resources to make some kind of a clean break. In their everyday lives, she was the one who devised the plan of action. He was the one to expedite the action. He could go to the grocery store solo, but not without some list that she had composed. Years ago, when they entertained the notion of going on vacation, he would call for the reservation, but she was the one who packed. They never lacked for anything as they made their way to their vacation destination. She had the peanut butter and spare toilet tissue roll. She had all of the contingencies covered. This day, however, was unlike any other and even Alicia was unable to devise a plan to return to normalcy.

"What are we going to do George? Are you going to go back there and fight?"

"Fight," George responded automatically. "Fight what? I was fired. They terminated me. I'm gone. They made me take my stuff. He pointed to the box of disheveled items on the kitchen counter. Years of dedication was now stuffed into a container that had once held reams of blank paper. "It's over. I'm done."

Alicia, sensing that George was beyond despair and was in a state of deep depression, changed tactics somewhat.

"Look, here's what we can do. I can go and look for a job."

Immediately, George replied, "No." His was an autonomic response, like the reaction when placing one's hand on a hot surface. The message never really made it to the logical portions of George's brain. Alicia's employment and George's unemployment would only further strip him of his manhood. He had been the provider and now he was going to be supported by his wife. Somehow it just didn't seem right. He knew that in most couples both halves worked. However, George felt like he was serving his family by allowing Alicia the time to do what she wanted. It was a way of expressing his love for her. She used to work as a waitress in a restaurant when they were first married. At the end of the day, she would collapse on the couch and he would rub her feet.

The couple decided that Alicia would stay at home when Daniel was born. For years they struggled as a family. But they pulled together as a team, making a good home for their boy. As Daniel grew and George rose in the ranks at *Run-Rite*, life got easier.

But with the loss of his job, George now faced the prospect that his wife would be supporting the family. For Alicia to return to the workforce would go against his principles as a man.

"Why not? You don't think I'm capable of work?"

Her defenses had started kicking in. She felt backed into a corner and was starting to show her claws. Her aggressive nature was beginning to surface as she, too, was going through the "what ifs."

"It's not that," George started. He paused. This would require a tactical response and he didn't have the mental acuity to spar with her. "I just want what's best."

"Well, under the circumstances, since you're not going back to Watsitumi, then the only logical alternative is for me to start looking for work. Don't you agree?"

She removed her hands from his forearm and folded her arms across her chest. The tension was growing. George just wanted her to hold him, stroke his hair and say "everything would be alright." He wanted comfort, not a solution. But that was not her way.

"Look, I don't know what to do right now. My world has just fallen...."

"Our world," she retorted. "I am in this with you, George. It is not all about you. I'm intimately involved in what happens next. Are you going to file for unemployment? Did you get a severance package?"

More questions followed, but George had no answers. He thought briefly about the unemployment office. He had no idea where it was, but he didn't want to go there. It would be like the Motor Vehicle Administration, which in his mind was the equivalent of Dante's hell. He would spend hours in line, only to realize that he needed some odd bit of paperwork that was printed on page four of an obscure request. The person waiting on him would look at him condescendingly as if he/she smelled something bad. He would need to sit and take a number. Usually it was "E241." The red light indicated "Now serving: D14." The unemployment office seemed abstracted to a few levels below the MVA. He wondered if it would smell. He didn't mind human smell. That was okay. However, these places had the smell of toxic plastic and metal, covered up by the smell of toxic antiseptic.

Sensing that George had faded into his own thoughts, Alicia grabbed his shoulder and looked him in the eye.

"Did you get a severance package?"

"I don't know," replied George wiping his face in frustration.

"What do you mean you don't know? Did they tell you about a severance package?"

"No."

"Did you ask?"

"No."

26

"Why not? What were you thinking?" Alicia was getting terse and it shut out George from being able to engage in any semblance of an adult conversation. He was an eight year old boy cowering in the dark room, wondering if there were monsters under the bed. He had no answers, and he feared even contemplating new ideas. While Alicia's mind was spinning out of control, he was trying not to be hit by the shrapnel.

"Okay, we need to make a list of our assets. We need to figure out how long we can survive without work. Maybe we can pull out some of the money from your 401K. I think you get a big tax hit if you do that...."

She was starting to formulate. George knew this would go on for a while. Whether it had any real bearing on reality, he didn't know. They each had their own response to crisis: George would focus on the potential downfalls (prefacing each thought with "oh my God") and Alicia would make lists.

"I'll get the employment section from the paper and we can go over..."

He replayed the insulting events over and over in his head.

"I am sure there are online resources. We can look at some websites..."

George thought about buying a lottery ticket: *The* lottery ticket ... and sailing away.

"If we need to sell the house, we can go live with..." Alicia rambled on. By now George only heard "whah whah whah" like the teacher from the Peanuts cartoon. But in his practiced husbandly way, he was able to offer a quick response if a question was darted his way. He would respond with a reply of least resistance. It was not the most constructive way out of this dilemma, but each partner managed in their own way.

There was dialog, but no conversation. There were questions and answers, but no resolution. George wanted to get on to the "next thing." But he had no idea what the "next thing" was. Alicia was formulating a plan. The scene had played itself out only a few times in their relationship. Most of these sorts of conversations occurred early in their relationship when they had nothing, and it was a struggle just to "make do." Up until now, the conversations were just a wade in the baby pool. Now they were definitely underwater.

It was Alicia who broke free from her shell, opening her arms. She had exhausted her line of questions. She had reacted and responded in the manner she had always done. Now that she completed her intellectual panic, she could open her emotional cupboard. This was what George was waiting for. George moved over and they held each other. It was an eternity of wordless union that only deep love can explain. After a while they broke from their embrace and moved toward the sink.

There came a point when routine kicked in. They both worked in the kitchen fixing dinner. They didn't talk. They had expended all their energy and were now in auto-mode. Fish sticks. Macaroni and cheese. Can of peas. They pulled out their folding tables and ate mechanically, not bothering to guess at the Jeopardy questions. They couldn't formulate their thoughts into the form of a question. They had no thoughts to formulate. After dinner, they sat on the couch and let the lethargy of the night's television programs lull them to sleep.

The next day George awoke in bed. He didn't know how he had gotten from the couch to the bed. At some point, one or the other had gotten up, turned off the TV, told the other they were headed upstairs, and made the trek, like extras in a zombie movie, to their room. It was something they had done for years. However, this was followed by George getting up, showering, eating some cereal while reading the paper, and then heading out to work. That last bit, however, was now gone. George was not sure how to fill the void. He thought about applying himself eight hours a day to finding a full-time job. Donning his slippers he headed out to the mailbox to get the paper, which was left dutifully on the sidewalk each day. His routine was almost intact, but instead of reading the headlines, he went straight to the employment section. It was shorter than he remembered. In the past, he remembered removing a vast section of the paper. Now the employment section seemed like a thin strip between the sports and comics. The despondent economic times only added to his growing angst.

Construction, nursing, receptionist. Construction manager, dental assistant, bank teller. Handyman, medical billing, office assistant. There was nothing in the paper for which George was remotely qualified. One entry made his eyebrows perk up. Mechanic. The idea of picking up a wrench again sparked his interest. He had no calluses, his finger nails didn't have grease buried beneath them. The only thing he was qualified for was answering phones for a call center. He felt very old and talentless. George's son, Daniel, had hope. Daniel was prepared, having developed the computer skills and training for this technological age. George was a relic. He circled the mechanic position, thinking that it was a long shot, but worth a try.

He put down the paper as Alicia shuffled into the kitchen. She made her way to the coffee machine, pouring the black joe into the "Happily isn't always ever after" cup.

"How's it going?" Her tone was much softer this morning. He felt a little "I'm sorry" in her voice, though she would never come right out and say it.

"Okay, I guess. It is just damn weird. I found something in the paper."

"Good," she said, with an equal measure of enthusiasm and fatigue.

"I'm going to the school today. I'll let them know that this will be my last week volunteering."

The words stung George a little, but after the defeat of yesterday, he had entered a stage of numbness. "Okay. I'm going to work on my resume after I call these guys."

"You may have to write a couple of resumes, depending on the kind of job you're looking for."

"Yeah."

The morning dragged on. George left a message with the mechanic shop. The boss wasn't in, but would call him back later today or tomorrow. The resume came out like a constipated crap. There was a lot of effort without much result. He contemplated how he could create a resume which would demonstrate his loyalty and commitment, but as he reread his composition, it sounded like an overweight balding man caught up in a dead end job. He had the desire to do something – anything – to work again. He went online, but the internet seemed a flood of bad information. He tried to submit his resume online, but it would not upload. He started getting a load of spam email and the whole process left him confused and out of touch. No wonder they call it monster –You submit your resume and receive a hundred Viagra emails.

He thought about taking a little time to go outside for a walk. But, he was supposed to be at "work." Walking wasn't "work." In fact, when the idea came to him, it heightened his sense of guilt. He surmised that he should not do any leisure activity until he had a job. Only then would he allow himself to relax. It was a kind of self imposed punishment for being "a bad boy."

He decided to try his hand at making a list of things he could do to get a job. Pulling out a memo pad and pencil he sat and realized he had no idea what to do next. He didn't want Alicia to come home and find out that he had done nothing. He tried to think of people he knew working somewhere that might put in a good word for him. But he had let his friendships dwindle to those co-workers still answering the phones at Watsitumi. For a millisecond he thought about calling Watsitumi and begging for his job back. This thought was soon replaced by the acid reflux shooting up from his stomach like an Apollo rocket launch destined for the moon. Still he persisted.

After taking a few yoga-style cleansing breaths, George picked up the phone and dialed the first four digits. He paused and the butterflies in his stomach turned to wasps. He put the phone back on the receiver. Walk – maybe he just needed some fresh air. He bargained with himself to go out for fifteen minutes and then apply himself with unbridled fervor to the task of employment. He felt the clock ticking.

The air was unusually warm and humid as George stepped out on the front porch. He left his sunglasses inside, knowing he was only going for a short stroll. He strolled to the edge of the yard and stopped at the end of the concrete driveway. He looked back. Their modest home was in good shape and he didn't want to have to give it up. His weekends were spent painting the garage door, or edging the sidewalk. He had only known the evening and weekend rituals that surrounded his humble abode. But the weekday morning world surrounding his home was a mystery to him. What time did the mail arrive? When would his neighbors come home? The Cape Cod style house had a new strangeness about it. He wondered if the house was considering divorcing him because of his lack of employment. He wondered if houses were really that fickle.

George opened the mailbox and saw the stack of letters leaning neatly inside. The mail had already been delivered. He cringed at the bills that lay angled in the white metal archway. He pulled them out, hoping that most of the stack was junk mail. It wasn't. The mortgage, electric and phone bill arrived simultaneously. He did a little mental calculation and figured they would not have a problem paying this month. He should get one more paycheck. Then he was in financial free-fall. Wrapped around the bills was one of George's trade magazines.

Industrial Spotlight was a magazine geared toward the industrial sector marketing. Normally, he took little notice of the magazine. He relegated it to bathroom. The magazine was a crescendo of articles, each one a little longer than the last. The magazine had an employment section located somewhere beyond the ad "You too can find financial independence by raising alpacas." The magazine might contain a position for which he was qualified. This was the answer he was looking for. He found his "next step." He might actually be able to put something on his list of things to do. Abandoning the idea of a walk, he took the packet of mail back into the house.

Discarding the bills on the kitchen table, he unrolled the *Industrial Spotlight* rag. Before he could even get to the employment section, he stopped at the cover. He couldn't believe his eyes. The cover was divided along an angle. Two pictures overlapped. In the top left corner he stared and blinked. He wondered if it was a figment of his imagination. Perhaps he had cracked and this was the opening gong of a lifetime of delusion.

George was on the cover of *Industrial Spotlight.*

3

George plopped down in the chair.

"What games are the gods playing with me," George thought. "Am I going insane?" The picture was indeed George, though not the George sitting down his current state of bewilderment. The George that was on the cover of *Industrial Spotlight* was a much younger, leaner and hairier George. It showed him with a broad smile. He was standing on the far left with six other people in the picture. His head was cocked to one side and one of the other people in the back had their arm on his shoulder. It was an old picture from his days at *Run-Rite*. The small warehouse had yet to be cleaned up. Some of the machinery was in place, but this was a very early picture of the crew. He vaguely remembered the picture. More than the photo itself, the image conjured up the smells of that building. There was a distinct smell of rubber, but it was tinged with the acrid smell of metal welding.

The bottom half of the picture showed the two original owners "present day" on a sailboat with their glasses lifted in triumph. The two founders, wearing outrageous Hawaiian shirts, seemed to be enjoying some joke. At Jim's feet was a briefcase – the only indication that any work was being conducted. Apparently they were embarking on a brave new adventure. The cover of the magazine had bright yellow lettering – "Visionaries from the past look to the future."

George scrambled through the magazine to find the article. Past the "What's Hot – What's Not" section was a short article about the founders of *Run-Rite*. The article started with a mysterious dig about some future project that promised to bring a healthy boost to the economy. There were no specifics, only vague talk of something grand. Whenever the author mentioned the "project" the text became dreamy and out of focus. George wondered if the author had signed some non-disclosure agreement and was unable to reveal the secret.

The article made George rise up from his twenty-four hour funk. This bridge to the past made a chill run down George's spine. This sign was not only unexpected, it was downright creepy. But, it returned power to George's soul. It ignited a flame of hope and inspiration. Perhaps he could leverage his past good work with these two wealthy individuals. They always trusted him. There seemed promise in this tidbit of good fortune. For the first time since yesterday, he felt like he could eat.

"Maybe they created a new engine," thought George. "Perhaps they will create a competitive market against Watsitumi." George tried to calculate how long the duo had been away from the company. He wondered if there was a non-compete clause in one of their contracts. Perhaps, only now, were they able to re-enter the marketplace. The thrill of the article sent sparks of electricity through George's veins. Had he still been working for Watsitumi, he would have cast the article aside. Perhaps he never would have glanced at the cover. Maybe he would have pitched it into the trash as he had done with others. But now, he felt he had the possibility of removing whatever curse had befallen him.

He read the article over and over. He tried to glean some tidbit of information about exactly what his two former employers were up to. But, with each reread, the article didn't divulge anything new. Even worse, the article didn't end with any kind of contact information. Some of the articles had references to websites, lists of emails, and a plethora of contact data. The mystery of this article made George giddy. It took the better part of an hour, but he was able to locate the fine print with an address and telephone for *Industrial Spotlight*.

"Hello, this is *Industrial Spotlight*," a voice on the other end of the phone blurted.

"Hello my name is Geor...."

"If you're interested in subscribing to *Industrial Spotlight* please press two."

George let the procession of options parade through his ear. None of them was really what he wanted, but having worked in the complaint department, he knew a few telephone shortcuts and pressed "O" for operator. There was a momentary pause and the voice came back on.

"Please wait while I transfer you to... that extension."

The phone went click and silent. George thought that he had been cut off. He started to hang up and redial, when the phone seemed to come back to life with a buzz. After it buzzed a while, a distinctly human voice came over the line.

"*Industrial Spotlight*, this is Sheila, how can I direct your call?"

"Hello Sheila," replied George in his best complaint department voice, "I'm George Forder and I'm trying to locate the author..." George paused forgetting the writer's name. He knew it was an odd name. He quickly fumbled through the now dog-eared rag."Umm... here it is. Samuel Sundergill." As he spoke these words he knew the author's real name couldn't be Samuel Sundergill. No mother in her right mind would call their child Samuel Sundergill, but there it was in black and white.

"One moment please...." Silence followed and then another set of tones.

A young voice came on the line. "You have reached the voicemail of Sam Sundergill. I'm not in the office right now. Please leave a message after the beep."

George hoped there was enough space on the machine for his message. "Hello, my name is George Forder and I'm actually on the cover of this month's *Industrial Spotlight*. I'm one of the guys in the old photo. Anyway, I was wondering if you have the contact information for either Jim Dalburth or Craig Lang. I used to work for them...."

George tried his best to lay out the history he had with these two fellows. He wanted to make sure that Mr. Sundergill knew that he had a prior connection with these two, and would never misuse the contact information. But with every step he took in that direction, he felt he was proving he was, indeed, a crackpot. The message became absurdly long. The length of the message was partly due to George's constant prefacing of each sentence with "I know I'm going on about this but..."

George hung up the phone and felt like he had put in a good day at "not work." No one had cussed him out. No one had threatened to "come down there and bust up every damn Watsitumi motor." In the midst of his angst over unemployment George found a glimmer of hope, and it made all the difference in the world.

George prepared dinner for him and Alicia. It wasn't gourmet – just spaghetti – but then he couldn't remember ever preparing dinner solo. It was the right thing to do. It was an olive branch that he could extend to his wife to let her know that he was trying. He was out of work and was going to make her life a little easier. Alicia smiled at George's attempt at a meal. The spaghetti stuck together and the tomato sauce was poured from a jar – cold – over the spaghetti. She ate it and made yummy noises, making sure that she would cook something in the crock pot for tomorrow so he wouldn't have to worry about it. George smiled as he ate the spaghetti, occasionally crunching into something hard.

George saw that she liked the meal, but sensed the worry that dwelt deep under her skin. They were both trying to console each other with light dinner banter. They had compensated their suppressed angst by becoming overtly polite. Between the "Would you like..." and the "Thank you..." as the salad, and the rolls were passed around. Alicia told George about her day's activities at school. George reminisced about *Run-Rite*.

Halfway through dinner the phone rang. It was Sam Sundergill.

"Hello, is this George Forder?"

"Yes, this is George," he replied as he tried to do some charades to Alicia to let her know who was on the line. He tried to mouth the words "Sam Sundergill" to her, but she only thought he looked like a fish out of water, its mouth opening wide and face contorting. She was totally mystified by his hand gestures, but suspected it was some good news by his reaction. George didn't expect a response this soon.

"Normally I don't respond to these kind of inquiries. You never know what kind of nut case is trying to get in touch with your source. Anyway, when you mentioned your name and your connection, I dug a little deeper and found your name in some of my background paperwork."

"I understand. My message was a little scatterbrained. Thanks for calling me back."

"No problem. I wanted to let you know, also, that I cannot give out any phone numbers or addresses. It really is against policy."

George could feel his heart pounding harder with each second. He wanted to get in touch with Craig and

38

Jim and felt if he could get past this reporter roadblock, he would be on his way back to normalcy. This one author with a silly name was keeping him from his destiny. His future hinged on a guy who probably lived on a diet of Twinkies and soda.

"I understand, but…"

Sam interrupted. "That is not to say I can't give the Run-Rite duo *your* address and phone number. I got your number from the message. Just wanted to call and get your other information: mailing address, email, etc. and I'll pass it on to them and have them get in touch with you."

George's spirits lifted, "Yes, of course. That would be wonderful. Thanks." George made a quick re-assessment of the author. He probably drank fruit juice and ate granola bars.

"No problem."

George hung up the phone. He kissed Alicia full on the lips. She was genuinely surprised at his response. There seemed to be a lightness and the spontaneous kiss was a pleasant surprise she hadn't had in years. She was used to only getting the "honey I'm home" kiss when George returned from work.

"Dinner? Kiss? You should have gotten fired a long time ago. I could get spoiled."

"The guys are going to give me a call. That was the reporter I told you about."

Two days later, George awoke a broken man. Craig and Jim had not called. He thought the connection would have been a sure thing. But with each hour, his hope turned to despair. He started out with the boyish "I can't wait" mentality of a kid waiting for a birthday present. It morphed into the "I can't wait" mentality of a desperate old man waiting for the impossible.

He got a response from the mechanic position, went in for the interview and totally blew it. George had hoped that the garage would have been like the warehouse at *Run-Rite*. This place was a mess. Tools lay strewn everywhere and a thick layer of grease and dirt covered every working surface. "Wilbur's Garage" was a trap for people who needed something done half as well at twice the price. Oddly, the exact calendar he had owned once adorning his six-by-six working space, hung on the far wall of the cluttered office. It still read February, but he remembered the image from a month's worth of daydreaming. The picture displayed the beach in the distance, all out of focus. The camera had been pointed downward at a star fish, its dark reddish brown tentacles set perfectly in the sand. It glistened in a few inches of water as refracted light beams criss-crossed the watery landscape.

He didn't know if the presence of the calendar was a sign or a warning. George wanted to go over to the calendar and slowly lift each page, advancing the images forward to the present month. He wondered why the owner wouldn't perform that sacred ritual with the honor it deserved. February lay exposed, the light and neglect bleaching the colors like a worn out shirt. This disregard set George in a sour frame of mind. Throughout the interview George fixated on the calendar. The owner saw George's eyes darting back and forth, wondering whether George could be trusted.

George seemed bent on telling the owner his shortcomings, rather than exploiting his strengths. The mechanic appeared gruff, with a three-day-old beard and the smell of beer. George wondered if the owner's shirt was red or brown. It was speckled with just about every fluid known to car and man. As the owner showed George around, he carried an almost empty can of peas that he used to spit into. Apparently the owner (whose name was Steve, not Wilbur) ran the last employee, "some kid too full of himself," out on his ear. The surly owner found out that the young man had been spending time working on his own car rather than the garage full of vehicles waiting to be serviced. George knew the pay would be next to nothing and that only seemed to exacerbate George's inability to put on a positive front. The owner could tell that George wasn't serious.

The owner dismissed him with a "thanks for stopping by and good luck...." George left the dirty garage dejected. George's first thought was to go home and shower.

He felt he had a talent for understanding things mechanical, but had never applied himself to picking up a wrench at home for an ambitious project. He maintained his own car, fixed things around the house, but he never tried restoring a car or building something from scratch. He was more the kind of person who would analyze what was already there, figure out what was wrong, and set to the task of fixing it. And, though he was upset at not being offered the job at the garage, he was in some way glad that it didn't transpire. He would have been miserable there and he would have taken time, way too much time, to try and clean the place up. The owner would, of course, dock his pay for not working on the cars.

As George got out of the car, he heard the phone ringing in the house. Under normal circumstances he would let the machine pick up the call, but these were not normal circumstances. Without even closing the car door, he raced through the garage to the kitchen, counting the number of rings. He had one ring to go before the machine picked up.

He snatched the phone from its housing and clicked the button.

"He...hello?" said George breathlessly.

"Hello, George?"

"Yes this is Geor...."

Before he could get his name out, the answering machine took over.

"Hello, you have reached the Forder residence... we..."

Raising his voice over the recorded message, George blurted, "Hold on a sec, I need to turn off the answering machine." As George neared the controls for the answering machine, he got the receiver too close to the answering machine and the whole system started a squealing feedback.

"Just a sec, just a sec..." said George over the chaos.

Then all was silent and George hoped that whoever was on the line wasn't calling for a phone interview. George paused to see if the other person had hung up.

"George? George? Is this George Forder?"

"Yes."

"Well, if it ain't a blast from the past! How are you doing? This is Jim Dalburth! I heard you were trying to get in touch with me!"

"Hey! I was wondering if you or Craig would call. I saw your article in *Industrial Spotlight* and was impressed. How are you doing?"

"Aw hell George, if life got any better, I think I'd bust. How about yourself? You still working for WhatTheFuck – I mean Watsitumi?" Jim laughed at his own joke. George knew that this was not the first time he had made that slip of the tongue.

"I was until a few days ago. They let me go."

"What?! You're a good man! Are they outsourcing everything to Taiwan or one of the other child labor whores over seas? What were you doing there?"

"Well, I was working in the complaint department."

"I thought you did marketing."

"They shuffled me around a couple of times. I think I became something of a boat anchor there. Finally they tossed me aside."

"How's your boy? God, last time I saw him, he was all into sports."

"He is in college now. Can you believe it?" George was impressed that Jim could remember Daniel and cared enough to ask.

Jim lowered his voice. "We're all gettin' old. But I found ways to get around that. Or at least forget about it. Drinking helps you know."

George chuckled, not knowing if that was another joke or advice. "I wanted to get in touch with you because..."

Jim interrupted. "Hey, you're recently outta work. You need a job. You read the article. Hey – that article was a piece of shit wasn't it? I mean I feel like we pulled the trigger too soon. I keep telling Craig to keep things under wraps... Oh well... sorry ... you were saying..."

"You pretty much hit the nail on the head. I'm out of work. We had some good times together. I felt like I did good work for you guys and wanted another opportunity."

There was an awkward moment of silence on the other line. Then Jim said, "George, I'll tell ya. It's big. Real big. We are about to do something amazing. I could hire a bunch of people that call themselves experts, but I have no idea if they can blow their nose or wipe their ass. I trust you. We did have some good times together and I'm willing to give you a chance. Things aren't happening right away. As you know, good things take time, but I'd like to talk to you about the project."

George could feel the blood pulsing through his veins, exceeding his internal speed limit. This is what he had been waiting for. He wondered about the timeframe. But if there was any chance that he could work again and build the company like he had with *Run-Rite*, then he was in.

"Terrific!" George exclaimed. "As you know my schedule is free. Where are you?"

"Well I think it best if you come see me. I'll set up a reservation for you down here. There's a place to stay within walking distance of my home. I'm in Key Largo, where the fish are big and girls are pretty —not the other way around. Say next week?"

Normally George liked to check with Alicia about any scheduling, but this was the opportunity he had been waiting for. He didn't want to put off lengthening his time without a paycheck any longer than he had to. The longer he waited, the more dire his circumstances.

"Sure... yes. That would be great!"

"Good, I'll set you up at the 'Marina Del Mar.' It is a few blocks from my house. Monday okay?"

"Yes. This is wonderful. I really appreciate the opportunity."

The two exchanged cell phone numbers, home addresses and concluded with some idle chit chat. But, through the whole conversation, George seemed to begin to glow. He was headed toward restoring the torn fabric of his life. Soon he might be able to say he worked for – well he didn't exactly know the name of the new company, or what they did. But, it was an American company. He was American. This would be as much his company as Craig and Jim's.

Alicia had put some meat in the crock pot. The smell permeated the kitchen. Having completed this call, things started returning to him – like hunger. Alicia told him to make the potatoes. She assumed he would get the potato flakes out of the pantry. However, George got the potatoes from the bin and stuck them in the oven.

George didn't know that baked potatoes took so long to cook. It was well after dark before Alicia and he were able to sit down and discuss the day. George tried to hold back his excitement, but Alicia read him right away.

"You got the call. I know you got the call." They hugged.

George beamed, "Yep. There is only one thing. I have to be in Key Largo on Monday."

"Key Largo? You're going to Key Largo? That sounds like a pretty big commute!" She smiled, "I guess you're going to write this off as a business trip. How long are you going to be down there?"

"He didn't really specify how long I would be there. I guess it will be a couple of days because he's putting me up at this place. Did you want to go?"

"No," Alicia replied reluctantly. "You go. I still have some time to put in at the school, and I'm going to start putting out some feelers about jobs in the area. I saw a sign at the grocery store. Maybe I could work the cash register. At least that would help."

"We haven't been on vacation in quite a while. We may not be able to get away once I start working. This might be our last chance. We haven't seen palm trees since – I can't even remember." George put his arm around her and squeezed.

"I know, but this isn't vacation. The last thing I want to do is go to some place only to find myself sitting alone in some hotel room. You go and I'll stay here and man the fort. I don't want to be a distraction."

"You are never a distraction."

Alicia blinked her eyes in a flirtatious manner. "Never a distraction? I hoped that at least sometime I could distract you." They both chuckled. Alicia thought about what she might hear on George's return. Curious to know more, she inquired, "So what is this project? What are these guys up to?"

George paused. "You know, I still do not know what is going on. He wouldn't talk to me until I signed a non-disclosure statement. I guess things have to be kinda hush-hush. As soon as I know something I'll clue you in."

"I hope they don't screw you over. You know, they could have treated you a little better at *Run-Rite*." She moved away from him and checked the potatoes. They were ready. She got the pot-holder and put the potatoes into a bowl, which she moved over to the kitchen table. George unplugged the crock-pot and put it there, too. They served up their meals. Apparently both had regained their appetite.

"Don't blame them. They were on their way out. They cashed in on their hard work. I guess they started getting restless and needed to apply themselves. From the looks of things they have been living the good life for a while. Maybe they realized they were getting soft. Maybe they needed a challenge. I just hope that I can help."

Alicia put two dollops of sour cream on her baked potato and twirled it into the deeper crevasses. She blew on a spoonful of the potato but didn't put it in her mouth. Pointing the white mound toward George, she pondered, "You think they're going back to building engines? If they do, what do you think your role would be?"

"I have been rolling that around in my head all day. I'm not sure about marketing anymore. When I was younger, it was a lot easier. If I had my choice, I would like to be out on the floor somewhere. Maybe I would work in the quality assurance department. Maybe I would be a project manager or something like that. What do you think?"

She smiled, "I think you could do anything you put your mind to." She paused, put down the spoon, and put her hand on his head, slowly moving it from his ear to the back of his head. "I've been worried about you. I was afraid you were going to settle for the first thing that came along. Don't sell yourself short – not to these guys or anyone else who comes along. I don't know if this is going to pan out, but I have already seen a change in you."

After dinner they did the dishes and then broke from their routine. The TV stayed off. They went upstairs and made love. There was a spark of joy that seemed to brighten the entire house. It kindled a fire that permeated the dark dusty corners of their banality. The love making was slow; each intensely aware of the other. Each was present in the moment – a shared place where they bonded in ways beyond the physical. It was an intimacy they hadn't experienced in years. They touched each other and explored each other as if they were young lovers. George held Alicia tightly and she relished the feeling of being entirely enveloped by him.

As they reclined in a state of semi-sleep, having shared that space where two become one, George looked into Alicia's eyes and said, "I love you." He had said those words before. In fact, it was a rule of his to say these words to her every day. But today, its wellspring came from deep within. From the special, guarded treasure in his soul he uttered those words. From a place that had been nearly abandoned, those words resonated from his core.

Alicia felt the depth of his love expressed in these words. A tear rolled down her cheek and she brushed it away, hoping that George would not misconstrue its source. In the midst of their crisis, she felt a resurrection of their spiritual union. She responded, "I love you, too." She couldn't have held the words back if she wanted to. George smiled with fuzzy warmth knowing that things would be all right. They both drifted off into a deep contented sleep that night.

The next day, they slept in. They shared getting a breakfast prepared, George manning the toaster and Alicia working on the eggs. As they sat at the table, the two discussed transportation arrangements to Key Largo. The expense of a flight to Miami and the cost of a rental car made them nervous. So, they decided that George would drive down. It was a long trek, but he could break it up with a nap, and perhaps stop somewhere for the night if he became too tired.

George liked this idea, not only because of the cost savings, but also because he dreaded the idea of just sitting idly in an airplane for hours as he rolled around all of the "what if" scenarios. Driving would give George something to do. He was getting fidgety around the house. Alicia was glad to help him pack and head out Sunday morning on his journey. The twenty hour drive was going to take its toll and George wanted to get underway as early as possible.

That evening they both decided to go to church. They hadn't gone to church in years. There was a special Saturday night "Contemporary Worship" at "First United Methodist Church."

The two had gone to a contemporary worship service back in the eighties and wondered how things had changed in the intervening years.

George pondered the church name. He wondered whether this was really the *First* United Methodist Church and what gave someone the right to give it that name. Was this the first place that John Wesley set down stakes? Didn't it all start because Wesley decided to forbid his girlfriend communion because she "wasn't that into him?" George's theological foundation was shaky and the only reason he chose to go with Alicia to church was to thank someone – anyone – for the opportunity that rose from his crisis.

They entered the church which looked like it hadn't had a facelift in a long time. It had a strained look, as if the church itself was saying, "C'mon people, we want you to come to the church more than two times a year."

The two sat three quarters of the way back in the pews. They fidgeted, feeling out of place, as if this was a mistake. Others took their seats and no one seemed to offer a hand or a gesture of friendship. For a contemporary worship service there were few contemporary people in attendance. Most of the congregants were white-haired or bald. The few children who came were immersed in hand-held video games or cell phone texting.

The band emerged with the pastor. George wasn't certain, but he believed the old man with the guitar in hand was the same person he saw performing back in the 80s. He started into a song that had the earmarks of a simplified James Taylor tune. The three chords repeated, ad nauseum, with a tempo that was way too slow.

George expected a contemporary service to be, well, contemporary. He thought the music would resemble and reflect the music of the day. In true church fashion, "contemporary" took on the look and feel of music thirty-years or more out of date.

The congregation clapped, as they must have done for years, and perfected when to start and stop with military precision. After too many songs and a forced "hey isn't this great" comment from the group leader, the pastor took the stand.

He read from Hebrews about running the race with perseverance. George's ears perked up and he could feel Alicia squeeze his hand, as though some divine

49

providence had picked out the scripture just for their circumstances. Perhaps God had hear their plea and taken notice. Perhaps this scripture was God's way of saying, "I am with you." The two glanced at each other and smiled.

The pastor cleared his throat.

"This passage speaks to our circumstances today. We live in a competitive world. It is 'dog eat dog' out there. But I am here to tell you that we are not created by God to try and beat each other in this race."

George's spirits were elevated by the opening remark.

"In fact, the only thing we need to beat is ourselves. I don't know about you, but I find, with age, I beat myself more and more."

The teenagers in the rows ahead of George looked up and snickered. Their parents "shushed" them, and they fervently went to town on their cell phones while they giggled.

The sermon went downhill from there. It wasn't a sermon. The pastor was both subliminally and overtly doing a personality dump. He was bemoaning his existence as a pastor and letting everyone know that he held the position only because Christ suffered on the cross , so he had to suffer too.

George and Alicia quietly snuck out before the pastor broke down into tears. They left embarrassed that they had walked through the doors in the first place.

ॐ ॐ ॐ

George only had one suitcase and it was not completely filled. He had his suit in a separate zip-up bag so it wouldn't get wrinkled. As George was loading the trunk of his Toyota Corolla, he thought, once again, about the decals on the back of his rear window. In fact, every time he was in view of his rear window he struggled with the decals on the windshield. George purchased the car used. It was a silver Corolla that seemed in pretty good shape for the miles that were on the odometer. When he bought the car used, he noticed, by the presence of the two decals, that the previous owner must have had a son and daughter. On the left side of the rear window was a caricature of a football player with the name of the high school displayed below. The cartoon character was holding a football and was headed toward the right side of the window. On the right side was a cheerleader in mid jump, with her legs spread and her pom-pom filled hands held high. However, the owner had applied the cheerleader decal at the same level as the football player. So, for George, it looked like this well protected football player was headed straight between the legs of the waiting cheerleader. It always made him uncomfortable. The sexual overtones were unmistakable and he wondered as he sat at every traffic stop, whether the people in the car behind him were thinking the same thing. He had thought about scraping off the decals, but wondered how much more perverse the scene would become if he couldn't remove all parts of each decal. He ruminated on the idea of an armless helmeted figure heading for a headless set of spread legs. So, once again, he dismissed the idea, left the decals alone, and hoped that no one would notice.

The trek down I-95 was one that George didn't relish. He began his trip filled with the energy and enthusiasm of reaching the goal. After a few hours, George settled in to the routine of driving. He listened to the radio to help keep from over thinking what was to come. The Eagles' *Hotel California* was followed by Peter Gabriel's *Shock the Monkey.* George hadn't heard those songs in a while, so they were refreshing. When he commuted to work, he listened to news radio. This was a delightful change. He had driven these roads along the northern part of his trek before, when they took quick family weekends to Maryland or Virginia, but had never attempted such a long drive south. George noticed that it didn't matter what time of day or night he arrived at this particular spot, there was always a traffic jam around Washington, DC. Perhaps this was where a convention of old people, who drive twenty miles an hour, stream to and from their hotel. After an eternity of brake and go, the accumulation the cars vaporized and the pace picked up. As the sky scrapers disappeared behind him, George entered the stretch of road that became hopelessly monotonous. On a short trip from one state to the next, George could handle the boredom of an hour long crossing with nothing interesting to see. But this was different. The road was the same for hours. Its hypnotic effect slowly infected George with fatigue and he had to play mind games to stay alert. George calculated the average distance from one Cracker Barrel to another at approximately one hundred thirty-five miles. Exxon stations were at around seventy. McDonalds were a mere thirty miles apart.

For a while George reminisced about his relationship with Alicia. He considered himself a lucky man. She was, in his opinion, way out of his league. They met in college. At the time, it seemed the right and natural progression to go from high school into college and then on to a well-paying career. He opted for a local college, knowing that his SAT scores would forbid him from attending a more prestigious place of higher learning, and that was quite alright with him. He really hadn't thought about *the future*. His parents wanted him to consider his future when he was in high school, but he chose to ignore their advice. He was quite happy with going along with the crowd and never really focused on anything that resembled a career path.

After a summer out of high school, no job, and no prospects, he eventually decided on a business degree.

He felt it would give him the widest possible opportunity to enter the career field when most of his friends were either joining the military, getting arrested for petty crimes, or becoming computer geeks.

He struggled his first year in college. George's largest failing was that he couldn't concentrate when reading. He enjoyed his fellow students, the parties, and a new group of friends with common interests and classes. The community was new and he wanted to be a part of everything. But, this desire to be part of the crowd sowed the seeds of his distraction. He would spend his day in classes, then most of his remaining time traveling the hallways of the dorm "catching up" with his friends. He opted to open a book only after eating and making a second set of social rounds. If he had eyes on his chest he may have had better luck reading, for this is where the book ended up after a few paragraphs of half-hearted concentration.

But it was a chance foray into the library that changed his life. He was looking for a book by someone named "Maslow" and, deciding to forgo the library card system which never made much sense to him, opted instead for a row of the library that started with the letter "M." After a frustrating fifteen minutes, deciding the library had no clue how to properly arrange books, he came upon a section which seemed to follow some sort of author-alphabetical order. Though he never found "Maslow" (in the fiction section of the library), he did find a beautiful brunette sitting in an overstuffed chair at the far end of the aisle. He considered himself well-known in school, and possessing a keen eye for women, he knew he had never seen her around campus before. George was sure that he would have remembered such beauty. She was in a white sweater, blue- jeans and brown leather boots. She angled herself in the chair in such a way that one leg dangled over the arm rest, while the other was curled beneath her. He wondered how that position could be comfortable, but she seemed totally immersed in her book and not about to move any time soon.

As he neared her, he noticed she was crying. She had a book in her hands, *For Whom the Bell Tolls* and as he walked, within what he would consider the "fight or flight" area (that was one thing he remembered from one of his classes, though he was not sure which one), she didn't even recognize his existence. He ambled to the edge of the bookshelf, pretending he had found his "Maslow" section. To further his point, he pointed to the books as though in search of the book of some great probing expedition he had been on for days. She still didn't recognize him, so he reached for the topmost book and with a feigned, 'oops' – dropped the book onto the floor. He bent over to pick it up and said, "clumsy me" hoping to engage in some idle chit-chat. Alicia, totally immersed in the text, didn't even register the noisy disruption.

He gave up, but not before noting the time of day on his watch. He would return, hoping she would be in a more present state of mind, in the future. He returned on many occasions, but she was never there. He asked around, but no one seemed to know who she was. With each passing week, his grades suffered. He spent more and more time in the library, searching for this vision in the white sweater. He wondered if she had been a figment of his imagination. He was restless and depressed.

Toward the end of the year, having barely scraped by with his grades intact, he saw this young, vibrant girl walking alone, along the quad, heading for the library. He ran, trying to stay out of sight. He didn't want to scare her. He slowed to an awkward looking fast walk, not unlike the strange walking competition in the summer Olympics, until he was within speaking range.

"Hey, don't I know you?" George asked.

Alicia seemed a little startled and a tad nervous. "Umm, I don't think so."

"I saw you in the library."

"Umm, sorry." She quickened her step, but George would not give up.

"Yeah, a few months back you were in the library, wearing a white sweater, reading..." George couldn't think of the book.

Then her eyes went wide. "Oh yeah, I was in the library. That was a long time ago. I was doing a paper on Hemingway."

"For what class?" asked George.

Alicia blushed. She hesitated, not wanting to respond. "For my English class."

She paused, looked down, and then gazed up at George with a look that made George's heart beat a little faster. "I'm a senior in high school, but I come here because the library is better."

George stopped short. There was only a year or so between them in age, but there was a social vastness that separated them. There was a social wall that seemed to go up. George was not supposed to date "high schoolers." Such a thing would bring him down a few notches in the college evolutionary scale. But she was so beautiful.

She thought he was handsome. He had a charm about him. When he smiled at her, she could feel that he wanted to be there with her. She returned the smile. George let out a sigh. He forgot that he had run to catch up with her and wasn't sure if he was sweating because of the exercise, or her radiant beauty. In the library, he hadn't noticed her dark hair which lay in gentle curves off of her neck.

She was not only thinking about this boy and their shared infatuation. She had already started dreaming about dating him. Dating a college man, for her, would put her in the upper echelons of Middletown High School. It was spring and she was planning on attending this college, but if she could get him to take her to the end-of-the-year dance, she would cause a stir.

Alicia decided to go out with George. They did date, and Alicia did attend his college. George dropped out midway through his second year. His grades were abysmal and he longed to set up a home for the two of them. He seemed to carry more desire to settle down than she did. She was quite content living in her world of American literature and got excellent grades, graduating in three and a half years.

She had thought of becoming a teacher, but things were put on hold because, soon after graduating, she became pregnant. Though unplanned, it was not unwelcomed and they both settled into the classic American family.

George relished those earlier years where they struggled, but always found ample time for fun. Yet, somewhere along the line, passion and the thrill of building a life together had drained away. Complacency led to banality and ended up in mindless repetition. Being fired, like being startled awake, jarred him to his senses. He was aware, not only of the financial crisis, but the thought that he'd taken his wife for granted.

Though his current world was a mess, he was staring at one chance to redeem himself in her eyes. George knew it was worth it. On this endless patch of highway, he started thinking how he might treat her better upon his return.

As the sun set, George started doing stupid things to try and stay focused while the car droned down this endless road. He pinched his ear so the pain would keep him awake. He counted the number of brake lights ahead of him. At one point he nodded, just for a second. The fear-based adrenaline generated as his neck snapped back to the alert position flooded him with enough energy to keep him going until the next rest stop.

The drivers who congregated along this highway each had their own driving style. Some drove like they were in a funeral procession, while others thought they were racing on the autobahn. Some drivers were so in tune with their car that they could wedge themselves between cars in a passing frenzy so close that you couldn't squeeze a fart between them.

For a while George felt as though he was in a video game. He reminisced about one of the first arcade games he ever played, predating the video era. An illustration of a red race car was stamped on a translucent film. Behind the car, an image of a road going by was projected. Other translucent cars would bang into his. It was a frustrating game, but he sunk many quarters in the machine until the arcade industry came out with such grand entertainment as Asteroids, Black Knight Pinball and Lunar Lander.

George was starting to feel depressed, resulting from a diet of junk food and lack of sleep. He knew that the lethargy was winning, until he entered a part of Georgia where he noticed that an exit ramp was lined with palm trees lit by the argon lamps spotlighting each one. Palm trees always made him feel better. He wasn't sure why. When a palm tree showed up on his calendar at work, he knew it would be a good month. He and Alicia had spent their honeymoon in the Cayman Islands. He loved looking at the palm trees. He noticed that there were different varieties. Some were bush-like, while others reached high in the sky before unfurling their light green canopy. He hoped that he could enjoy some of the scenery of Key Largo when he arrived.

Another technique he used to stay awake was engaging in mock conversations with Jim Dalburth. He pretended to make small talk.

"Why of course, I'd love to have another one. So do you think there will be many hurricanes this year?"

"I think it will be generations before the gulf is cleaned up. But I believe in a firm political policy that supports jobs over the environment…. Of course it is all important, but we have to invest in people…I will support a candidate who favors small business deregulation, and tax incentives…."

"A bonus check? But I have just been hired!"

George had become delirious by the time he reached Key Largo. The sun was well over the horizon, heralding a Florida-hot morning and marking a twenty-four hour day spent in the suspended reality of travel. Those few hours when he napped at rest stops provided no real recovery, just a way to fend off the danger of trying to drive with your eyes closed.

He didn't really see Key Largo. It just sort of appeared with the first few mom and pop shops. He missed his turn for the Marina Del Mar. There was a huge dive shop where he was supposed to turn, but his reaction time was slow and he had to do a U-turn and double back. Key Largo claimed to be the "dive capital of the world." For a moment George wondered how many "dive capitals of the world" there actually were. He wondered, "What were the qualifications to be the 'dive capital of the world?'" Was there a U.N. council where all of the "dive capitals of the world" gathered together to squabble about their claim to the title? Did they hold their summit underwater? If Key Largo was the "dive capital of the world" then the large dive shop, with its red flag with diagonal white stripe blowing in the morning breeze, must surely be its capital building.

George thought he had made yet another wrong turn because the road leading back to the Marina Del Mar looked like it was going through a residential area. There was a park on one side where children happily swung from monkey bars or kicked a soccer ball. He was about to turn around, but at the end of the road two large yellow structures appeared nestled close to the canal. The hotel was bookended by a restaurant called "Coconuts" and a dive center called "Ocean Divers."

Coconuts was a bar and restaurant run by the Marina Del Mar. It bore the overpricing of a hotel-run libation factory, but the food was good and the fish was fresh. The chef could simply walk out the door and drop a line into the canal which ran along the backside of the hotel, if necessary. The cloth rooftop showed signs of age; the dark red rich tint had faded to a light, but not pink, coloring. And, it had a few spots where it had been torn by tropical storms.

There was both an inside and outside portion of the restaurant. There were two bars; one inside and the other outside. The exterior bar was larger. Wisely, the owners knew more people would be spending their hours lounging outside, watching the boats on the canal, and feeling the fresh tropical breeze.

Boats were moored along the back side of the hotel which faced the restaraunt. The boats ranged from lean sailboats to pregnant catamarans. Motor sailors occasionally fired up their diesel engines, sending a cloud of putrid smoke to the group of people gathered around white plastic tables and chairs that lined the edge of the canal.

George entered the lobby. There was a gathering of people in line for the free continental breakfast. He noticed the obligatory coffee machine and juice dispenser. However, this place was not very creative with the rest of the fare: cereal, toast, muffins, cinnamon rolls and pastries. The carb overload made his stomach feel ten pounds heavier. A young man stood in line wearing a Nike shirt with the sleeves cut out and sun glasses that looked way too expensive. When he got close enough he grabbed the entire tray of cinnamon rolls and dumped them into a plastic bag. He turned, headed out the door and loaded the rolls and his SCUBA gear into a waiting SUV. "He won't be able to float with all of that in his belly," thought George.

George, weary from the journey to the point of losing all common sense, got his key and headed to the room, not bothering to fetch his suitcase. He needed sleep and he needed it now. In a few hours he would be paling around with Jim Dalburth and he wanted to bring his "A" game.

He passed the first of two buildings, heading for his room 127 on the first floor. Actually, from his vantage point, the room was on the second floor. However, in Key Largo, where everything is built at sea level, the "real" first floor is left for garage space, human resources and other expendable space that could be washed away during a deluge. The "Key Largo" first floor was up a flight of steps.

Before ascending the stairs, he could see that "Ocean Divers" – the Scuba shop and dive center on the far side of the building complex - was already bustling with divers scrambling to get rental gear sized up. A palm tree half covered the large wooden sign for the building. George pondered the large hammerhead shark the company used for its logo.

"I would think that a shark would be a bad idea to promote diving," George ruminated. However, he figured these were the kind of people who wanted to jump into a pool of sharks, bungee jump off a bridge, skydive, or eat an entire tray of cinnamon rolls before jumping off the back end of a boat.

After a quick scan of the room, George called Alicia to let her know he arrived safely. He closed the hurricane shutters to restrict the light streaming in from the already hot morning and grabbed a nap before his upcoming adventure.

4

He slept all morning and part of the afternoon. The air conditioner betrayed the incredible heat and humidity outside. A shower passed through the area unnoticed by George. The morning sunshine turned to midnight in an instant and pelted Key Largo with rain droplets the size of God-spit. George didn't hear any sound of the water as it fell in undulating sheets. His snores mingled in a dissonant duet with the rolling thunder. As soon as it had begun, the downpour turned to a light mist, which did nothing to relieve the sweltering tropical atmosphere. A rainbow appeared off-shore as the black cloud drifted out to sea. The aftermath, however, left its evidence in huge pools along the roadside. George was startled by how late he slept. It was four o'clock.

He called Jim to let him know that he was in Key Largo.

"George! I'm glad you made it okay. Did you have any trouble getting down here?"

"No, I made it without a hitch."

"Wonderful! How 'bout I pick you up, we do a little sight-seeing, and then have dinner. Does that sound okay?"

"Sure! I look forward to seeing you. I'd love to catch up, talk about old times..."

Jim interrupted, "... and get back to work, eh?"

George chuckled, "Yeah, and get back to work."

"Good, I'll see you in an hour."
"Perfect," replied George.

ও ও ও

George was waiting in the parking lot as a large black Hummer came rolling in. It glistened with shiny chrome and a paint job that reflected the surrounding landscape. It looked recently washed and polished. For some reason, the truck reminded him of the sheen of Mr. Ishiri's shoes. The vehicle artfully avoided the larger pools of water that had collected in the netherworld between parking lot and road. He wasn't sure if it was Jim, but as it neared, the horn blared. Except it wasn't really a horn but a loud obnoxious rendition of "Who Let the Dogs Out." The black behemoth stopped and the dark tinted driver's window rolled down with a whirr. Jim was behind the wheel wearing sunglasses and a Hawaiian shirt.

"Hey George! Damn, it is good to see you! Hop in!" Before George could reply, the window started closing.

George rounded the large beast of a vehicle and could feel it radiating a nuclear heat from the engine. George wondered how far Jim had to drive to get to the Marina Del Mar. The increased temperature rippled off the grill consuming breathable air. He had to step up into the vehicle. In contrast to the outside oven temperature, the AC inside was blowing arctic cool air at a temperature just less than a winter gale.

Jim Dalburth used to be a silver haired inventor, working in his garage, wearing a red flannel shirt. The Jim Dalburth that greeted George in the Hummer bore little resemblance to the man George had once known. He had doubled in size, lost most of his hair, and looked like dough that had risen on a warm afternoon. Jim held out a large hand with stubby fingers. George shook his hand. There were no calluses on what used to be the rough hands of a factory worker.

"It is good to see you again," said George.

"Boy, you bring back a lot of memories, George. You look good. Hell, we are all getting old, aren't we?"

"Yeah, I suppose we are."

The cab of the Hummer had a sickly sweet smell to it. George couldn't tell if it was air freshener, Jim's aftershave, the smell of alcohol, or some combination of the three.

"Lemme show you around," Jim said, as he spun the Hummer out of the parking lot, sending a shower of spray from the small lakes that lay around the edge of the road.

Jim headed north on Highway One. He must have assumed that because his vehicle was larger, black, and traveling way over the speed limit, he had the right of way whether signs, lights, or screaming bicyclists indicated differently. Jim treated driving as ancillary to other tasks such as fixing George's seat, demonstrating the heated butt options, or bragging about the display panel on the dashboard.

Jim careened off the highway, with a spray of gravel and barreled into John Pennekamp Coral Reef State Park.

George hadn't noticed the park on his late-night arrival into Key Largo. He didn't notice much during the last 300 miles of his trek, except that his eyelids were staging a sit-down strike. The park was invisible behind the trees. George was surprised by the length of road leading to the ranger's welcome station. Mangroves and other trees intertwined in a chaotic and dense forest. George had always assumed that the land was a small strip, not much wider than the highway they had just exited. This road indicated otherwise. The welcome area at the end of the lane looked much like those found up and down the East Coast. Even though the outside felt like an Amazonian rainforest, the park ranger at the station still wore long pants and boots. The dark haired ranger appeared oblivious to the sweltering weather as she reached up to the driver's side window to hand off a set of pamphlets to Jim.

The surrounding vegetation quickly cleared to a few well placed palm trees as they approached the main building, a large parking lot and water. It was a pleasant park with a playground and snorkel areas. George saw that the site was well planned, with large maps indicating sites of interest as Jim momentarily slowed for a small red car with three sea kayaks bungeed to its top. George noticed an old couple kayaking around the mangroves that grew in abundance across the water's edge. Even though it was late in the day, there was still activity as far as the eye could see. To his right, George saw what appeared to be fishing boats docked near a building. A group of passengers had spent the day on the water. Many of them appeared quite red from an inadequate application of sun-screen. A little further along George spotted a rack of kayaks, like the one the old couple had been using. A young man, in full park ranger regalia, sat in the heat on a picnic table, next to the rack.

"George, this park was started by a newspaper editor back in the sixties. If you head out and snorkel in the water over there, you'll find the remains of an old ship wreck. Cannons litter the sandy area where all those people are," instructed Jim, pointing to a spot quite close to land. "They call this the coral park, but you have to really take a boat or something to see anything like coral. Most of this is sea grass and muck. But a lot of people come out here to play."

The parking lot was emptying out, as people, some with strawberry tans, headed back to their cars looking for a meal after a day at the park.

Jim continued, "During the day this place is packed. That building there is the hub of this place. They have a couple of aquariums, some interactive displays, and a visitor center manned by the rangers."

Jim didn't slow down. George had to absorb the view quickly because Jim was racing through the park.

"This is what makes Key Largo. People come here to get into the water. Hell, my wife thinks she's a fish. She goes out on a boat just about every day."

Jim did a U-turn in a parking lot. He stopped the vehicle. There was a pier on the water and boats were moored, bobbing up and down. In the distance a boat was returning from a snorkeling excursion. A few people were sitting on the bow as the boat drifted perfectly into its awaiting slip.

"That is a glass bottom boat coming back. They head out twice a day and the park has three of them."

"Interesting," replied George, wondering where all of this was going.

"Key Largo is now dependent on tourism, especially diving and snorkeling and crap like that," Jim continued as he headed for the park exit.

"I know you've come here for a job, and I want to offer you something, but it is all about this place. The better you know it, the more you will understand."

"Yeah, I was upset that I was fired. I panicked at first, but now that I'm here, things seem to be better. I wasn't happy at Watsitumi."

"Those fuckheads," said Jim as he slapped his palm against the steering wheel. "They don't know a good thing when they have one. They took *Run-Rite* and turned it into Run-Wrong."

George chuckled. "You got that right. It is good to see you, though. I miss the old days."

"Well then, we will have to make some more!"

They went over a bridge toward the back edge of the park. From this vantage point George could grasp the size of the place.

"What you may not realize," Jim continued like a tour bus emcee, "is that the reserve extends way beyond what you see here. Out there, a few miles, you can sport fish, but within the limits it's all for the public to enjoy. Because they set up fishing restrictions, there are all kinds of critters out there swimming around."

George noticed an incredible diversity of people. Most were dressed in the standard shorts and Hawaiian shirt, but not all. One woman looked like she was ready to head to a bridal shower. Some of the older men wore khaki long pants and a white shirt. The children ran around in bathing suits.

Jim spun the hummer around in the parking lot, surprising a young family. The mother in a one piece flowered bathing suit grabbed the little girl who had bent over to examine a small shell and wasn't paying attention to the maniac behind the black four-wheeled beast. Jim kept the tour going as he backtracked out of the park. George would have liked to walk around and absorb the vibe of the park. But Jim, scaring only a handful of pedestrians with his disregard for the difference between "roads" and "parking area," took the most efficient path through the mass of cars toward the exit.

Back out on the highway, Jim crossed two lanes and took a hard left. People heading south honked their horns. Jim paid them no regard.

They passed a few boarded up shanties. Many of the smaller shops had succumbed to the downturn in the economy. George was surprised that this place wasn't exploding with retail outlets, galleries, and mom and pop shops. For some unknown reason, the desire to make Key Largo the final destination for a vacation had waned over the years. People seemed to use Largo as a quick stop on their way to Key West. Key Largo seemed to live up to its name. "Largo" — a place where people slowed but didn't stop.

One aspect of the vacation scene, however, seemed to be thriving. The large black auto crossed lanes to a building with a large dive sign. The building was painted with fish and coral but the paint was chipped and faded. The previous owner had an adult video store, and the "other" painting behind the fish was a scantily clad woman. George looked at the building and was reminded of one of those childhood pictures that tricked your mind into seeing something that wasn't there. If you looked at the building directly, you couldn't make out the girl, but if you tilted your head just slightly and squinted, she started coming into focus.

Jim pulled into the lot as the Hummer kicked up a plume of dust from the gravel. Jim rolled out of the big vehicle like a tentative kid sliding down a hot slide on a summer day.

Successfully landing on terra-firma, Jim smiled and said, "This is my favorite place, for more reasons than one!" Jim raised his eyebrows over his sunglasses and the two of them headed into the dive shop.

The place was playing music way too loud, to the point that the speakers couldn't keep up, turning the music into a static frenzy that didn't seem to abate. Behind the counter were two young men with long hair and deep golden tans, seemingly oblivious to the cacophony of blurting and snorting music. They were incredibly muscular, but without the heft of musculature artificially created in a gym. The two could have been from California, Florida, or a thousand different beaches

68

where the waves were sweet and the curls awesome. They punctuated their discussion with the word "dude" and seemed oblivious to the customers who entered the store.

But their conversation didn't center on "catching the tube," but rather, "the guy came up with DCI and I took out his regulator and he spit blood all over me, dude, like something outta horror movies. I knew he was headed for the chamber. He had set his dive computer to nitrox thirty-two but was only sucking the standard twenty-one. Those things should have reset, so I don't know what planet he thought he was from… "

Jim tugged at George's shirt and led him away from the two who babbled on, speaking with a lingo that defied George's comprehension. There were racks of tubes, things with dials, suits that looked like astronaut underwear, flippers of all size, shape and color, and masks. George looked at the price tags on all of this stuff and took a hard swallow.

"A hundred-fifty bucks for a scuba mask? I saw one at Wal-Mart for ten," said George. "You have to be rich to do this!"

"Yeah, but people do it. They do it all the time. On the weekend, the Marina Del Mar is packed with divers. And from what I hear, that Wal-Mart mask won't do when you dive."

Toward the back of the shop was a young woman pushing a broom. She had jet black hair that looked like the wind had just reshaped it into a perfect tousle on her head. She too was tanned, unlike many of her white skinned counterparts who lived in the North, where snow, sweaters and shelter were necessities. She must have been in her late twenties, but could have been younger. She didn't notice Jim and George approaching. Her head was bobbing to the chaos coming over the speakers as she swept. A beautiful silver necklace danced around her neck in the opposite direction to her gyrations. George could understand why Jim wanted to come here. This young woman was dressed in incredibly short shorts and a translucent white top, which barely hid the perfectly formed breasts and firm frame that made men go stupid.

Jim put his hand on George's shoulder and squeezed a little too hard. As he did this, the girl emerged from her music induced transcendental state.

"Buster!" yelled the girl, dropping the broom and running into Jim's arms. George couldn't remember exactly, but he didn't think Jim had any children. This was confirmed when they both kissed in a way that was definitely not familial. She had a hypnotic effect any man within her view, with power that radiated out from somewhere within and exuded a sexual cloud enveloping anyone in her midst. She seemed built for one purpose and Jim was the focus.

Jim broke from the hold, turned to George and said, "This is Trish. She's my..." Jim stumbled awkwardly. "Well, we are *really* good friends."

With that, Trish giggled and bit her lower lip in a way that indicated that "good friends" was not a proper description of their relationship. There seemed to be a real disconnect. George couldn't reconcile that these two had anything in common, could ever be seen as a couple, or find any mutual compatibility. It was like ketchup and ice cream. They worked well separately, but no one would combine the two. Trish was the epitome of youthful exuberance bundled in the ripe fruit of sexual desire. Jim, aka "Buster," was the poster child for American decadence wrapped up in the Pillsbury dough boy.

"Trish, this is an old friend of mine, George Forder."

Trish held out her hand. It was an extension of perfect skin, retaining all of the feminine qualities of young womanhood, but had the strength of one who didn't languish in some upstairs reading room or lounge around watching hours of television. Her grip was firm.

"It's nice to meet you." She gave a quick smirk that showed a set of perfect teeth. Had George not been married, and maybe had he been a few years younger, he would have melted like ice cream on a hot sidewalk. For an instant George wondered how many doctors had prescribed Viagra to Jim in order for him to keep up with such a female.

Just then another "song" came over the blaring speakers. Its energy seemed to cause Trish to go into a possessive fit. She jerked to its rhythm, not unlike a Pentecostal tirade.

"Oh Buster! This is the one I was telling you about. It is the greatest!"

She closed her eyes and her head started banging to the beat of the music. She stopped to see what kind of reaction Jim had. He forced a slight bobbing of the head, but would have been sent to the hospital with whiplash if he tried to imitate her.

"It's the latest from the *Taliban Monkey Elite*."

"Excuse me?" George blurted.

"The *Taliban Monkey Elite* – it's a band out of North Carolina. The lead singer is David Blade. He was in the band *We're Closed,* but left them after being inspired by some news report. This is my favorite song. It's called *Revenge*."

George paused, trying to make sense of what she just said. The music rant caused waves of disassociation with reality. He could barely make out the words.

Revenge, revenge it's you we will avenge.
You smashed them down, you think....

71

At that point the singing crumbled into something that resembled more animal glutteral noises rather than human vocal tones.

"So you listen to a band whose members belong to the Taliban?" George asked, interrupting the furious movement of this possessed goddess.

"No, silly," she responded with a giggle. "They are against the Taliban. Listen to this song."

"I'm trying," George said sarcastically.

"David Blade was watching the news and he heard this report about the Taliban training monkeys to kill American soldiers."

"What?!" George looked to Jim to see if he understood what she was saying. Jim just nodded, more interested in making carnal headway, overlooking any quirks that required conversation.

"Yeah," she continued."The Taliban show the monkeys pictures of American soldiers. They learn what they look like, and then they train the monkeys to use a gun. They send them out into the desert and the monkeys shoot the Americans. It's real. I saw it on a news report," she added to bring home the point.

"I never heard that" replied George, adding this to the list of Yeti, UFOs, and Santa sightings. (Did Trish still believe in Santa? She seemed young and naïve enough).

"So David Blade left his old band, *We're Closed*, and started this one. It is a patriotic band that sings all these upbeat songs about how we are going to destroy the Taliban and stuff."

George remembered being that age, living in a Baltimore apartment. He shared it with two other guys. Between the three of them, they barely made ends meet. There was a band out of Frederick, Maryland called *The Skeptics*. Wherever they happened to play, George was there. Their music had as much energy and was as zany

72

as the *Taliban Monkey Elite*. He remembered the rhythm guitar player rolling up a page from the Washington Post, sticking it out of his zipper like a political penis, and setting it on fire as he played. Their claim to fame was an album they put out that got a little notoriety overseas. The radio played their hit *The Ghost of Abraham Lincoln.* George was brought back to reality as the song *Revenge* faded with a drum and bass car-wreck.

"Buster, what did you think?" she asked.

"It was my fave," Jim responded.

"*Fave?*" thought George. The word echoed from some deep place from the past, when Mr. Brady was talking to Jan about being a cool dad. Trish didn't seem to notice. She was happy he accepted the music. She nestled closer to him giving him a hug. The two were connected in a way that would make anyone, young or old, feel uncomfortable.

"He's so cute. You know, he bought me this necklace." She lifted it off of her chest. For a moment, George could see one of her breasts. There was something intoxicating about her. George wondered which of these two was playing the other. If Trish hung out with those two "diver dudes" at the counter, her life would be relegated to old cars and fast food. Jim could put her into a lifestyle of luxury no ordinary male her age could match. Jim reaped the physical reward of having a young wood nymph by his side. It certainly wasn't a match made in heaven. Beyond that, Jim was already married. In fact, he was on his second marriage.

"The necklace is beautiful." George replied.

"It was hand made by Indians who used to live in this area. They have moved to Miami." Jim winced a little. George smiled, knowing that the necklace was purchased in a mall somewhere.

Jim gave Trish a squeeze, "Yeah, she is a gem, and I try to treat my women well."

That statement made George cringe. George had been a faithful husband. That is not to say that he had not been tempted, but he enjoyed growing old with Alicia. They were both showing the signs of their age, but they relished the experiences and history they shared and invested in together. George remembered that Jim had divorced his first wife when he sold the company to Watsitumi. Perhaps the corrupting nature of success ultimately depleted Jim of dedication to his relationships. People, like Jim's first wife and George, were the fallout of success. George wondered how many others were left behind in the wake of Jim's success. He hadn't kept up with the others who help grow *Run-Rite*.

"Well, hon, we gotta go. I'm showing George around a little."

"It was nice meeting you," said Trish. She gave George a quick hug. She put her arm around Jim's neck and they kissed. She turned her eyes up and looked at Jim like a lonely puppy and asked, "When will I see you?"

"Soon, real soon." Jim responded with a more serious tone than any other time in the dive shop. There was some hidden intent in that statement which eluded George. "Let's go."

The two men headed back to the black Hummer. They drove south along Highway One and for a minute or two, no words passed between them. There was an awkward silence that neither was willing to cross. Finally Jim broke the barrier.

"Okay. So you may think that was wrong. But I think there is something between us. I really do. She is incredible. I mean, come on, a guy my age with someone like that? God, she just about kills me in bed, and... well, it seems perfect."

George found himself in an awkward position. If he told Jim what he really thought, there would be no chance of getting a position in this new business venture. But to acknowledge the relationship between Jim and Trish was not in George's fiber.

The best that George could muster was, "I guess you have to follow your heart."

"Exactly!" replied Jim, smacking the steering wheel. "God... you know, I wanted to show you everything, because unless you see it, you won't understand. We're guys, you know? We can't be chained down, caged up, and tossed aside like day old meat. We have to hunt! I forgot that for awhile. The good life spoiled me. I mean, look at me. I'm fat because the good life tried to destroy me. Not anymore – nope. I'm striking out with something brand spanking new."

Even in the frosty air conditioning, Jim was red-faced and sweating, like an overheated car that was on its way to a total meltdown. George wondered if that speech was for George's benefit, or a self pep talk.

"We get stripped of our manhood. Look at you." Jim turned and looked at George. George hoped he would turn back and face the road. "Watsi-fucking-tumi stripped you of your manhood. They fired your ass and sent you packing. What does that do to your manhood?"

At least at some visceral level, George agreed with this logic. He understood how big business slowly destroyed the internal fiber of self-dignity. He also knew he wanted to regain that quality.

Jim instinctively turned off to a bar called "Diver Down," which was located in a small line of shops. The barber, insurance, real-estate, and shell shop looked exactly the same.

Though the bar looked non-descript on the outside, inside the bar was adorned with antique diving gear and photos. There was something quaint about this place. It looked like it had been there for a while. There was a stale odor reminiscent of a time before 1970 when everyone smoked as they knocked back rum and cokes.

The walls had inhaled the community holding Pall-Malls and Salems, and were now slowly exhaling the decades of nicotine. Along one wall, two spear guns and an old mask were arranged in such a way as to look like a coat of arms. A long rubber hose snaked its way to the corner where it was connected to two tanks which seemed precariously perched over a booth. A few framed black and white pictures of Jacques Cousteau, with autographs, hung proudly behind the cash register. A man in a cowboy hat clutching a small glass was at the bar. A couple, trying not to be noticed, sat at a small table, eating fries and drinking a few beers.

The two new arrivals took a seat in a booth in the corner underneath an old wetsuit. The suit had some plastic attachments. George craned his neck backwards, looking at the odd fixtures on the suit. He couldn't figure out their purpose. The bartender came over to the table. He handed Jim a drink. Turning to George, he asked, "Whad'll ya have?"

"Um, I'll have a beer, you got Yeager?"

"Sure, coming right up." The bartender turned away.

"See? That's service. I don't even have to ask." Jim took a gulp of his drink. George could smell the alcohol from across the table. Jim put the drink down with a quenching, "Ahh, that's better."

The bartender returned with George's beer and a small bowl of pretzels.

"Not a lot of folks come around here anymore. I mean, you got the 'Key Largo' song and the whole Beach Boys thing. But Key Largo ain't what it used to be," Jim said.

George didn't know any history of Key Largo, so he had no comparison. Jim continued, "Most of the folks just use this as a stopping point on their way to Key West. Hell, go into any of the shops around here and half of the postcards are for Key West. It's as if Key Largo doesn't even exist."

Jim rolled the glass around the swiftly forming condensation which pooled on the table. "But then, Key West ain't what it used to be either."

"What do you mean?" asked George, tipping back his beer. It was cool and refreshing. George only drank on occasion, and even though they had been in the air conditioning, George was parched from the heat of the evening. The breeze, which seemed constant before, had stopped on their trek from the dive shop.

"Used to be that Key West was all head-shops and transvestites. It was an 'anything goes' kinda place. It was where the pirates lived. Now it is just a fucking tourist trap. Used to be that Key West had wild parties every night, and you could get pretty much whatever you wanted. But if you wanted to get laid, you had better check under the skirt first, if you know what I mean."

The bartender had anticipated Jim's need for a second drink and brought one as soon as the first one's ice cubes tinkled with no liquid to hold them in suspension.

"Now they're building hotels and setting up all the crap that goes along with it. In a few years it's going to be a country club."

"Is this part of your business idea?" George decided to push the issue. "Is this why I'm here?"

Jim put up a hand. "Not so fast. I want you to get to know this place first. There is more here than meets the eye. I got something planned for you tomorrow that will knock your socks off. But tonight, we celebrate. "Raising his fresh glass, Jim offered a toast. "To good times – old and new!"

George and Jim clinked glasses. In a gulp George drank the rest of his beer.

"Tommy – another one for George here!" Jim yelled at the bartender.

"That's okay, I'm fine."

"Nonsense – I know you are, but we are celebrating!" The bartender brought back another beer and another drink for Jim. George hadn't eaten in a while and could feel himself getting fuzzy. Watching the way Jim drank, George wondered whether Jim would be in any condition to drive.

"So, have you been in touch with Craig?"

George wondered whether the two *Run-Rite* owners had been working together on this project, or had kept in touch at all. All of the photos had the two of them together, but Jim hadn't mentioned Craig's name since he arrived.

"Craig is a dick," Jim responded, sucking down the third drink as quickly as the first. "He's keeping to himself pretty much. I don't understand it. He is a no good asshole who wants to stay fat and sloppy. He has moved to Tortola and just wants to sail."

George thought about that lifestyle and would probably side with Craig. He would love to spend his days sailing. He thought about Tortola, Virgin Gorda, and the nearby islands. While sitting in a cubicle, he would take a few moments between each call, look at the calendar on the wall and imagine himself, barefoot, walking hand-in-hand with Alicia as they strolled along together.

"I'm trying to get him involved in this project. He thought it was a good idea at first, but he's being a little chicken-shit about it now. I don't know why. He never could commit."

George thought about what transpired in the dive shop and considered how Jim could talk about commitment.

Jim continued, softening a little in that drunk, love you/hate you, emotional rollercoaster. "Craig is a good guy, but we have kinda gone our separate ways, you know? We had a good thing, but he didn't want to sell *Run-Rite* in the first place. I told him that he was nuts. When Watsitumi put the money out there and Craig didn't want to bite, I thought he had gone out of his mind. That was the beginning of the end for us. We get together occasionally, but that is mostly for interviews or photo shoots."

George could smell the alcohol exuding from Jim's pores. It was a similar smell to the cabin of the Hummer. He noticed that Jim had become a little redder around his cheeks. Jim ran his hand through some imaginary tuft of hair. He stared at his glass.

"But we did it – you know? We accomplished our dream. But that was both a blessing and a curse. Astronauts…"

George waited for Jim to finish that thought. But nothing came after that. Wondering if he had heard him right, George said, "Astronauts?"

"Yeah – astronauts. When I was a kid growing up, we always looked up to the astronauts as our heroes. The Apollo program pumped out astronaut heroes. I mean with a name like 'Buzz' Aldrin how could you not be a hero? But you know what?"

Jim paused for dramatic effect. He stuck his stubby finger in his glass and moved the ice.

"Most of those heroes turned into a bunch of alcoholic nobodies. After they shut down the moon program, what happened to the heroes? They had ticker tape parades and now they speak in elementary schools to a bunch of kids who have no idea who they are. They lost their edge. I guess I lost mine too."

There was a deep sadness in that last statement. Jim had been seduced by his own success and was paying the price for it. He was now lashing out, grasping for something tangible, fighting for something which would shock him back into that existence of adventure and fortune that he had when he was a young man. George wondered what kind of a man Jim would have been if he had not sold out to Watsitumi. Perhaps Craig suggested the right course, though it may not have netted them the fortune they now possess.

"Aw fuck," said Jim, snapping out of his pity. He belched and a plume of sickly sweet aroma surrounded the table. "We gotta pick up the missus. She should be getting back about now. We'll get her, head over to the house and then go out to eat. Sound good?" Jim looked at his watch and confirmed that he was probably late.

George took a hard swallow. He figured since he was hitting on Trish that Jim was either divorced or separated. Knowing now that he was still married to his second wife hinted at Jim's life as one of the reckless decay of success. However, George was playing the game to find work and he had to put up with Jim's peccadilloes in order to help save his family's future. Putting on the mask of the enthusiastic child, George played along.

"Sounds great to me. I'm getting hungry."

George stood up and felt the effects of the beer on his sense of balance. The two headed out. George didn't know where they were headed, but it appeared that Jim had changed his mind and was dropping George off back at the Marina Del Mar hotel before collecting his wife. He headed past the hotel and pulled into the "Ocean Divers" parking lot. The two got out and Jim continued his rant against his wife.

"We gotta get the queen bitch of the universe. She hates me, you know. But hell, isn't that the way it is with any marriage? She spends all her time out there so she doesn't have to be with me." Jim pointed, waving a finger in the general direction of the Atlantic Ocean.

"I don't know about you, but I think to myself – 'you stinking bitch, you ruined my life' – and then it comes out and all I can say is, 'pass the salt.'"

As they headed toward the dock, George could hear a guy with an Australian accent saying, "You can wash your gear in the fresh water in the tub over there. Thanks guys."

A stream of people, tanned and tired, carried loads of black gear toward the parking lot. They were energized by what they had seen and were talking about the day's dives. They were in their bathing suits, throwing their equipment in their trunks and hatchbacks. Those who had made reservations at the Marina Del Mar hoisted their equipment on their shoulder and headed along the dock toward the elevator.

There was a lot of activity on the dock. Gear was being piled up. Tanks were being carried from a boat to the air "filling station." There was a large tub of fresh water. Some were rinsing off their cameras and other dive equipment. As they approached, there were cute signs like "Divers do it deeper" and "No crying while diving." George stepped down the short flight of steps toward the boat. He was in front of Jim, curious to see all the activity.

There was a streamlined efficiency to the crew of the boat as they took off the coolers, tanks, and other gear. It looked like heavy work, but these folks had it down to a science. The name of the boat was "Santana." A beautiful woman was lifting the tanks from the boat to a blond haired man on the dock. She was in a turquoise bikini bottom and a tight-fitting black shirt with what looked like the logo of a wave. Through the long sleeve, skin-tight shirt, you could see that she was strong yet curvy. Her reddish-brown hair was tied back in a pony tail. She didn't look up as her husband and his friend approached.

Without breaking her stride handing over the tanks to the mate on the dock, she said, "Hmmm... you're here early. I usually have to wait an hour before you get here. Today – only half an hour. You must be trying to make a good impression."

Putting on a face of overt politeness, Jim responded, "Donna, this is George. He used to work for me. He's the one I told you about."

A little embarrassed, Donna looked up. "Hi, sorry about that, I'm Donna." She kept unstrapping the tanks from the boat and heaved them over to the deck hand. "I'll be done this in a sec. I have to go to the office and then I'll be ready to go."

"Can I help?" asked George.

Donna smiled. "No, thank you. We have a system here and it goes quicker if we just handle it ourselves."

She glanced up at George. George noticed that her blue green eyes matched the water around her. She was not young like Trish, but she seemed more beautiful. Where Trish was cute and sexy, Donna looked stunning and regal. In another life, she might have been a silver screen actress whose beauty didn't fade with age. The beauty seemed to radiate from within. Because of the hard work at the SCUBA center, she retained a figure that other women her age might envy.

Tossing the last tank overboard, she turned toward the bow of the boat. There was a bunch of gear that she hauled over the side. With a whip of her neck, she simultaneously dumped the equipment gracefully to the ground and grabbed her pony tail, wringing it out. She crossed her arms and took off the black shirt. Underneath was the matching turquoise top, which didn't do much to hide her breasts. She was an incredibly beautiful woman who momentarily took

George's breath away. He tried to hide his reaction from both Donna and Jim.

George wondered how anyone could cheat on a goddess like Donna. She was in her late thirties and had a mature elegance. As she walked up the stairs to the office, George noticed both sophistication and a self-assured gait that seemed the opposite of the girl they left in the dive shop.

"There she is," said Jim shaking his head. "She thinks she's a fish — always SCUBA diving. Sometimes I just wish she would stay at the bottom of the ocean. Maybe I need to make a remote control that cuts off her air supply. She makes my life a living hell, you know."

George countered, "She seems pretty nice."

"I suppose to someone on the outside, she is. But we fight all the time. There is nothing left between us. I'm ready to move on."

"That's too bad. I'm sorry to hear that."

"Well, you gotta do what you gotta do."

George turned and picked up some of the stuff that was in the pile by their feet. Jim picked up a vest of some sort. Donna, returning from the office, followed behind with two tanks labeled with yellow and green.

"I understand you're here to talk to Jim about his latest project. Correct?" asked Donna. She sounded both formal and terse. It sounded more like a military command than a statement.

"That's right. I used to work for Jim years ago."

Jim pressed a button on his car key and the back of the Hummer flipped up. Jim, George and Donna threw Donna's gear in the back. He pressed the key again and the back slowly closed and latched. "I just got laid off at work and am scrambling to try and find something. I got in touch with Jim and – well – here I am."

"Well it is my understanding that I have you for the next few days, right?"

This caught George off guard. He looked at Jim who smirked. "That's right. I have some business to attend to, so I'm leaving you with 'Donna, the mermaid.' Don't worry. She's harmless."

"Hah!" exclaimed Donna. "That's what you think." They all got in the Hummer. The drive was less than a minute. George expected them to pull up to some mansion villa on a hill somewhere, but then realized that nothing in Key Largo qualified as a 'hill'. They turned down one of the side streets near the Marina Del Mar and stopped in front of a nice sized, but not ostentatious house. It was a concrete structure that was painted to look like a Spanish style home. Jim pushed a button on the dashboard of the Hummer and the gate in front of the home slowly slid aside. As they drove in, George realized that the backyard ended at a canal.

Other homes, nestled side by side, had boats. Some of them were pulled out of the water, others bobbed in the gentle wake, securely tied to the dock.

"Home again, home again, jiggity jig" said Jim to himself. At the back of the garage, facing out toward the canal was a little tiki bar that obscured the view of the water. It seemed a later addition to the property – some necessary outside libation center. There were two side doors. The first was opened a crack, which allowed George to see that the "first" floor was a small workshop. It looked as if no one had worked in it for years. All of the tools were in their place. The workbench had no stains or dings. George pondered the sight and wondered if Jim had ever used this space. It seemed like a museum replica to the original Jim who, by the end of the day, had grease up to his elbows. Jim and George entered the house through the second door which led upstairs to a kitchen.

The place was immaculate. A large window in the breakfast nook looked out onto the canal. Pictures of coral reefs, fish, and other underwater landscapes hung throughout the house. The floors had throw rugs, but no wall to wall carpet. The floors were tiled except for the living room, which had a dark wood floor.

Jim opened the fridge, popped the top off of a beer and handed it to George. "Here ya go."

The effects of his beers at the bar had just started to wear off. It seemed George was constantly thirsty in this place of sun and fun. He wondered, however, if beer was the adequate tool to quench his thirst. Maybe he should be on a diet of water and fruit juice. Jim made another mixed drink lightning fast and was sipping away when Donna entered. She had rinsed and stowed her gear. She was still wearing her bathing suit as she made her way into the kitchen.

"I see you're at it already, Jim. George, tomorrow we are going to be in the water, so you may want to hydrate with something other than alcohol. It doesn't do a very good job when you exert yourself in the sun. I would hate to have you pass out on me."

"Are we going SCUBA diving?" George asked, a little alarmed at the thought.

"Jim didn't tell you? No, tomorrow we are going to be in a pool. He wanted me to show you a little of what it is like down there. It is all part of his 'grand plan.' But if you have a fear of water, or claustrophobia, or anything like that, then we will do something else – go shopping or something.

George thought a moment. This was totally unexpected. He was tentative. He had been snorkeling throughout the years, mostly at state parks when he took the family on vacation, but he never had been SCUBA diving – even if it was in a pool.

Donna sensed his hesitation.

"Don't worry; we aren't going to do anything dangerous. I'm going to take you on a "Discover SCUBA'

85

adventure. We won't be deeper than twenty feet. Just about double what you would find in a pool – if all goes according to plan. I'm a dive instructor, so you'll be with me through the whole thing. Trust me; it will be an experience you'll never forget."

"Okay" said George, a little uncertain about putting his life in the hands of a total stranger. He felt his hands go clammy. He pondered and realized he had not pushed himself physically, nor had he done anything out of the ordinary for any reason, over the last few years. His life had been devoid of the word 'risk.' This day had been the first day that he had been willing to let go and trust others, so why not take it a step further?

"Good," she replied. "You know where the pool is at the hotel? Be there at 8:00 a.m. tomorrow. We'll start then." Jim grunted and Donna headed down a hallway.

"You know I hate that woman," said Jim under his breath.

In a lowered tone, George replied, "You seemed to have made that perfectly clear."

Jim finished his glass and started pouring another one. "She is so…. I dunno. We have grown apart. I met her when I came down here. She was younger then, and seemed so full of life. Now she spends her time working at the dive shop. That's where I met her. When I moved in here I walked over there one day and there she was behind the counter. I knew she was the one for me. Yes, I was still married at the time, but there was chemistry between us."

George found these statements a tad ironic. After seeing Trish and Jim together, George wondered if Jim was somehow trying to replay events from his past.

"I figured once we got married, we would travel – see the world – give up on this place. But no, she never left. I guess it is in her blood. She used to sail all the time. I figured the two of us could sail the Caribbean or something. I'm not sure what happened, but here we are. She traipses out on a SCUBA boat all day, and I make all the money. Things didn't turn out the way I planned."

George understood a little better the adage, 'money doesn't buy happiness.' Though George went through the stress of his current employment crisis, there was always harmony and peace in his home. And that peace was the fertile ground for the relationship he shared with Alicia. Perhaps that was the main difference between Jim and himself. Jim was always looking for the next big thing – he was expecting something that he could never achieve and therefore was never truly content. It had nothing to do with wealth; it had to do with the myth of the American Dream. For some reason George recalled the lyrics from a Grateful Dead song, "What a long strange trip it's been...."

"Yeah, I even bought her a sailboat. Want to see it? I have two."

"What? Two?" George felt that this was totally unfair. He longingly looked at a boat picture for years and Jim had two.

"Yeah, I recently went to a boat show and found a sweet deal on a boat. Let's check it out."

They headed back down the kitchen stairs, through the garage, and rounded the other side of the tiki bar. There, sitting in the water, was a blue hulled sailboat with a tall mast reaching for the sky. George's heart leapt and his jaw dropped. There, before him, was his dream boat – the Tartan 4100.

5

"No not that one, George. That is the old boat. I don't think they even make that one anymore - this one."

Next to the Tartan 4100 was a newer, all white boat. Its chrome shone brilliantly in the setting sun. The waterline showed no signs of age. The halyards were unfrayed, their tight weave had a show-room look. George had read about some of the innovations the Catalina Corporation had launched with this craft. But, George's heart (and glances) strayed back to the Tartan.

"This is the Catalina 445. It's a new design, new boat, and I had to pull a helluva lotta strings to get this puppy." It was obvious that George was more curious about the Tartan, but Jim pulled him toward the Catalina. The Catalina was called the "Fickle Girl." The Tartan was called "Property of a Lady." He wasn't sure about the name of the Catalina, but he believed the Tartan was named after an Ian Fleming/James Bond short story. They strolled onto the "Fickle Girl."

"You know, George, in this economy you can wheel and deal. Not like a few years ago. In the past, I never would have been able to lay my hands on this thing. But apparently, some asshole with no brains and less money ordered this thing up. They had a one year waiting list. In the process, this guy loses all he earned and had to sell the boat before it even came out of the factory. He took a loss just to save his shirt and stay out of jail. I paid a 'used boat' price for this. Isn't it sweet? It's got a full Raymarine setup and you can basically single-hand this from the cockpit."

George was impressed. He dreamed about Alicia on the bow of a sailboat sunning herself as the boat gently rocked, anchored somewhere where the palm trees swayed gently with the breeze. He imagined that Tartan sailboat ad that said, "Be the dream." He was close. Jim opened up the collapsible wheel. He turned on the touch-screen display attached to the binnacle. George was transported back years, to that moment when he and Alicia made their wish list at the boat show. They had mapped out their course to one day sail the blue water.

"Yeah, I think this was a good investment. I didn't have to pay the depreciation cost you get when you buy a new craft like this. Of course, it isn't like buying a new car. When you get something like this, it has its own quirks. The refrigerator coils don't work and there is a small leak around one of the fresh water seacocks. But other than that, I think she is pretty nice."

George had spent years dreaming of sailing a boat like the one he was on. He had taken a few classes, but it was cost prohibitive. He wasn't willing to sacrifice his son's future for something so frivolous. But at this moment, he barely heard his former boss as he rambled on about this or that feature. George put his hand on the wheel. It was locked, so it didn't turn, but George was intimately aware of the minute changes under his feet as the boat lifted, if only an inch, as the water gently lapped against the hull. He looked up and saw the wind vane and anemometer. Halfway up the mast was the radar and satellite. The rigging was pristine. The lines were coiled and wrapped by a pro.

They went below and looked at the spacious master cabin. The galley appointments were sparkling and the whole thing smelled new – not like car-new, but a new boat smell. There was nothing spoiling the bilge hold. The sea had not taken its toll on this new toy.

"I wondered what it would be like to live on one of these things, until I realized with 'Property of a Lady' how much trouble they are. Still, I think at one point or another every man dreams of being-one-with-the-sea in one of these things, right?"

George nodded. "Amen. This is amazing. It is a showcase boat."

"Yeah, I thought about doing that, too. You know – keeping it sparkling and sailing it to boat shows around the country. You can make money taking these things to various boat shows, you know."

George interjected "I used to go to the Annapolis Boat Show. They always had the best boats out there. Man, I fell in love with them then. I'm still in love with them now." Suddenly he felt a few years younger. He was a teenager in his friend's first car. He was looking at a Babe Ruth baseball card. As he snapped back to reality he realized that he had been smiling. George wondered how long the grin was plastered on his face.

"Well, I think you'll get your chance. Donna would be happy to take you out."

"Really?" George couldn't contain his excitement.

"Yep, though she'll probably take you in the other one." Jim wagged a finger in the direction of the Tartan. He let out a sigh. "I bought this thinking it might help heal our relationship. She hasn't set foot on this boat, damn her. I'm trying to work things out, but she digs in and is set in her ways."

George wondered if the way Jim tried to 'work things out' was to buy his way in, or out, of a relationship. He seemed to have no skills in actually communicating with his wife. George couldn't understand exactly why Jim would want to work things out anyway. It seemed, with Trish, he had already made up his mind to move on.

Jim showed George the aft compartment that could be either a workbench or sleeping quarters. This boat had no tools on board, nor had anyone set up the space as an aft bedroom. Jim opened the top hatch. It was a spacious opening that George had not seen on any other boat. This piqued George's curiosity for other innovations that he would like to see, first hand.

George made a mental note to take Alicia back to boat shows when he returned. It was years since they had done anything like that. This sparked a fleeting longing for his wife. He missed Alicia and wished he had brought her here. He felt that this moment would be much richer if it was shared with the one he loved. George had no idea that, while he was job hunting, he would get the opportunity to sail. He wanted to call her on his cell phone, but thought it inappropriate while he was getting the "tour."

They went topside. Donna was waiting for them on the dock. She was dressed in a blue blouse with a white flowing skirt that had a pattern of multicolored flowers around its base. George thought she was beautiful in the turquoise bikini. However, in this outfit, she brought not only beauty, but also a regal yet carefree aura that enveloped her. She was simply stunning. The wind took hold of the hem and blew it lightly as if the skirt decided to dance.

As she stood there on the dock with the dying embers of twilight, she didn't get near the Catalina. She kept her distance, as if the boat gave off a repelling force field. The men stepped off the boat. Jim asked, "Whaddya think?"

"It is an amazing boat. You know I have always dreamt of sailing." He turned to Donna, hoping she would take the hint.

"Well, I'll take you out, but not in that thing." She turned away from 'Fickle Girl' with a look of contempt.

91

"Donna!" said Jim, frustrated.

"Hey, that is my boat. You bought that one for me." She pointed to the Tartan. "This one? I guess that is for your girlfriend."

The pause that followed took on dimensions of discomfort that would make thumbscrews seem like mere hors d' oeuvres. George looked at Donna. He didn't know if she was kidding or if she knew about Trish. Jim blushed, but shrugged it off with a "whew – women! Can't live with 'em. Can't kill 'em."

Jim looked at George with a "shut the hell up" face. George could feel the electricity in this awkward moment. Jim finally changed the subject. "Let's eat, shall we?" He clapped his hands together and seemed to be washing them of this moment.

Donna shot a glance at George. It was as if to say, "I am not that stupid." George couldn't hide the fact that he knew about Trish. With his return glance, he acknowledged, wordlessly. George could sense the bitterness in Donna. He wondered if the same sharp, biting attitude would be present tomorrow when they were alone and she was in control of his air supply. If so, it was going to be a long few days. George hated being in the middle of this squabble, but his hands were tied. He would need to ride out the storms between these two if he had any hope of obtaining employment. He had not anticipated these kind of games.

They all headed for the Hummer. As the sun started to sink, a breeze had started to pick up. Donna looked less like she was walking and more like she was floating toward the black metallic monster that awaited them. George offered to let Donna sit in the front seat with her husband.

"Oh, no. You boys stay up front and talk. I'm just here for the food. We will do this Italian style; men in the front, girls in the back."

92

They headed south, past the point where Jim had conducted his tour. They left Key Largo by crossing over a bridge into Islamorada. There seemed to be an abundance of northbound traffic. As they travelled south, they passed a building painted by Wyland, the marine artist. A large stingray, one story tall, glided past a window while a sea turtle tried to make its way to the second floor. When George lived in Baltimore, he remembered that Wyland had painted a mural for the National Zoo in Washington, D.C. George wondered how many other buildings were adorned with sea life by this artist.

George noticed the green mile marker signs ticking down the numbers as they headed away from Key Largo. Near marker eighty-eight, there was a large sign with the same number. George didn't know that this was a restaurant until they headed down to a parking lot that looked like it was actually below sea level. At the end of the parking lot was a white building. To its left was an outside bar where some young couples were throwing back drinks.

Crossed tiki torches were strategically placed along an outside eating area, waiting and ready as a backdrop for a photographic moment. At the main entrance of the restaurant, a waitress dressed in a white lace summer dress waited patiently for customers. She stood behind a wooden podium rechecking the seating for the patrons located both inside and outside the establishment.

The three were escorted to an outside table with a priceless view of the burgundy clouds. The vibrantly colored sky looked as if the divine artist was painting it with a large palette knife. The reflection on the water below them made it glow with a magical vibrancy. Jim plopped down in his seat and George waited until Donna sat before he took his chair. She smiled and nodded to him with silent thanks. A muscular, Africa-American waiter gave them their menus and filled their glasses with water. The waiter's name badge read 'Apollo.' George found the name fitting for a man with his build and stature. Perhaps he looked larger because the three were seated, but George doubted it.

George thought the sun had disappeared earlier as they made their way south, but its remnants still lit the horizon as they ate on the terrace of this fine dining establishment. A white archway, used for weddings, framed the orange and purple hues of the last rays of the sun as twilight slid into night. A pier jutted out from the edge of the restaurant and a few boats were tied alongside.

As soon as Apollo had put down the menu, Jim ordered a rum and coke. The handsome waiter asked if anyone else wanted drinks. George remembered what Donna had told him about being hydrated for tomorrows SCUBA adventure. He shook his head 'no' and the waiter went to the next table. The menu was filled with a variety of wonderful choices like crispy yellowtail meuniere, key lime seafood penne, or broiled Florida lobster.

The bartender arrived and placed the drink in front of Jim. Without hesitation, he chugged the glass and told the man he wanted another.

The two drunken couples at the bar were being a little loud. The men hugged each other in a bromance embrace and the women laughed, pointing at the men's foolishness. Some of the patrons looked on and shook their heads with varying combinations of amusement and bother. They laughed as one of the men slipped off the bar stool. He looked like he was on a boat in a storm being tossed to and fro across the deck. They all started singing a song, but couldn't remember the lyrics and, therefore, created their own slurred language to suffice.

"Roxanne, you wa han in mah so... Roxanne!"
They laughed like children who were doing something
bad and were getting away with it.

"The Keys can turn into quite a party town on
the weekend. This is nothing." Jim turned his attention
back to the menu. While he was inspecting the choices,
he continued, "If you had been at the Marina Del Mar
during the weekend, you might not have gotten much
sleep. You see, a lot of the divers will come here on
Thursday night, spend the night, and then dive Friday
and Saturday. Saturday night – watch out – they're done
with their weekend dives and party like crazy. They're
not your typical party crowd. They have no etiquette. I
think the tank air makes them go nuts." Jim looked at
Donna, baiting her for some response. She simply turned
her head away, as if simply wanting to look at the fading
light, but biting her tongue.

George wondered, "Jim, do you dive?"

Donna let out a chuckle without turning back to
the conversation. Jim replied, "No, I don't. That would
require a moment where you're alcohol free, and – as
you can see – I prefer to stay medicated. It makes things
easier." He shot a glance at Donna who was smirking.

She turned her attention back to the men. "Jim
prefers to stay in the glass bottom boat where he can
wave to all of us groupers under the sea."

Jim laughed. "True, true. I don't like getting my
feet wet. I don't like jumping out of planes either."

Donna came to the defense of her aquatic
passion. She wanted to set the record straight, so George
would not think he was doing some silly, life-threatening
activity tomorrow. She paused, so it wouldn't seem that
she was reacting emotionally. She placed her hands,
palms down on the table, unclenching them in the
process.

"SCUBA is relatively safe. You have to be cautious, but it has a wonderful track record. If you're going to 'buy it' underwater, it's because you most likely did something stupid. In all my time SCUBA diving, there has never been a single fatality on the boat. The worse we had were people with DCI, or someone getting bent. That was their own damn fault."

"Excuse me? DCI – bent?" interjected George.

"Sorry – DCI - Decompression illness hits someone who didn't monitor their nitrogen levels. You see, nitrogen builds up in the body when you're underwater. If you don't take care to let it release slowly, and get it out of your body, you can get sick. Most of the time, you have to send the diver to a hyperbaric chamber where they can release the gas out of their system slowly."

"So nitrogen builds up in your system. What happens if you don't let it out slowly?" George was getting nervous, thinking about what might happen to him.

"It forms bubbles. This can hurt and cause nerve damage. You ever hear of a diver getting 'the bends?"

"Sure," replied George, though he never considered what that really meant.

"If you let the nitrogen bubble in your system, it gets in the muscle tissue and nerves around the spinal cord. It is very painful. So much so that people double over in pain. They can't stand up straight. That is why they call it 'the bends' or 'getting bent.' I have never experienced it to that degree. The worst that happens to me when I do extensive diving is fatigue and aches in my joints – like a mild arthritis. We have dive computers which help regulate how much time we can spend diving down there."

George was getting nervous about doing a 'discovery dive.' He blurted out, "I don't know if I'm cut out for something like this."

Donna put her hand on his arm. "Don't worry. I'm not going to do anything that you do not want to do. We are going to take it slow. Tomorrow we are in the pool. Bring a t-shirt and plenty of sunblock. This Florida sun is intense."

"That's what she does to me. She scares the hell outta me and then says, 'It'll be alright.'" Jim's speech was a little slurred, but the evil intent was not.

Donna ignored his remark. "Diving isn't for everybody. I know that. Jim wants me to take you out because his 'grand plan' has something to do with diving." She paused. George tried to read her face but couldn't make out the wheels that were spinning in her head. There seemed to be a great deal more going on in the conversation than he could fathom. He was observing the conversation like two antagonistic chess masters saddled up to the table.

The two young couples stumbled arm in arm through the terrace and onto the pier. They leaned on each other, staggering to its edge. George could see the name 'Nitro' printed on the side of a racing boat that was tied up at the end. It sat low and sleek like an alligator with its head just breaking the water's surface. The black motor dwarfed the craft. It must have been at least 300 hp of raw power. He wondered if it was some repossessed drug smuggling boat that these four had picked up on eBay. The larger of the two men tripped into the boat and helped his female companion off the pier. The smaller man and his mate hopped in with less difficulty. Once in the boat, the smaller man turned and removed the dock line mooring 'Nitro' to the wooden pier. There was little current this close to shore, yet the boat started drifting as the four settled in for their sunset trek to parts unknown.

The food arrived. George couldn't believe how much seafood stared back at him. It all looked fresh and tasty. He had ordered the captain's special and was delighted by the portion. The aroma that wafted up from the fish draped in a creamy wine sauce over pasta surrounded him and set his taste buds on alert. It was a pricey dish, but he was hungry. He caught a whiff of Donna's yellowtail and it had a wonderful citrusy overtone.

Jim kept at the mixed drinks and the waiter made sure his glass never ran dry. Donna had lost count of the refills, but knew she would have to drive the trio back to Key Largo. George stuck to iced tea, following Donna's advice.

Trying to keep the conversation alive, George asked, "Donna, you sail?"

"Oh yes, I love to sail. It is great sailing around here, whether you're on the Atlantic side or the Gulf, it is all good here. I have been sailing since I was a little girl. My father said I was a born sailor. My grandparents lived in Grand Cayman and taught me to sail before I could read. They were always taking me out. When I was old enough, my parents took me to sailing camp. I fell in love with it immediately and have been sailing ever since."

"You haven't been going out lately. Even when I want to go out," said Jim spitefully as he shoveled a forkful of food in his mouth.

"When I go out, I want to enjoy the experience. You want to motor the whole time, drop anchor and drink yourself into a stupor. Where is the fun in that?"

"I am a man of destina – deintination – destinations. If the process is too slow, I come up with new ways of figuring it out."

Donna decided not to delve into the conflict. She was about to change the subject when she noticed activity on the water.

There was an electronic whirr, a click, and then nothing as the foursome tried to start the motor. It didn't kick over on the first try, so the large man tried it one more time. This time it sounded as if it would start, but then a loud pop emanated from the motor and a large plume of blue smoke rose into the sky. The firecracker-like explosion caught the attention of most of those who were on shore enjoying their meal. Those seated on the outside dining terrace turned to see the new entertainment near the shore, now that the sun had disappeared below the horizon.

"Assholes," said Donna under her breath, looking at the drifting boat. She turned to George. "When we got married Jim bought me 'Property of a Lady.' It's a great boat and sails wonderfully. It points well and can move with just a whisper of wind. I don't get out on her much anymore though. We used to sail all the time."

She had a look of reminiscence. Jim seemed oblivious to the statement. George detected a sadness and wondered if Donna would do things differently if she could turn back the hands of time.

"But I guess we got busy. Didn't we Jim." She patted his arm. George could see that it didn't matter how much money you invest in a relationship, there is still the human factor where both parties have to work together. He thought about how decay had entered into his relationship with Alicia. They weren't as biting and bitter as the Dalburths. George wondered what was worse: the couple who let the ordinary routine ruin their relationship, the fighting couple who went out of their way to disrupt the other, or the couple who simply gave up and went their separate ways.

The boat, 'Nitro,' had drifted beyond the point where the smaller man could throw a dock line back to the pier. The larger man went aft, cursed and took the cover off of motor. The complex engine was an artistic work of metal and chrome. The innards of the motor seemed to reveal nothing to the large man and he went back to the ignition switch. A second time, it sounded as though the motor would start. It turned over a couple of times, caught, sputtered, and another cloud of blue smoke lifted to the wind like a sacrifice to Poseidon.

The fourth or fifth time, the motor caught. The crowd on the terrace clapped, and as the larger man took a bow, the motor sputtered and conked out. The boat had drifted from the innocuous eddy of the pier into the current of the gulf and the boat was heading out to sea, all at the will of the ebbing tide. Jim laughed at the befuddled crew. Both women started screaming at the larger man.

Under his breath Jim muttered, "Sounds like the carburetor is clogged. He could fuck with that thing all he wants… it ain't gonna start."

The other two thought Jim was rambling, and continued their conversation.

George's eyes went hazy.

"I have always wanted a Tartan 4100. For years I kept a poster of that exact boat over my desk. You really think we can sail her?" George's tone had taken on that of a boy of about fourteen. He tried to restrain his enthusiasm. "I took some classes, but never got far."

"This boat basically sails herself. We made a few modifications. She has a self tailing jib, a new genset…"

George heard these nautical words, but didn't know what they were. He would remember to ask her for a private tutorial.

The crowd had quieted, amplifying the cursing of the female crew on "Nitro." George turned his attention back to the folks drifting out to sea. There seemed to be a palpable curse that descended on those struggling in the water. The observers could sense that things would soon get worse.

"What the hell..." said Donna. The smaller of the two men had jumped into the water in an attempt to push the boat – swimming – back to the pier. The current was way too strong. The amusement of the crowd turned to worry as the boat receded from shore. George saw how drunk they were. The women fell as they maneuvered out of the way of the ranting larger man. He could still hear the cursing of the women whose vocal pitch went higher with each tirade. The smaller man had made his way toward the back of the boat and was trying to turn it around. The larger man started fiddling with the ignition as a woman slapped his back and cursed like a sailor.

"Oh God no!" said Donna. George knew what would happen if the engine started. There was a likelihood that the small man in the water, trying to swim the boat back to shore in a futile effort of desperation, would be chopped up by the 300hp engine if it went into gear and the prop started spinning. They could hear the whirr and click of the electric starter and the motor tried to kick in, as the larger man, in total disregard for his semi-submerged passenger, opened the choke and hit the starter. Luckily, the motor was still locked up and didn't budge.

Apparently word got to one of the cooks who'd arrived to work at the restaurant in his Sea-Doo. He came out of kitchen, still in his apron, lifted the seat of his Sea-Doo and pulled out a tow line. He fired up the small craft and a fountain of water spurted out the back. Without a pause he was on the water headed toward the floundering "Nitro."

Seeing help was on the way, the three got the smaller man out of the water, avoiding a larger catastrophe. The women had started pummeling their respective partners and letting loose with expletives between hits. With this crisis averted, the terrace seemed to settle back into a buzz of everyday conversation.

George turned to Jim. "It is amazing how one small error can cause a cascade effect. If that guy hadn't casted off when he did, they would still be at the pier, safe and sound."

"Yeah, you gotta be careful around here," said Jim in a low, ominous tone. He nodded toward Donna. She knew he was drunk and opted to ignore his veiled threat.

The three finished their meal. George was hoping that Jim would open up about the position, his idea and the prospect for employment. However, Jim was now far too gone to broach that subject. He had become a silent morose drunk who was self-absorbed.

Donna and George helped Jim to the Hummer. Twilight had given way to a gallery of stars that stretched to the watery horizon.

George returned to his room tired and confused. He received a number of mosquito bites back at the restaurant. He didn't realize, as he was feasting on a scrumptious meal, that he was their target. He started counting the number of bites around his ankles and gave up, choosing to simply scratch. He called Alicia and told her the news of the day, including his potential sailing trip on the Tartan.

"I'm jealous" came the voice on the other end of the line. "You are going out with some woman I don't know on *our* dream boat? Are you ever going to come back?"

That was not the response that George expected. He thought she would be happy for him, but realized that it was their shared dream to sail together. Going out on the Tartan without her seemed to violate some unspoken marital rule. He had let the cat out of the bag and was unable to do anything about it. They rarely spent time apart. With no promise of income and George seemingly taking more vacation than business, a palpable tension grew on the other end of the line. Alicia was alone, at home, and that only added to the bad karma that was building.

With nothing better to say, he only admitted, "Hey, I wish you were here with me."

Not wanting to engage in a spat over the phone, Alicia changed the subject. "I talked to the school board about our situation. They're looking into a position at the elementary school for me. They want to expand their special needs department. I told them that I don't have much experience in that area. My major was English, but I told them I would give it a try. The only problem is that I need to get certified, which means that we would need to spend some money for me to go back to school."

"That's great!" George was happy that they were willing to work with Alicia on this, but that feeling was also tinged with a hint of remorse that she had to go through any of this at all. He wanted to see her face. The phone could lie, her face could not. Did she really want to do this, or was it putting her in position she would later regret? George didn't know.

"I'm not sure I'm up to it, but I think it would be an opportunity for me to get into the system."

"Of course." George thought about the books in the living room. Alicia was an avid reader and her specialty was American literature. Yet, she never flaunted her skills and depth of knowledge. She lived simply, but there was another side to her that she kept private, which only George entered when Alicia allowed. She was incredibly intelligent and had a memory for literature. George couldn't talk to her on that subject because he found it difficult to read a book of any depth. He liked the trade magazines and newspapers.

"Oh I almost forgot..." said Alicia. "Craig Lang, the other half of the *Run-Rite* duo called. I thought he would be down there with you two. I told him where you were. He said he would get in touch when you got back. I'm not sure what that was all about. He wouldn't leave a message."

George talked about his upcoming plans. They exchanged pleasantries and, like kids with a high school crush, neither one wanted to end the call.

☙ ☙ ☙

George woke early the next morning. His stomach didn't feel great and he wondered if it was the beer, or the fact that he would be donning SCUBA equipment and attempting to breathe underwater. He went down to the continental breakfast but found nothing that suited his need for real food. He made some toast and had a cup of hot tea. With both hands occupied he had difficulty lifting the latch that separated the pool area from the outside breakfast buffet.

Donna was already at the pool. She had a black t-shirt on over her turquoise bikini. She had connected a vest to the tank and had some hoses running off of the tank. She waved to him as he entered the pool area.

"Are you sure this is okay?" asked George.

"Sure, the bar, the dive area, and the hotel are all owned by the same people. Ocean Divers regularly holds classes here."

George finished his tea. "I gotta tell you, I'm not so sure about this."

"That's fine. We'll take it one step at a time. If at any time you don't feel comfortable, we'll stop. I want

104

this to be a good experience for you. I've had over a thousand dives and taught hundreds of people."

They began the lesson with just a mask. George had snorkeled before so that was not an issue. He was told that the vest was called a Buoyancy Control Device or B.C. for short. She demonstrated how the vest had air pockets, which could be inflated from the tank. They sat in the shallow end of the pool and he donned the vest. He was surprised that it would float with the heavy tank. She talked about how things float or sink, and it all made sense. Because of her professionalism, George was starting to feel at ease. He knew he could simply stand up if things got out of control.

Step by step, she methodically told him about the equipment. She described the connector to the tank as the regulator and the different stages that allowed you to breathe from a high pressured tank. She stressed that the trick was to simply breathe normally. He started to visualize how the regulator worked. He imagined the mechanical process of the valves and how, if a failure occurred, the design would fail in the 'open' position, allowing air to come out in a worst case scenario.

The moment had come for him to go underwater and breathe through the regulator. He closed his eyes and instinctively held his breath. She was underwater also, and squeezed his arm. He opened his eyes and saw that she was smiling, even with the regulator in her mouth. He exhaled and tentatively took a breath. The air came into his lungs with little effort. He started breathing normally. She gave him a 'thumb up' which meant to rise to the surface.

Taking the regulator out of her mouth she said, "Congratulations, you were breathing underwater."

"Yeah there really wasn't anything to it." George smiled. This was going to be fun.

A few hours flew by as George's curiosity claimed dominance over his trepidation. As a child he lived near a pool, so he knew he could swim. He hadn't gotten in a pool in years and it felt refreshing. Others looked on, and the two carved out their space as young families brought their children to the pool before beginning their daily activities. Some divers passed by and gave a cheer or thumbs-up sign as a way of affirming George's decision. Or, perhaps they were congratulating him on being with such a beautiful woman. George didn't care. He enjoyed learning something new. He started asking a ton of questions.

"Okay, so how do I know when to put air into my B.C.? How much weight do I need if I'm in salt water? What do I do if my air starts running low?"

Donna did her best to answer his questions. After a while she exclaimed, "Boy, you're really taking to this! I didn't think you would be this interested. I've shown some of Jim's other people the ropes, but they either bailed after the first five minutes or seemed like they had more important things to do. Only one or two actually went through with the training. I think you're going to do just fine. Let's take a break and get some lunch.

George didn't know that so much time had passed. He had been totally focusing on what to do. When it was lunchtime, George's fingers had shriveled to raisins. As he emerged from the water, George realized that he was famished. They both made their way, dripping wet, to the Coconuts Bar. From their perch they gazed down on boat after boat coming and going along the canal. Each boat carried different clientele.

One catamaran carried snorkelers. The boat had a large sign that said, 'Snorkel, Sunset and Snookered' in multicolored letters. Below was the 1-800 number and departure location. The makeup of these folks varied the most. Some were just children. Others seemed way too fat to float. Some looked like they had already had too much to drink. Jamaican Reggae/Rap was blaring from the speakers. A few of the folk were dancing to the beat, making sure that one hand was on the boat as they gyrated.

Another boat was close behind. This boat had a canvas cover over the top. In contrast, the people seemed much more sedate. It was a small boat and only four or five people were working with dive equipment that resembled the kind that George had been playing with in the pool.

"Hey I recognize that stuff," he said enthusiastically.

"You're different from Jim's other friends," said Donna, brushing back her ponytail. "Most of them are business types who drink too much, have bad breath, and want to grab my ass."

George chuckled. "Yeah, I don't know any of them. All I know is that I came here looking for work and Jim sends me on this weird excursion."

"Sorry about that. I think he's getting eccentric in his old age. I want to apologize for the way I acted last night. You know he asked me for a divorce."

George was stunned by her candor. "No, I didn't know that."

"Yeah, he puts up this front for 'his people.' He collects them, you know – people – he collects people. He's trying to collect you as well."

"What do you mean?"

She responded cryptically. "You seem to have a good head on your shoulders, George. Just use your common sense. Think things through, okay?"

Without fully understanding, he replied, "Okay."

They finished lunch. George felt a little guilty having lunch in the middle of paradise with a beautiful woman who was not his wife. She seemed more sad than bitter today, but there was an inner strength and beauty that he could appreciate. She seemed to be more like the "old Jim" he knew. She was the strong-willed, aggressive person who had her head on straight. George wondered if the "business" that Jim was attending to had anything to do with Trish and the fact that he had asked for a divorce.

There seemed to be two modes to Donna. When she was in the water instructing George about the proper SCUBA techniques and usage, she was authoritative and clear. But there was another side of her that was lonely. She wanted a companion to talk to. George felt that if Jim would just open up to Donna and give her a chance, she would reciprocate and the two of them might be able to work out their issues. But Trish was Jim's second drug of choice and he was hooked.

Donna had George dismantle the equipment and reassemble it. He had to don the outfit by the side of the pool. When he was on land, the equipment was bulky and cumbersome. The mask limited his field of view. The flippers made it nearly impossible to get around. But in water, the B.C. felt like it wasn't even there. Donna took him to the deep end of the pool and they tried everything from clearing the mask underwater to taking off the weight belt and putting it back on. He was gaining confidence. Knowing that he was with an expert helped, but he wondered how different an ocean dive would be. In the pool, he could surface and swim to the side. In the ocean, it was twice as deep, there was current, and he had no idea how to get around in a boat while wearing flippers.

He felt like a helpless novice and hoped that he would not forget everything by tomorrow.

"You've done a great job today. We covered a lot of territory in a short period of time. Remember your hand signals. Tomorrow when we dive, if you feel hesitant about anything, you can let me know like this,: she said showing the hand signals for "Things aren't quite right."

"We can always come to the surface," she said demonstrating the "Thumbs up" sign, which meant that they needed to ascend. George made sure that he knew those two signals.

The next day, he got up early and headed over to the dock. Other divers had assembled and were helping to get the boat ready. They put their regulators on the tank they would use for their first dive. They stashed their other equipment beneath the seat, trying to get a "prime" spot on the boat. Some put on a shirt. The water was too warm for a full SCUBA wetsuit. Most just wore a "rash guard" – a tee shirt or something to protect their upper body from the Velcro cummerbund and other straps that held the B.C. vest in place.

"You ready for this, George?" Donna was already in the boat. She was wearing a red two piece that was just as charming as the bikini she was wearing yesterday. Some of the men looked at him with envy and he stepped aboard with the saunter of an alpha dog.

"Yes I am." George looked around and was surprised by the people on board. He expected the boat to be filled with adrenaline seeking twenty-somethings that were looking for the day's thrill. Instead, he found a mishmash of humanity.

One couple looked like they were in their sixties. They leisurely went through their gear. Though moving at a slower pace, George could tell they were well practiced. Their suits were worn and frayed. There was a peace about them that George, at this moment, would never reach.

A man with an expensive looking camera looked too big to be a SCUBA diver. A large beer gut hung down

109

as he tweaked a lens. The two flashes extended well beyond the framework of the camera.

Four Italians donned what could only be called, designer SCUBA gear. The wrist dive computer looked like a multicolored video game.

The boat held an eclectic slice of the population which made George more comfortable. He would not be singled out as the odd man in this game of underwater exploration.

A boy, fourteen years old, seemed as much an expert as the guy donning the large SCUBA knife. Each had their own system – their own ritual – in preparing for the morning dive. The elderly couple checked each other's equipment. One of the Italians was programming his dive computer with the expertise of a NASA ground control technician. Some spit into their masks. One family reviewed advanced hand signals.

The first mate settled the crowd and the captain started the large twin diesels. The growl and the vibration was the signal for those still strolling about the boat to head aft to the two rows of seats on either side of the craft. After running through introductions and performing the required Coast Guard safety check, the crew shoved off and the boat headed down the canal. Million dollar boats and derelicts sat side-by-side. George wondered how much the houses cost along this stretch of water. Many of the homes along the canal had closed hurricane shutters as the wealthy owners took comfort in cooler and less volatile spots around the globe.

Last night, when going to the Dalburth house, George noticed that many of the places down the street had "for sale" signs. The economic distress hit both the wealthy and the poor with equal vengeance in this tropical wonderland.

The vessel made little wake as it made its way through this aquatic backyard neighborhood. The water tour distracted George from the task of getting his equipment ready.

Donna helped George fasten his regulator to the tank. He repeatedly checked to make sure he could breathe through the mechanical device, putting the regulator in his mouth and remembering his poolside adventure. The boat sped up as it exited the canal and entered the channel. The weather was perfect. Other boats followed in line. George was surprised at how many dive boats were heading out this early in the morning.

He had heard that this was a big fishing area but saw fewer trollers. He remembered that Jim had indicated that there was a large area of protected water as part of the park. He wondered if it extended out this far.

Donna pulled him aside to review some of the commands and to keep his mind from spinning with "what if" scenarios.

"Do you see that house over there?" Donna asked, pointing to the large pink house that dwarfed the others in the area.

"Yeah."

"That whole area was a landing strip. All of those houses used to be a concrete runway. The government shut it down because this private airstrip was used for drug smuggling. The original owner still lives in the big pink house. He made millions building and selling those houses."

Finishing up with the equipment, Donna led George to the bow, where others had found an area to park while they headed toward their first diving destination.

Sitting, Donna spoke loudly to continue her story over the thrum of the motors, which had revved now that they were clear of the no-wake channel.

"In the mid-seventies, there was a terrible storm. A small private Cessna Skyhawk had to ditch in the water somewhere right around here. The current was strong and the pilot had no chance of swimming to shore until the current changed. He did make it, though."

George nodded.

Smiling, Donna continued. "When the pilot reached shore, the authorities were waiting for him. His explanation to the police was that he ran out of fuel but by some miracle - 'Praise Jesus' - two garbage bags showed up to help him float to shore. The bags were, of course, filled with prime marijuana."

The two laughed. The stories put George at ease until they got the ten minute warning from the first mate. It was time to suit up. George felt like a child as Donna helped him with his gear. He had butterflies in his stomach. He didn't want to disappoint Donna. She had worked hard with him yesterday, but things were happening so quickly now that he considered backing out. She kept reassuring him that she would be with him the entire time. Everyone around him had different equipment. Some of the people wore dive computers on their wrists; others had sophisticated gauges attached to their pressure gauge. Some people wore thin suits that covered their bodies; others were going out in swim trunks and a t-shirt.

The captain cut the engines and the first mate attached the boat to a mooring. Four other boats were already there, creating a large circle about two hundred yards wide. Their divers were already in the water. They were diving in a place called "Molasses Reef." The divers, suited and ready to get wet, sat and listened to the first mate.

"This area has an incredible density of fish. The current is running southwest to northeast, so after you get in the water, I recommend swimming past the bow of the boat and heading in that direction. There are a number of channels. Each one is unique. Yesterday divers spotted three leatherback turtles. Of course you will also find schools of grunts and angelfish."

Divers nodded, but George was too busy getting the heartbeat drum roll running through his head to slow down.

Donna sensed George's worry and spoke to him, wondering if George would back out at the last minute. She put an arm around him.

"We're going to wait until everyone else has entered the water. That way we can take our time getting in. They're going to be entering the water using the 'giant stride' method. I haven't shown that to you yet, so we are going to get in the way I showed you at the pool, okay?"

"Sure thing." George was glad to know that no one else would see him flailing about. As the boat emptied, George became more and more nervous. Donna reviewed the hand signals as she put on her flippers and B.C. vest.

"Hang on to the dive rope once you get into the water. I don't want the current to send you away. I'll talk you through from there. You ready?"

George stood up and started walking, taking baby steps because it was difficult to maneuver with the flippers on. The first mate held his elbow and double checked the pressure valve on his tank. The first mate started quacking like a duck as George waddled toward the dive platform. Everything was awkward and heavy, but he remembered how that would all change when he was in the water.

George had seen the other divers make the big step. He knew he could sit down and do the entry as he had been instructed at the pool. But he felt that the 'giant stride' was in his capability. He put his hand on his mask and regulator and took the plunge. He gasped as he hit the water. He held his breath, ignoring the instruction from Donna. He regained his senses when he surfaced. He saw the blue line that floated on the surface and he grabbed it. His first rational thought, after "I'm still alive," was "the water is warm."

Donna was already on the diver's tow line. He didn't see when she entered the water, and didn't care. She gave him some last minute instructions. He adjusted the regulator in his mouth. It had moved when he bit down on it during his entry, so his first breath tasted a little salty. He breathed short and shallow out of nervousness. He didn't want to hyperventilate before he even got started. Two days ago he didn't know Donna. Today he trusted her with his life.

She held the valve on his B.C. over his head and slowly let the air out. He started breathing more quickly as the water rose above his nose. He was descending. He felt a momentary panic as the water went above his mask, but Donna was taking things slowly. She never let go of him. She had a firm grip on his B.C. vest as the last of his head submerged.

He was diving.

His mind was going a million miles an hour. He was reviewing all the emergency procedures that he learned yesterday. He breathed in short quick breaths. Donna got in his face to get his attention. She took two fingers and pointed at her goggles, indicating that she wanted him to watch her. She demonstrated long slow breaths. George forced himself to slow his breathing a little. He relaxed.

114

She pointed up. George didn't want to take his eyes off of her, but he looked up. The sun showed through the meniscus with pulsating, undulating, dancing strings of light. He saw the hull of the boat about ten feet away. He had no idea he had descended that far that fast. He took a long breath of air realizing that he could still swim to the surface if he had to. Donna, again, got his attention.

She pointed for him to look down. Below him was a patchy spot of sand surrounded by blue-green growth. Noticing he was descending, he started kicking his feet to slow the descent. It was an automatic reaction and nearly caused Donna to lose her grip of him. She gently pulled him along so they would come to rest on the soft sandy spot among the coral. Other divers were swimming around. "It seems so natural for them," he thought. He felt awkward, not gliding through the water like the others. He squeezed his nose through the soft plastic that formed a seal around his face and equalized his ears, as she taught him in the pool. She gave him the "Okay?" sign and he responded with the same hand gesture.

Donna let go of his vest and indicated that she wanted him to kneel. He wasn't sure how to do this at first. His flippers were so big. But he swam up a little and then put the flippers behind him. He came down on his knees. She again signed to him "Okay?" He nodded his head and accidentally gave the thumbs-up, but changed it to the "Okay" sign, remembering that the thumbs-up meant he wanted to surface. For a few seconds they just knelt in the circle of sand as the underwater world swirled around them.

Donna wanted George to relax in the environment. He didn't take his eyes off of her. There was a tension in doing nothing. He had to learn to trust the equipment he was wearing. She indicated that she wanted him to look at her. She rose off her knees and swam around him and returned. She then pointed at him with the hand signal to do the same. He was flying solo. He circled above her and returned without a hitch. She gestured the "okay" sign and he returned the signal. She then gestured that they would now swim together with her in front.

George thought he would have felt claustrophobic in all of the equipment with the pressure of the water bearing down, but everything seemed to work. As he rose off his knees and followed Donna, he didn't feel the weight of the tank. He didn't have to work hard to kick with his flippers. The two of them lifted a few feet off the bottom of the ocean and headed toward the coral.

George could see that Donna was looking back at her student frequently. They came to an area where the coral ridge was built up on both sides of a sandy channel. Donna flipped all the way around and was somehow managing to swim backward, her front fully facing George. She moved her legs in a frog-kick motion, effortlessly navigating against the current. She slowed and pointed to one of the ridges now rising well above their heads.

George had been so busy with the exercise and mechanics of diving that he didn't take time to look around. He paused and took in the landscape – or seascape – and it hit him. Hundreds of fish were swimming, foraging, and darting around. Coral was waving in the underwater breeze. It was simultaneously foreign and recognizable. The underwater wilderness was teaming with life. Scale had little meaning. Donna took him past a large dome of brain coral. It reminded him of the Fiore Dome at the cathedral in Florence, Italy. It towered over the neighboring fan and branch coral. She gestured for him to get closer. He was awkward, not used to the additional mass of the gear on his body, and didn't want to run into the massive structure. Donna wiggled her finger around the structure. He wasn't sure what he was supposed to look at until he realized that there were hundreds of tiny orange fish cleaning its surface.

Donna pointed to something that looked like two flowers growing along one side. The flowers had fingers emanating from them that seemed to pulsate with the small current that ran over the brain coral. Donna took his hand. He wasn't sure what he was supposed to do. She pulled his index finger and wanted him to touch the flower. Reluctantly he stretched out his finger to the tentacles that blew in the aquatic breeze. As soon as his finger touched one of the appendages, the whole flower snapped shut inside a rocky cocoon. The flower, which had once been open and swaying back and forth, was completely hidden. She held out her hand in a gesture to wait. Slowly – incredibly slowly – the flower started opening back up.

They looked under a coral ridge and saw thirty fish with yellow and blue stripes idling, as if waiting at a bus stop, for some undersea transportation. Fish were everywhere. Donna paused at one coral outcrop which loomed over their heads. She ran a finger around her head in a circle and pointed at a large fish coming their way. He didn't get it at first, but then understood; it was an angelfish. The dark body was framed with yellow striping. It seemed large, but was thin. George had no idea something so beautiful would approach them with no fear, only curiosity. Donna smiled. George could see her eyes squinting with delight.

It was one thing to see the angelfish foraging along the coral, but unexpectedly, an entire school swam right past them. George was startled and took a quick breath. He jerked back. There were so many and their

117

combined power as they rocketed past created an underwater wake that George could see. They passed by seemingly unaware of the presence of their two human observers.

A couple of divers were swimming back from the venture against the current. One stopped, pulled out an underwater camera, and snapped a picture of an interesting creature lodged in the rocky outgrowth. Donna pulled his arm and indicated that they were to get on their knees in the sand. George wanted to continue swimming. There was a whole new world to see. But, he followed his instructor's orders and knelt in the sand. It was a little easier maneuvering this time. He was getting used to the mass on his back and the extensions on his feet.

She checked his pressure gauge and gave him the "okay" sign. She made a gesture of something hopping. She pointed down at a rock. He looked back at her with a questioning look. She indicated to continue looking at the rock. Nothing. Nothing. Then it hopped to another spot. This "rock" was actually an animal. Its ability to blend into the environment was phenomenal. Donna then had him turn and she showed him what appeared to be a giant slug making its way across the sandy floor.

George realized that everything down here was alive. Even the rocks moved. In the woods, George would spot the occasional deer, squirrel, or chipmunk. But the underwater world teemed with life everywhere. In every direction, the dense population moved in a three dimensional dance. A large fish with deep purple and blue coloring came up to George curiosly staring directly at George's mask. It swam around him and then darted off. As George rounded a corner filled with purple fan coral, a school of about fifty silver fish swam between Donna and George. Their scales reflected the sunlight.

To George it seemed like they had walked out to a group of paparazzi, with cameras going off in random flashes. The two divers looked at each other in amazement as the fish disappeared into the hazy blue distance.

They swam on. After scanning the variety of coral, Donna stopped and made three slicing motions across her arm. She pointed overhead. George didn't quite understand. She pointed and moved her arm. He tried to focus and then spotted a thin needle-like fish with razor sharp teeth.

"Barracuda!" George jumped in surprise. The fish reacted to George by darting off. Donna pushed her hands in a "calm down" motion. She checked his gauges and they started back the same way they had come. Donna got very close to an overhang and motioned for George to draw closer. Until now he hadn't noticed the current, but now that they were heading back toward the boat, the current was noticeable. It took much less effort to travel the same distance moving with the current. However, the invisible force of water made it difficult for him to remain stationary. He struggled to maintain his position as Donna pointed to a hole where something green was moving around. It looked like an underwater snake. George assumed it was some kind of an eel. The small writhing ball came partially out of its hiding space. From movies, George thought of an eel as an imposing monster. This was actually cute. Its small eyes seemed aware of the divers gazing back at it.

As they drifted down the sandy channel, George heard the sound of someone munching potato chips. He instantly realized this was impossible. Potato chips would instantly go soft. But somewhere ahead, there was the definite crunching. The "munch – munch - munch" continued. Floating by, the two spotted a large parrot fish chomping away at part of the coral. Before this dive, George thought that the underwater world was a quiet place, but this was not so. The rock-eating parrot fish shit out a tan plume that slowly made its way to the ocean floor. Donna pointed to the detritus. She scooped up some sand and let it float, in the same way as the parrot fish crap. George made the connection.

George pondered the incredible vastness of this landscape. A number of SCUBA divers entered the water from the boat, and there were several other diving boats. However, he only chanced upon a few SCUBA divers in his time under the water. Donna and George had only explored one of many trenches that fingered out from the mooring area. They could have taken any number of channels that diverged from this main artery.

Donna took another look at George's gauge and gave the "thumb up" signal, but pinched her fingers together. They were going to ascend slowly. She indicated that he needed to look up as he surfaced. The boat hull seemed far away from their current location and he wondered why they were coming up at this spot. He started swimming up and she grabbed his vest, slowing his ascent. As he rose, he looked down to the fading landscape and looked forward to returning. He was hooked.

The current was drawing him closer to the boat as they came up. She grabbed his B.C., pressed the valve to release air and stopped his ascent. She looked at her watch and they hovered under the water, looking down at the landscape. He felt like he was a satellite in outer space, looking down on a miniature Earth. This was the 'safety stop' she educated him about. There was no way to demonstrate this in the pool. Though the adrenaline rush was still coursing through his body, his heart rate and breathing were calm and regular.

By the time they broke the surface of the water they had arrived at the boat and were grabbing the diver tag line. George took the regulator out of his mouth and said, "Wow! That was Incredible! I couldn't believe..."

Just then, a small wave smacked him in the face and caused him to choke on the saltwater. Donna took the regulator out of her mouth. "Keep the regulator in your mouth until you're back in the boat. Take off your flippers and give them to the mate. George did as he was instructed. With a heave, he pulled himself up the ladder as the first mate grabbed his vest to keep George from tumbling back into the water. George leaned forward to maintain his balance. He spit out his regulator and swallowed. His mouth had gone dry breathing the canned air.

Back on the boat he felt clunky and heavy. He sat down, placing the tank in the empty holder. He undid his B.C. vest and put the flippers under his seat. They were among the first of the divers to return. An older couple sat drinking some fruit juice and talking about all the sights they had seen.

"So, did you like that?" Donna asked as she came over to George. She was wringing the saltwater from her hair.

"Oh my God, that was incredible. Wow! I have never seen anything like that. There is *so* much down there. What was that jumping rock thing?"

"Oh, that was a conch. That is how it gets around."

"Wow."

"What about that flower?"

"Oh, the sea anemone? That isn't really a flower."

"I never would have believed it if you hadn't shown me. Thank you. Thank you."

Donna replied, "Hey, you did all the work. I have to congratulate you, though. You're the first one of George's cronies to make it to a dive. Everyone else stopped at some point. This is all part of his job offer - or grand scheme - or whatever you want to call it. He usually ends up taking "his prospects" on a glass bottom boat – but now you know that a glass bottom boat is not the same. Funny, though...," she paused for a moment of melancholy reflection, "Jim has never done SCUBA. He's relegated to the glass bottom boat."

"So, this job has something to do with SCUBA? I like it and everything...."

"Don't panic. This is an above ground thing... at least for now."

"What does that mean?" George wondered whether he could get any more out of Donna. Both she and Jim seemed tight-lipped about the job opportunity. The fact that he seemed to like Donna more than Jim might not work in his favor. Was aligning with Donna was a good political move? George didn't know.

"Jim actually made me sign a non-disclosure statement. You know he's paying me for this. But that is not why I'm doing it. I have my own agenda. Don't worry, it will make sense soon enough. Just enjoy the ride."

"Well, I have to hand it to you. You have a great job. There was a big silver fish, I'm not sure you saw it. It had a snub nose..."

"That was probably a 'permit'. Hold on a sec...."

She rummaged through one of her bags. She pulled out a sheet of thin plastic. There were pictures of fish, their names and brief descriptions. They were organized by size and color. He had seen many of the fish that were printed on the page.

"Wow, what about that slug?" George was trying to remember all of the detail of his dive.

"That was a sea cucumber. They're all different. They're really incredible animals once you get to know them."

"Wow."

"Funny, most of the first-timers use 'wow' or 'incredible' or 'fucking intense' after their first real dive. You're a 'wow' person. I like 'wow' people." She failed to mention to George those with a claustrophobic nature that sent them over the edge. There were a few more categories - "Get me the hell outta here" and those who just whimpered for their mother. Luckily, George was not in the latter category.

Divers arrived casually on board. The first mate plucked them from the water and all seemed to enjoy the dive. As they took off their gear, they shared stories of the array of life that teamed below them. The older couple took off their equipment and sat in silence. They seemed to have entered a transcendental state. Unlike the others, they simply breathed deeply and smiled at each other.

"I guess we came back early," said George as he put a bungee cord around the near-empty tank.

"Yeah," Donna responded. "Like most first-timers, you're an air hog." She went over to one of the two fresh water showers and rinsed off. The white shirt she was wearing allowed her red bikini top to show through. While she was showering off, men who had come aboard stopped their idle conversation. A couple took a swig of water, their mouths suddenly becoming dry. Donna took no notice of them. She had seen it all before.

"So I'm an 'air hog?'" George wanted to engage in conversation because his mind was wandering like the others.

She let go of the pull valve and the water shut off. She swung her hair around and wrung it out on the deck. Lifting her head up she replied, "Yeah, the first few times you go in, you have a tendency to suck down a lot of air. Did you find yourself trying to catch your breath? Sometimes newbies will experience a little mini hyperventilation when they realize they're sucking air from a tube."

George admitted that he had done that. Donna came over and helped him change his regulator from the spent tank to a fresh one.

"Thanks."

"No problem, George. I think you're getting the hang of this."

The last few divers ascended the steps of the boat. The first mate took a head count and performed the obligatory roll call while the captain fired up the engines. Couples huddled together talking about their explorations as the boat unmoored and headed out to sea. Donna took George by the hand and they headed to the bow of the boat.

Donna turned to George with a serious look on her face. The wind was blowing and the motors made it necessary for them to speak at a "crowded bar room" volume. "You are different from the rest. You know that?"

George didn't know where this was coming from. He wanted to talk about the upcoming dive, but apparently Donna's wheels had been spinning in another direction. There was a long pause and she continued. "I trust you will do the right thing."

"What are you talking about?"

"Look, I can't tell you things I want to tell you. But I don't want you getting hurt. You're Jim's friend and I respect that. In fact, other than Craig, you're the only person I've gotten to know from Jim's past. You seem like a really nice guy and I just don't want you doing something you might regret." There was an ominous tone in her voice.

Not fully understanding, George confided in her. "I need a job. That is why I'm here. I don't understand all this hush-hush, but I'm a patient man. I'll listen to Jim. Right now, I have nothing to lose. But I'm not stupid."

"I never said you were..." Donna interrupted.

"... but I have my family to think about. I'll listen to his offer. If it is any good, I'm going for it. You sound like I need to be wary. I respect that. I'll keep my eyes open."

She smiled. He wasn't sure if it was the wind, but her eyes were watering. She smiled and looked at him with a face that he couldn't read. Her smile hid a deep pain. George wanted to reach out and hold her and tell her it would be all right. But he thought that might be inappropriate. He wanted to say something pithy that would break this barrier, but he could think of nothing.

It was Donna who changed the subject. "Spanish ships used to come here from South America and Mexico filled with gold. On their way to Spain, they would often travel along the Gulf Stream before setting out to the Atlantic. This coral ridge, and the coral farther inland, would catch the ships during storms. Natives would come out and help the foundering ships. They would get supplies, gold, and whatever else they could get from the ships. The natives would paddle out in canoes and bring back the supplies and stranded crewmembers. Soon small towns, like Key Largo, started to emerge. This became a pirate outpost. So you and Jim are in good company."

George, wanting to join Donna in lightening the mood, closed one eye and said, "Arghh matey."

They both laughed. Donna closed her eyes and felt the wind. George did the same. The air was warm and humid. The boat came across another boat's wake and the craft started porpoising. The first mate gave the "ten minute warning" for them to prepare themselves for their next dive. They were headed to "Eagle Ray Alley." George and Donna left the bow and joined the rest of the divers aft. The captain came down and briefed them on the layout of the terrain and specific features to observe.

This time, George had a better idea of what to do. They entered the water and headed for the bottom. This terrain was different than "Molasses Reef". The trenches were much wider and taller in Eagle Ray Alley. As before, Donna had him find a sandy spot and kneel. They ran through many of the same drills and then were off to explore. Around one bend, a large anchor and pieces of a ship lay strewn across the sandy bottom. Small fish fought for territory over the encrusted objects. The objects from the ship were half submerged. Many of the large cogs that once worked a huge propeller shaft had their teeth shorn away. Other parts were unrecognizable. Time was wearing these man-made pieces back into the fray of the underwater seascape.

Unlike "Molasses Reef", large coral cliffs jutted over the path. Antler coral seemed to spread its fingers, reaching over the ledge. As before, the spectacle played itself out in a living, dancing, chorus of life that spread into a blue infinity. Around each turn there was something new. George wanted to soak it all in. He was a blind man who had just been given sight. He wondered if Donna had ever lost the wonder of this place. It hardly seemed possible. Though the fish were territorial, the place never stood still. No amusement park, movie, or play could match the entertainment found in Neptune's realm.

Donna checked on George regularly. He had gotten into the habit of looking at his pressure gauge and could relay to her the latest reading. She would smile and give the "okay" signal.

Donna motioned for him to stop. She indicated that she wanted him to swim around and look at things. She used hand gestures, indicating that she was ascending a little but it was okay. He didn't really understand, but indicated with an "okay." She started swimming up and he stayed close to the sandy stretch between two corals. With Donna out of his field of view he could absorb the grand scope of the landscape. He explored some crevasses that housed small lobsters and crabs. One underwater plant sent up small balloons along its leaves to keep them facing ever sunward. He could hear the "munch munch" of a parrot fish, somewhere out of sight, tearing the coral with its sharp teeth.

Donna rejoined him after a while. He was getting tired. At one point his right leg started cramping. He remembered the training from the pool and grabbed the tip of his fin and started pulling it toward him. The muscle didn't seize up into a full-blown cramp, but he could feel that it wouldn't be long before it happened again. He was down to about three hundred psi of air when they started to ascend.

Back in the boat, George took off his gear. Donna said, "You did great that time. We were down there for about forty-five minutes. Good job!"

"Really?" George hadn't taken notice of the time. "Why the time difference? The first dive was only about thirty minutes."

"I think you finally relaxed. This dive is a little shallower, too. But not so much that it would be that different."

"Wow, incredible," George said mindlessly.

The last diver came aboard and the first mate started handing out oranges that he had cut while the spectators were submerged. Divers thronged to grab a few slices. The boat headed back leaving a large white wake behind them. George didn't notice. He had reached that place, both mentally and physically, where he was

127

drained. He ate a few orange slices but didn't speak much.

Donna sat with him after stowing her gear. "You're not saying much. Everything okay?" She gave him an "okay" signal, made a goofy face and crossed her eyes. In that moment she looked like some of the fish he had seen. They both laughed.

"Yeah, I'm doing great. I'm tired. That was exhausting, but it was exhilarating at the same time."

"Oh..." she said. "You're in the zone..."

"Yeah, I guess that's what you call it. I'm just replaying the day over and over in my head."

"Zone..." she repeated, like a Buddhist monk meditating on a mantra.

"Zone..." he imitated.

He sat for a while and just stared into space. Across from him, some of the young divers watched as the first mate took one of the unused tanks and cranked open the air valve. He took an uncut orange and carefully placed it on the air stream. It hovered and started spinning wildly. A girl giggled with delight as it defied gravity.

"I've gotten it to spin so fast that the air column actually skinned the orange."

The tank gave out and the orange toppled to the floor rolling aft, off the dive platform, and into the big blue. Donna, at some point, had gotten up and retrieved some sunblock. She grabbed George's chin and dabbed some around his forehead, nose, and cheeks. He didn't realize that he was getting so much sun. He thanked her and they both headed to the bow to reclaim their spot. Others were sitting around sunning themselves or just enjoying the sea spray that came over the bow.

One of the divers stood up and pointed, shouting excitedly. Some dolphins were playing in the wake of the boat. The vessel, which had seemed filled with divers who were content to idle back to the dock, suddenly reanimated as they scrambled through their bags to find their "land" camera, cell phone, or other picture taking device. The glistening grey creatures had no trouble keeping up with the boat as it sped toward shore. The animals danced through the white froth of the wake. Their swimming seemed effortless, as if in an eternal state of play.

George and Donna moved over to the starboard rail to get a good view.

"Why do they do that? Why do they follow the boats?"

"Could be a lot of reasons." Donna replied, her hair blowing dry in a wild pattern around her face. She reached with her left hand across her face and tried to tuck the free flowing locks behind her ear. "Some of the fishing boats will get rid of the excess chum, or throw the remnants of their catch overboard on the way back. The dolphins are looking for a meal. Sometimes they follow the boats because other fish are following too. As the prop churns up the plankton, fish swim to eat them. The dolphins follow close behind. But in this case, I think they're just playing."

"Really?"

"Yeah, look at them. They're looking at us when they surface. They're braiding."

It was hard for George to distinguish one dolphin from another, but it appeared that they were regularly changing position. They did appear to be "braiding."

"Wow, incredible."

"You have been saying that a lot today."

"Sorry, I'm at a loss for words."

"I understand."

The shoreline came closer. The captain throttled the boat down a notch as they entered the channel. The wind died down and the afternoon heat landed on the boat. It was a sauna. The sky seemed to be crying out for some relief in the form of rain, but no clouds were in the area. A subdued air descended on the vessel as the divers slowly collected and packed their equipment.

"Whew, I'm tired," said George as they entered the canal that would lead them back to the "Ocean Divers" dock.

"Just think. On a normal day, I would go out and do it all over again. Well – not exactly. We would go to different locations. Sometimes, it makes for an incredibly long day."

"So how much is out there?"

"The area we visited is all part of the protected area of the park. Up here, around Key Largo, there is really good coral. As you head south, the ridges get fewer and farther between. So you have really seen some of the best of Florida. There is plenty right here for a lifetime of diving."

"Do you ever get tired of it?"

"Never." George waited for more of an explanation, but it never came. They entered the dock in silence. Other boats were heading out. Large catamarans loaded with snorkelers and boats with SCUBA divers were maneuvering through the narrow channel. Some of the sunset cruises were departing with tourists prepped and ready for a few hours of drinking before the golden dome closed over the darkening blue sky. Divers unloaded, soaking their gear in a large tub of fresh water before departing. George got his gear off the boat and laid it neatly on a post. He returned to the boat and helped Donna, the crew and helpers from the dive shop to unload the tanks. In his exhaustion he still found the strength to assist. George wanted the full experience. Being a part of the crew to refit the boat for the next dive somehow made the day complete.

"Did you see the shark in Eagle Ray Alley?" asked the captain.

George's eyes went wide. "No. You mean there was a shark that lives there?"

With his Australian accent, the captain knew he had George hooked. "Sure thing mate, but don't worry – it only goes after the fresh meat of new divers."

Those around laughed. George relaxed and chuckled as well.

With the boat ready for the next excursion, the crew changed hands. Donna led George up the stairs to the office. She took her dive computer with her. Using it, she filled out a log of her dive. She had to prove to the owner that she had not exceeded her maximum exposure time on any given day. There were some who tried to "double dip" in order to make more money. This increased their probability of getting "bent." The dive computers didn't lie. They told both the length and depth of the dive. However, some of the less honorable divers would use two identical dive computers and switch them each day. That way they never recorded the fact that they had exceeded their maximum dive time many times over. They were willing to risk their lives for a better paycheck.

George looked around at some of the items for sale in the office/store. One wall had a rack of "Ocean Diver" tee and polo shirts. The other wall was filled with the latest in dive gear. It was a much smaller store than the one at the edge of the highway, but everything was arranged and placed with professional retail expertise. Behind the counter was a rack of PADI books. Some were general "open water" diving manuals, while others were more specialized. There were books for boat diving, aquarium diving, night diving, etc. The glass case had bumper stickers, earrings with SCUBA divers, and key chains. He wondered what he should get for Alicia.

The grey-haired man behind the counter held out his hand.

"Congratulations! I hear you had a couple of good introduction dives. So you going to sign up for classes?"

George didn't know what to say. "Yeah, I have to talk to my wife about it."

The man behind the counter snickered. "Okay, pal. Have a good one!"

Donna and George headed to the little cantina next to the office. It was mid-afternoon and the sun was blazing hot. George wondered why he wasn't sweating more. He wondered if he was dehydrated to the point that he had stopped perspiring. He wondered if the salt water had clogged his pores.

The two sat at a small table overlooking the water. It was a quaint spot that seemed to typify 'tropical.' The dark wood and rustic tables and chairs seemed to belong there. A crowd had gathered downstairs as a kid was tuning up his acoustic guitar and setting up a small PA system for the evening entertainment. George sat down and Donna disappeared. He thought she was right behind him. She soon returned carrying two Coronas.

"If you were diving again, I would advise against having a beer. Alcohol and diving do not mix. But we're done. Do you think you'll do it again? Do you think you'll get certified?"

"Yes! I would love to take Alicia on a dive so she could see what I saw."

"Bring her down here! I'll take her out."

"That would be great." George took a swig of the beer. The day was incredibly hot, he was incredibly tired, and the Corona was *incredibly* delicious. It seemed to slake those demons deep in his parched soul. He realized that until today, he had been in torment about his job. But something about Key Largo, the promise of work, and the excitement of the dive made him forget his worries. The land seemed to cast a hypnotic spell over George and anyone else who stayed for more than a day.

"You have that look," Donna said with her elbow on the table and head in her hand. "I've seen it before. It is a waking nap. I'm kinda there myself."

"Another beer and you'll have to scrape me off the floor."

"Cover your beer!" Donna said suddenly, looking up. She put her hand over the mouth of the beer. George looked at what she was doing and did the same. "Hey Charlie!"

A man came up from behind to their table. He was spraying some blue cleaning fluid. The man must have been about ninety years old and was in charge of bussing the tables. His eyesight wasn't so good, so he started spraying about four feet from the table. A fine mist of the chemically laden cloud wafted in their direction and would have nuked their beers had it not been for Donna's keen observation.

The old man, who looked like a gnarled old tree, bent down and kissed Donna on the cheek. He reeked of sweat, but didn't appear to be sweating in this heat. George wondered if the old man was capable of sweating. Perhaps his shirt hadn't been washed this year. It was a faded blue work shirt that housed a colony of smell producing microbes. So Charlie was not necessarily an individual but a living and moving colony of body odor.

"Charlie, this is George." The old man turned and bowed.

"Charlie doesn't say much, but he's a hard worker." Charlie, having gotten his kiss, moved on. Without regard to those around him, he started spraying and wiping other tables. He continued spraying until the entire cantina smelled like the YMCA.

"Doesn't he get high with that stuff – spraying all the time?" George asked.

"Hey at his age, wouldn't you?" They both laughed.

For a moment they just took in the landscape. Beyond the railing, boats traveled back and forth along the canal. This was a busy time of day. The two seemed suspended in time. Donna broke that magical eggshell of suspended reality by saying, "We're not done. I have a surprise for you this evening."

George didn't know what to say. The statement made him feel awkward. It sounded like she was making a pass at him. He knew she wasn't happy in her marriage. He blushed.

"Oh hell no. Don't go there." She said responding to the look on his face. "Look, don't even think…"

"I'm sorry. This has been a fun day. I'm not that kind of …."

"It's okay. After today, I think we can say we've become friends." She put her hand on his arm. He smiled, relieved that this awkward moment had passed. They finished their beers. Donna took George by the hand, stood up, and pulled him out of the cantina. "We're running out of time. We have to go."

Donna seemed to have a sudden burst of energy. George would have loved a nap, but her exuberance, which sprang up from some unknown source was infectious. George laughed as he was pulled from his chair and they angled their way through the maze of tables and chairs toward the parking lot.

Feeling like a kid again, George asked, "Where are we going?

"You're going to love it… I just know it."

They headed back to house. Donna threw a pair of pants at George. "These never did fit Jim. They have a drawstring so they should work. Get out of your bathing suit. Donna picked up the phone and ordered a pizza. She disappeared and returned in a pair of Capri pants and a polo shirt. Her hair was combed. The pizza came quickly. Opening a few more beers they devoured the pizza in record time. Donna showed no effort toward maintaining a lady-like attitude with the consumption of four slices. George had trouble keeping up.

"I saw that look in your eye," she said as she let out a deep and vibrant belch.

"When? Today? During the dive?"

"No silly! Yesterday when you were with Jim - I was watching you out of the window."

George struggled to remember the moment she was talking about.

"C'mon. We have work to do."

Still wondering what was up her sleeve, George followed obediently out the door. They rounded the back of the house and stopped.

"Jim had to show you his new toy. But I saw you. You were looking at *my* boat. This one is *mine*. This is the 'Property of a Lady'."

The Tartan 4100 sailboat seemed larger than the Catalina. It wasn't a matter of size; rather it was a presence that made it seemed to loom larger. The outer hull was a royal blue, offsetting the white and chrome. The Catalina, though a fine boat, was all white and seemed like a little sister to the Tartan. The "Property of a Lady" glistened in the sunlight. The Catalina seemed to bob and dance in the slip. The Tartan seemed to roll more slowly. George wondered if it was a matter of ballast and rudder, or just personality. Donna hopped from the pier to her boat, effortlessly.

"Welcome aboard!" She stood straight and waved for George to join her. George paused. He was about to board his dream.

6

Donna wore a wide grin while waiting for him to board. George was wearing the same smile. He wasn't as nimble as Donna and didn't hop onboard. Grabbing the rail, he pulled himself up and onto the sailboat. The last time he was on one like this was many moons ago when he and his wife dared to dream about sailing. Now aboard, he looked at the lines, all carefully laid and coiled. He wondered if Donna was the one who took care of the boat, or if a hired hand scrubbed it down. If it was up to Jim, he would hire someone; if it was up to Donna, she would do it. Donna and Jim seemed worlds apart. George had a hard time reconciling how those two ever got together.

"She is beautiful." George continued to marvel at the workmanship and detail. He noticed how the winches were pulled farther aft from the one in the picture that hung on his wall. There were additional lines for another sail. He wasn't sure if that was for two jibs - a cutter rig, or if it was for a spinnaker. He imagined a multicolored spinnaker leading the boat downwind.

"She is indeed. Follow me." Donna led him below deck. Unlike the Catalina, this sailboat was decorated in cherry wood. It was much darker than the standard light teak. Blue curtains and ivory colored pillows accentuated the brass fittings. A decent galley with a double sink and gimbal mounted stove gave an indication of some wear. Food had been prepared here. There were some chips in the wood along the counter. There were a few scuff marks on the floor. Unlike the pristine Catalina, this place had been lived in. The guest quarters housed some additional sails, boat hooks, a bosun's chair, and odds and ends that a boat out to sea might need in a pinch. No one would be sleeping there.

The master suite was large and accommodating. There were drawers under the bed. A door led to the combination shower and head.

"Very nice," George said after the initial inspection.

"Yeah, I'm sure it isn't as nice as the other boat." She swatted her hand in the direction of the Catalina.

"You haven't stepped foot on 'Fickle Girl?'"

"Are you kidding me?! Jim bought that for his latest tart. I'm old news – I get the old boat."

George didn't deny her statement. "But I mean he paid...."

"Fuck that." There was pain in her voice and George could tell he had crossed some invisible line.

"I like this boat better. It has character."

Donna softened. "Yeah old boats have character, but when they get old they're often ignored."

"I dreamed about sailing a boat like this," said George. "This boat is perfect just as it is. There is nothing wrong with it. Really." Donna started crying. George held her. She had seemed strong while swimming during their SCUBA adventure. Now, she seemed like a scared girl.

"It's over. It is really over. He's with her now. I don't know what I'm going to do."

Pulling back and holding her by the shoulders, George looked into her eyes and said with deep conviction, "After what I saw today, you're an incredibly strong, self-reliant woman. You have a beautiful light that shines in you. Maybe you haven't had to tap into it for a while because you've been living the..." George

138

paused. He was about to say 'the good life' but knew that was not the right thing. "...the soft life."

Through her tears she chuckled. "Yeah, I've been living the 'soft life.' I'm just afraid."

George contemplated the intersection of their lives. He pondered that moment when he wondered how he could go on in light of his unemployment.

"The other day, I was sitting in my car thinking my life was over. Today you showed me that it is really just beginning. Today you may be afraid, but tomorrow you'll find that strength that is buried deep inside you and you'll be all right."

The two moved to the settee and sat down. Donna reflected, "When it all started, I was so young. I didn't have anything." She turned her gaze back to George. "I was dirt poor, living in a rented room. I wanted to dive and sail. That's what I knew. Then Jim comes waltzing in. Before he got fat and ugly, he was quite charming."

They both chuckled.

"He offered me the world and I bought it. I did what he wanted me to do. I dressed like he wanted me to dress. I drove the fancy car. I quit my job. At first it was great. We went to parties and he showed me off. I was a star. I was their 'little darling.' But that world came with a price. There was a dark side to it. It wasn't long before I found out that Jim was cheating on me. I talked to some of the other women about it and they didn't seem to care. Their husbands were unfaithful, too. But they didn't care... they told me 'well that's just the way things are done around here.' They would cover up their pain by going out and buying things that were more and more extravagant. They lavished crap on their kids and bound them up with schedules that would make an ER doctor cringe."

Donna swallowed hard. Her mouth went dry. "Then I realized that these people were nothing like me. I wasn't like them and there was no way I could fit in. Maybe if I was willing to give up my soul, I could become them. Maybe today, I'd be drinking by the pool all day, backbiting so-and-so. But that is not me. I went back to work. Jim was furious. He threw a fit. He smashed things. He was about to hit me, but I didn't flinch. I wanted him to hit me. It was then I realized he was no longer Jim and I was no longer me."

George saw the strength that lurked deep in her soul. He said, "But then, when you went back to work, you found your freedom again."

"I did. It seems every time I start rebuilding my life, something happens and I have to start all over. But I'm prepared. I have money and a lawyer. I'm putting up a fight."

"I have no doubt," George replied.

Donna pulled George close and they hugged. She broke off. She knocked on the wall behind her. "Let's find the wind. This girl knows how to tame it. She can sail with a napkin and turn on a dime."

They both got up and headed up the short stairs by the galley.

On deck, they prepped the boat. George had read enough sailing magazines and had taken a few classes, so he wasn't a total novice. He struggled tying a clove hitch knot. Donna showed him with ease. Donna explained the boat to him, its quirks and nuances. Donna fired up the diesel and let it run. She checked the winches and the furling systems. She went aft and unhooked the power line that kept the batteries charged. George followed as she showed him where all of the filters were located.

She demonstrated how to light and set the stove. She took up the floor covering, which exposed the bilge,

140

and showed George the hidden piping underneath. She demonstrated how to open and close the three main water tanks with the seacocks. She went over controls for the manual pump in case things got a little out of control. Back on deck she opened a hatch behind the captain's wheel. She demonstrated how to steer the rudder using a tiller that you could insert, should the chain between the rudder and wheel become broken.

It took about two hours. George wondered why Donna was going through so much detail. In his few classes, he had not gotten such a intimate explanation of the various systems. Nevertheless, Donna persisted, checking and describing every facet of the boat. Donna had George change the filters. She had him manually raise the sail and unfurl the jib. She was careful to explain each line. At the helm, she demonstrated how to bring up the GPS, wind direction and speed, radar and a host of other electronic monitoring systems. These instruments were redundant of those found down below at the navigation station. The boat could be sailed without leaving the wheel.

The sun was just starting to change from silver to gold as they got underway. Though George had been tired after his dive, the thought of sailing the Tartan rejuvenated both his body and spirit. He had looked at the poster on his cubicle wall for years. Today he was starting to live the dream. Donna gunned the motor and the boat slowly started forward. She eased off, the inertia now beaten.

"Take the wheel." She turned to George and let go. George had no choice. He sprung to the wheel, his heart pounding. She laughed. "We're goin' thataway." She pointed down the narrow channel. "Try not to hit any other boat, unless you have a spare million bucks to give away."

That did nothing to put George at ease. He was gripping the wheel with white knuckles. The boat seemed like it knew where it was supposed to go. At one point, he drifted a little and overcompensated. The boat hesitated in its movements, but veered toward a large Hinkley sailboat with glistening woodwork.

"Relax... you only need to make little adjustments. We haven't even gotten to the fun part yet. If you want to wreck into a boat, you know how to pick 'em. That one is about three mil..."

George tried to relax. "It's like driving a car.... It's like driving a car... It's like..." The mantra didn't work. They were coming to the end of the canal and what lay before them was the open ocean. Donna got up and helped him navigate the channel. Green and red signposts indicated the lanes of safe passage. Speed boats surged past them. They bobbed in the small wake. There was some "funny water" as the current of the larger ocean met the placid water of the canal. The sailboat bobbed in strange ways and George could feel his legs acting like shock absorbers as he headed into the big blue.

"We're heading south." Donna grabbed the wheel and the boat spun about immediately. She revved the motor and the boat responded creating a small white trail of foam. After a tour along the banks of the island chain, they picked up another channel that headed back toward land. George could see a bridge spanning a small strip of land getting larger as the boat carved its way through the water toward it.

George couldn't tell if the mast was too tall for the bridge. It looked like they were headed for disaster. Donna took the wheel. There were some tricky currents that wanted to beach the sailboat. The mangroves were drawing ever closer, threatening to snarl the 'Property of a Lady.' George was certain that the mast would snap and the boat would founder, but Donna piloted on without a care in the world.

He looked up as the steel girder supports arched overhead.

"That was close!"

"Yeah, I've done this before. You have to know the tides. If there was an extremely high tide, I wouldn't do this, but we cleared it by a few feet. You were right under the mast, so your perspective was a little off. We're swimming in the gulf now. They motored for a few minutes and Donna put the boat into idle.

"Well, we don't have much wind. It usually dies down around now. Let's raise the main sail!"

They opted to avoid using the power winch and pulled the lines by hand. The sail came out and the jib opened up without any problem. As they luffed, the main sail barked softly in the calm evening whisper of a breeze. Donna turned the wheel and the sails started behaving. They filled slightly and the boat listed to port. She cut the motor.

"Trim the jib a little." She straightened the rudder and the boat's bow nodded as if in agreement.

George had to remember which line was the active jib line before he pulled it. There was more resistance now as the wind tried to push the sail. He got the winch handle out of a nearby pocket and pulled the line tight. The craft picked up a little more speed. Donna gave George the wheel. He was thrilled. The boat was quiet as the wind carried it westward on a close-hauled starboard tack.

"Do you know how to come about?" asked Donna.

"Ummm…. Not sure I…"

"You have the easy part. You just say 'ready about' and I'll respond with 'ready.' Then you say 'helm's alee' and you turn toward starboard. Got it? I'll help you the rest of the way."

"Okay." George could feel a rush of blood going to his head. "Ready about." George almost started turning before Donna responded but caught himself.

"Ready!" She turned to him and smiled.

He turned the wheel and the boat started turning into the wind. As soon as the jib started coming across the bow, Donna pulled the opposite jib line. The jib ruffled, puffed out, and the sailboat responded by regaining the speed lost in the maneuver. Donna came over and stopped the turn.

They practiced this routine until George could feel when to turn and when to stop. He could feel the wind on his cheek and neck and was able to make minute changes that kept 'Property of a Lady' happy. They came about on a beam reach and the boat entered a galloping stride across the water. George couldn't contain his smile. Another sailboat was performing opposite maneuvers at a distance. He remembered the dolphins and understood their sense of play in the water.

George imagined himself being photographed for a calendar that would hang on the wall in a cubicle somewhere. Palm trees, setting sun, a beautiful woman, and the boat of his dreams combined in a picturesque montage worthy of June or July. A puff of wind came and the boat listed a little to starboard. There was a faint spray of salty mist that brushed the side of his face. He tasted it, and it tasted good.

They turned back, heading for a dead run back toward land as the sun was setting. Until then, he was cooled by the breeze, but since they were running with the wind, the heat returned and he started to sweat. He could see they were closing in on a cove. Close to shore

Donna took the wheel, started the motor and dropped the sails. They coasted to a cozy spot and set anchor.

"There are a few beers in the fridge. How about getting a couple?" Donna was the captain now and this sounded like a direct order. He went below. The fridge had a layer of frost and the beers were the only thing that weren't frozen.

The sun was setting. Yellow-orange bands stretched out to infinity, turning the water into a metal pool of liquid gold, purple and blue. Frigate birds circled overhead checking their territory before heading to their nests deep in the mangrove forest. They looked silver and black depending on how the light played off their feathers. The birds seemed to linger on the unseen waves of wind far overhead.

The two sat in silence, listening to the sounds coming from land and hearing the gentle lapping of the water against the boat. Donna held out her bottle. "To another perfect sunset."

"Yeah, perfect." They clinked bottles and returned to nature's show. The glow had turned a deeper red and the water was afire. It was a serene moment of pure bliss. The evening breeze didn't abate which kept the two comfortable and kept the boat free from the bugs that would otherwise smell blood and start to swarm. Altair, Deneb, and Vega were just staring to sparkle high in the early evening sky.

A moment of peace washed over the sailboat as a refreshingly cool breeze kissed the two with a barely perceptible passing.

"So why did you get with Jim in the first place?" asked George out of the blue.

"Huh…" Donna started reflecting on the past, playing reruns in her mind. "When I first saw Jim, he wasn't like he's now. But then again," she chuckled, "Neither am I."

She turned in her chair. "You see, I was always looking for adventure. That's why I took up sailing and SCUBA. It was a man's world, so early on I learned to take care of myself. I was working the desk, scheduling the boats, when Jim waltzed in. I didn't even look up. He said, 'So here I am. I'm new in town and I'd like to take you to dinner.'"

She opened her mouth, feigning surprise, in an attempt to recreate the moment. "Of course, I said, 'Sir, I'm here to schedule dive trips. If you would like to schedule a dive, I would be happy to help you.'"

"So he says, 'Do you go out on these boats?'"

"I answered him honestly, 'Occasionally.' So he keeps asking me a bunch of questions. 'When do you go on the boats? What kind of boats are they? How deep is the water?'"

"I figure he's a diver who is maybe a novice or something. I answer his questions and he signs up for three dives – all when I'm on the boat. The next day he boards the boat in shorts, sneakers, and a white shirt. He doesn't have a wet suit or a mask or anything. I wondered if he was a stalker or something. But he paid hundreds of dollars to just sit there on the boat."

George laughed. "I would have thought he would have started taking lessons or something."

"No," she replied. "He became known as the 'mascot.' For two weeks, he spent his money foolishly, and at the end of each boat trip he would ask me out. So, finally, just to get him to stop, I made a deal that he stop buying boat time and I'd go out with him – once. He agreed."

George responded. "That doesn't sound like Jim. He was always one to bargain for a better price."

"Well, I didn't know him then. So I thought I was solving a problem. So, I asked him where we were going. He says to dress in jeans and a shirt. Casual – that was okay with me. What I didn't know was that he rented a jet. So he picks me up and drives me to the airport where we take off in a jet and have dinner in New York City! Remember, I was young, so this was a tad scary. He takes me into Manhattan and buys me a dress and shoes and takes me to an upscale restaurant. After that, we go dancing. We hop back on the plane and I thought I'd gone to heaven. But we didn't come back here."

"Really? What happened next?

"He takes me to a place in Pennsylvania – a horse farm where we watched the sun rise over the mountains. He whips up a breakfast and we pack a picnic basket lunch. Mind you, I'd never been on a horse, but he tells me that they're trail horses and quite tame."

"Weren't you tired?"

"Well, I had gone from reality to fantasy at that point. He said, 'If I only get you once, I'm gonna make it count.' So we take off on the horses. I'm dead tired so we lay out a blanket on a hill overlooking farm country. We both nap until noon and then open the picnic basket filled with wine and cheese. It was surreal. We return the horses, head back onto the plane, and come back twenty-four hours later."

"Sounds like he was really trying to charm you."

"He was. It was wonderful at first. We made plans, and he lavished me with whatever I wanted. I guess I fell for the dream."

George wondered whether or not he should ask her this next question. "So when did things change?"

"I never realized that I was his 'project.' That's just the way he is. He gravitates to one thing. He obsesses over it. What I didn't know then, but do know now, is that when he has totally conquered his 'project' he moves on to something – or someone – else. "

"I'm sorry." George said.

"Don't be. It's not your fault. Look – I got myself into this and I'm going to get myself out of it. In the mean time, I'm trying to put some of the pieces of my world back together. It's kinda like this boat. You treat her right, take care of her, and she'll last a lifetime. But if you fight her, you'll lose. Jim is going to lose."

"You're a very special person. I hope it all works out."

The conversation had waned along with the daylight. Both sat there in their own contemplations. George had done more new things this day than he had done in the last six years. He, for a moment, was able to suspend the reality of his concerns, focusing on the concerns of another, and realize the value of a single day. Donna pondered where her future would lead without Jim in the picture. Donna took a swig and turned to George, "You have five dollars?"

"Ummm...," the question seemed an odd way to break the silence. "Not with me. These are Jim's pants. I left my stuff back at the house."

"...but you have five dollars, right?"

"Yeah."

"Good! It's yours."

"What's mine?" George was confused.

"This." She stretched out her hand like Vanna White on "Wheel of Fortune."

"The.... 'Property of a Lady'?" George laughed. It was a good joke. "Oh my God!" He closed his eyes, tilted his head back, and laughed hard. It was contagious. Donna couldn't help herself. She couldn't remember the last time she really laughed. There had been the polite chuckle, but this was a belly roll laughter that came from deep within. They were both punchy and tired and the laughter released from inside them like a waterfall.

Once George had regained his breath he said, "Oh that was great."

"What?" Donna said innocently.

"You - selling me the boat for five dollars. I can see it now…" George spread his thumb and pinky in a mock telephone. "Honey, I have something to tell you…. Just bought a $300,000 boat for five dollars. Hope you don't mind. Shall I swing by and pick you up?"

They both laughed a little more.

"So what is your wife going to say?"

"What?" responded George.

"When you tell your wife that you bought a boat for five dollars."

"Oh come on…" George was suddenly realizing that this wasn't a joke.

"I'm serious."

"You can't be… the Tartan 4100…" He stopped and looked in her eyes. There was no madness. There was no prankster lurking within. She was serious. For an instant he imagined being the owner of his dream. But something prevented him from moving from fantasy to reality. The leap was just too far.

"George, I like you. I like you a lot. You're the first person I've met in a long time that I could say that to. Most of Jim's 'buddies' hang around because they're out to drain him. They want to eat him alive. You're not like that. You have a kind face."

"But…."

"Let me finish…" She stood up, leaned against the rail and continued. "It's over between Jim and me. I know that. You know that. This boat was a symbol of our love. It was the physical representation of the dreams we made together. Now those dreams are gone. I want a sailboat, but I can't hang on to this one. I want you to have it."

She turned and faced him. The sunset reflected on her face with deep golden hues making her look more like a modern day Rembrandt painting. "I'm going to get

149

a lot of money from the divorce. And I'm going to make Jim pay for it. He's an asshole to let me go. I'm the best thing he's got. So I want him to know what our love is worth to me. Five dollars."

"Look, that might...."

"... put you in an awkward position? Trust me, if you work for Jim, he'll put you in a worse position. What happened when Jim sold out *Run-Rite*? Did you get a bonus? Did you get compensated for your years of service?"

George couldn't remember ever getting a bonus from Jim once they sold the company. He wanted to defend his old employer, but was feeling uncomfortable.

"Well, I stayed on at Watsitumi..."

"Yeah, and look where you're now. You're right back where you started."

The words stung but George couldn't deny her logic. The thought of coming between his potential employer and his new friend was irreconcilable. He also had a hard time fathoming how Alicia was going to take the news.

"Okay, George. Since you're such a hard man to bargain with, I'll sweeten the pot a little."

George wondered what was going to come next. A bead of sweat formed on his forehead. He wasn't trying to bargain at all.

"What... the house? How about a million bucks," said George trying to diffuse the situation.

"Slip fees can break your back. Just finding a place to put the boat can take years. I have a slip in Key West. I'll give you the slip contract for free. You have the slip for a year. If at any point during the year this deal seems bad, I'll buy the boat and the slip back from you. Okay?"

George's mouth felt like he had just tried to eat an entire peanut butter sandwich in one huge bite. There was no more beer in his bottle. This was too good to be true. He had a quivery feeling in his belly. Reality had slipped away with this offer. Nothing seemed to make sense. Key Largo was like a drug and today he had totally lost touch with reality. Donna persisted.

"Tomorrow you're going to get an offer from Jim. You already know that. We don't have to tell him about our deal. It'll take a day for the lawyers to draft the paperwork for the boat. You don't have to sign it until after the employment offer. I'll hold your five bucks in escrow if you like."

She chuckled. George just tried to swallow.

"Oh, you're out of beer. Let me get you another. She traipsed down the steps and out of sight. Only then did George realize that he had been holding his breath. He was probably turning blue. He didn't want to hyperventilate. It was as if the involuntary reflexes of his body had given up and he was in command of everything: heart, bowels, saliva, breathing, and all those other minute tasks that kept a person alive.

He stood up to find his knees weak and shaking. George knew that it wasn't the sailing adventure that caused this phenomenon. Regaining his strength, he ran his hands along the chrome. He could see his distorted reflection in the winch. He walked along the length of the boom and felt the cool metal. His touch made the boom rock a little. It creaked against the lines that held it in place.

This could be his. It was almost his. He had come for a job, in the face of utter financial defeat, and found his dream boat. It was almost his. He could sell it and be financially... George second guessed that thought. If this boat was his, he would never sell it. But he also felt that he couldn't own such a craft. He had a notion of what the monthly costs would be. He also had the reality that he lived nowhere near water, so the boat would go largely unattended. But then, if he got the job offer here in Largo, and he accepted, then he would probably move. He thought of living on the boat with Alicia. He went forward and looked back, the boat's lines seducing him.

"I see you two are getting to know each other a little better." Donna appeared with another cold brew. George stepped aft. He took the cold bottle and upended the bottle in a long draught.

Donna asked, "Still trying to get your head around it?"

"This is a dream."

Donna corrected him, rapping her fingers on the boom. It made a muted metallic pinging sound, as if church bells were ringing in the distance. "No – this is reality. You can touch it. You can feel it. I saw the look in your eyes. Hell, tomorrow your cheeks will hurt from smiling so much."

George didn't deny it. There was a point where he felt at one with the Tartan. But he still couldn't grasp the situation. There was no reply. George had been so dumbfounded by the offer that he wondered if he could remember the English language.

"We'd better get back. Jim will be returning from his 'business trip' tomorrow." She made quotation marks with her fingers and then rolled her eyes. "So, what do you think of your new boat?"

"I hate to use these words again, but 'Wow – incredible.'" They both laughed.

"We are going to have to work on your vocabulary."

Donna piloted the sailboat back, more comfortable than George with navigating, as the embers of sunlight faded and the tropical night consumed the last remnants of the day. George was totally spent. He had packed two life-changing events into a single day.

He wondered if he would make it back to the room before he passed out.

They secured the 'Property of a Lady' and said their goodnights with a hug. He headed back to the Marina Del Mar with a throng of mosquitoes haunting his every move. He could hear the music playing from the hotel bar and restaurant. He also heard the young man still wailing away at the Ocean Divers Cantina. Looking up he saw dive gear draped across the railing from a fellow diver who, apparently, also had a good day.

Heading down the hallway, he heard a man moaning in the throes of passion. He didn't, however, hear a female join him in the duet of consummation. He laughed and stifled, thinking he might have been heard. George stumbled into his room. It seemed an eternity since he had left.

He grabbed his cell phone and pushed the speed dial for home.

"It's about time you called..." his wife said playfully on the other line. "How was your day?"

"Incredible. I have something to tell you...."

7

George woke at 9:30 a.m. To the party-going crowd in Key Largo, this was the time when you stopped snoring and entered that deep sleep your body craves after a night of debauchery and cheap liquor. For George, whose habit was to rise at 5:30 a.m., this was the latest he had slept in years.

He was tickled at Alicia's sarcastic response to the purchase of the boat, once she finally gave in and realized that George was not kidding. "Hey, you'd better take it now before she changes her mind! You didn't have to do anything else to get that boat, did you?"

Unlike yesterday, this was a day of relaxation. George didn't fully understand the lengths to which he had to go merely to get a job interview. He saw no purpose for yesterday's SCUBA dive. It seemed strange to expect every potential employee to go to such extremes.

The experiences of the last twenty-four hours were transforming. He recounted, in detail, the events of his underwater adventure. When he closed his eyes, he could feel the current of the water flowing around him. He enjoyed the way he felt floating underwater. It was an alien world that now beckoned for his return. This was combined with the feeling of the rocking of the boat. It was as if the water had somehow permeated his entire being, working its way through him and replacing the land-based George with one in harmony with the water. He remembered the older couple on the dive boat. They seemed to *know*. Like a Christian convert, he felt like his world was altered in an indescribable way such that he would never be the same. He had become one with both water and wind. The water cleansed him and the wind refreshed his soul.

At lunch he headed over to the Coconuts Restaurant. Some vacationers were sitting around the bar. Their large combination motor/sail boats were barely able to fit in the slips. Unlike the Tartan George sailed yesterday, these behemoths had two stories, complete with folding chairs, hibachi, bicycles, and fishing poles. The owners woke up early and scrubbed down the deck and hull. It was now lunchtime and they were making their transition from bloody marys to whiskey sours as the sun crossed the zenith.

A wealthy owner of one of those larger vessels, after more than enough drinks, had taken his bar stool podium and was lecturing anyone within earshot. "Hell, I don't have to follow the law anymore. You see, because our president ain't from America, we don't have to follow the law. So I just do what I please." He paused, trying to clear some of the mental haze that built up from his morning libations. "I worked my way up from the stockroom to become....so I say goddam this country, we should all get dual citiz... citizer... citizenship."

The balding man tending bar gave him another round and shook his head.

George sat down and ordered a burger, fries, and a soda.

"So, whaddya think pal?" The drunk had a new audience in George. George was now held captive until his order arrived. "We all goin' to hell?"

"Are you an evangelist?" George said, deciding to have a little fun while he was waiting.

"Hell no! But they make millions on T.V. and don't have to do a thing but sell themselves. I'm talking about the good ol' U.S. of A. I don't have to pay taxes, because this country doesn't have a president."

155

"What do you mean, of course we have a president," George retorted. He had seen this man on his large boat called "Oasis." It was a motor sailer, which meant it wasn't very good at doing either, so it basically sat in the dock.

"He is an illegal *alien*." The man said leaning forward. He said the word "alien" like someone from one of those conjecture style shows from the seventies, trying to connect aliens, pyramids, Stonehenge and the Bermuda Triangle all in a sixty minute parade of "What ifs?"

"I think all politicians are *aliens*," George responded trying to match this man's statement with the same innuendo filled intonation. George wondered when he would get his food. George questioned whether this man was truly insane, or whether the alcohol had warped his mind temporarily. The man pondered George's statement and had a look not unlike a computer with its hour glass tipping and the hard drive spinning away.

"Nah. Couldn't be. We got some republicans in office who are red, white, and blue. Got some of them who fought in wars...."

George's first reaction was surprise. The man at the bar had actually taken his statement seriously. His second reaction was disgust. George wondered about the connection between fighting in a war and holding a potential office. George almost blurted out, 'Oh, you killed someone? Then you would make a good politician!' But he held his tongue.

"There is a conspiracy, you know. They're trying to sell America right out from under our noses. That is why I bought a boat. I figure they can have the land, but they can't take the sea. So I bought..." The man raised his glass, the ice tinkled in tribute to his next statement... "the 'Oasis.'"

"So you're seeking political refuge and refusing to pay taxes because we are being invaded by foreign forces?"

The man belched a little. The pungent smell had an overtone of alcoholic sweetness. "Damn skippy..."

It was an interesting answer to an illogical premise. George thought that the man had actually put thought into the process — paranoid thought that extended beyond his drunken state. Curious, George decided to challenge the man.

"Sounds like you're running away from the problem."

"Running away? Running away?" The man chortled. The man sought an immediate response, but he couldn't focus long enough to put an argument together. He had rarely been challenged. "I am merely seeking the best vantage point when the shit hits the fan. This country is going down blazing. Can't you see it? Can't you see it.... You never told me your name..."

George didn't want to give this guy his real name – drunk or not. "Alexander..."

"Alexan.... Alxean..." Strike two. The man opted to bunt. "Alex... *we're different. We know...*" By offering the man his name, George was suddenly in this guy's club – some secret society – which set him apart from his responsibility to country. He was now a member of the drunk, rich renegade club. "I mean. It is not just the country. Everybody depends on us. So when we go down. The world goes down with us."

The man had transitioned from an annoying drunk to an annoying drunk who was trying to be an apocalyptic prophet. He grabbed George's shoulder. This was their secret drunken handshake. "We *know!* Luckily we have the money to do something about it. We can get on our boats and find safety until this whole thing blows over.... The government take over... the land… hell, global warming… with a boat…. No problem…."

The inebriated man was migrating from annoyance to delusion to incoherence. George wondered if this man's partner who shared the 'Oasis' was now out shopping for a new set of clothes until nightfall when she would join him in his stupor of paradise. The man seemed out of breath, as if he had run around the bar three times. Proclaiming doom and gloom apparently took a lot of energy.

"You don't think global warming is a myth?" George asked the question because weather seemed non-political.

"Hell no! I'm a sailor! I see the weather every day."

George pondered that statement and wondered who on the planet had not seen the weather every day. Perhaps there was someone who lived in a cave who never emerged. The man slapped his hand on the bar. "Hell… all we got is weather. All we got is weather. They're changing it."

Now curious, George had to ask. "Who?"

The man looked around like he was secret agent number nineteen about to pass off important documents to secret agent number eighteen. He licked his lips. George leaned forward. The man had forgotten how to whisper, but this was his best attempt.

"The *democrats*. They're seeding the clouds. They're making it warmer so they can say they were right."

George thought it was an interesting use of political funds. The man continued, his speech slurred. "They are seeding the fucking clouds to melt the icecaps. They want to bring on flooding because most people live on the coast. Those people? *Republicans*…"

George had not seen that one coming. He also didn't see his lunch coming and really wanted it to arrive so he could get away from this inebriated prophet of doom.

"It all has to do with population control. They kill the millions of people on the coast because of the flooding." This was the Albert Einstein of Key Largo. "They instill fear and panic which leads to world domination."

The man got way too close to George's face. "That's it. When people are afraid, they become like sheep.... sheep don't ya know. Sell ice to Eskimos. Democrats... democrats... damn.... World is going to hell."

George's food came and he decided to eat it by the pool. It had taken too long to arrive and the man was getting creepy. George needed an excuse and lunch seemed the best one he had.

"Well, I got my lunch and I gotta go. Nice talking to you," George lied.

"You are a good man... Fred... er Sam... er... What was your name?"

"Hassid," George replied with a combination of sarcasm and distaste for the drunk.

"Hassid?" The man leaned back as though he had been shot with a paint ball gun. Secret agent nineteen had been double crossed. Then he looked at the white features and German/Irish heritage of George and began to laugh. "Hassid! Ha! I get it.... That is a good one pal! Yeah – Ha –fucking – sid! Ha!"

George left the man in his fit of hysterics. He glanced over his shoulder to make sure his new found friend wasn't going to follow him. That was unlikely. The man was glued to his bar stool, looking for the next victim to impart his political insights. A little kid in blue swim shorts and water wings came running across the deck, and George had to lift his food high so the kid wouldn't be wearing a French fry wig. The young one quickly turned and did a cannonball by his older sister who was now screaming.

He made his way to a blue folding lounge chair, straddled the chair and sat. He placed his plate in front of him and put his drink on the hot concrete. A little lizard ran past on its way to the darker, moister part of the landscape behind George.

Picking up a fry and dipping it in the small mound of ketchup, George wondered about that drunk. Was his disassociation from reality born out of decadent success? Or, was it somehow tied to this place? Maybe it was some combination of upbringing, media, and alpha dominance. The man at the bar was still talking, though everyone around him had scattered.

George wondered if he would turn into a bar toad in light of success? Would he find someone young enough to be his daughter and try to seduce her with jewels and a fancy car? At this point in his life he could easily say no. But then he didn't have any money to speak of, so he had no real frame of reference. He loved Alicia and he cherished their relationship. He was not the most attractive man, so no woman after seeing a ring on his finger had ever made a pass at him. But then, he didn't have any diamonds, Armani suits, or a Lotus car as a plaything. He did have a boat - or at least he would after he signed the paperwork. Was this the beginning of his downfall? He shuddered at the thought. "It couldn't happen to him," he thought. "Could it?"

George tried to stop thinking about that possibility by rehearsing responses to some questions that Jim might ask during the evening's upcoming interview. It was difficult because he didn't have a clue what he would be offered. He went over his work history. He imagined questions relating to his personal life and involvement in the community. George could only draw responses with broad paint strokes. He couldn't whittle down a detailed game plan.

He finished his meal and moved his plate from the reclining chair to the ground. He adjusted the chair so he could lie down and feel the warmth of the Largo sun.

He was never good at test taking, and quickly abandoned the task of trying to come up with pat answers for hypothetical questions. His mind went back to his wonderful dive and sail experience. It wasn't long before the details faded to blissful blackness. Under the afternoon Florida sun, George fell into a deep sleep.

ও ও ও

He returned to the Coconuts Restaurant that evening clean and shaven. The drunk from the afternoon had disappeared. The place was filling with the evening mealtime crowd. Men in Hawaiian shirts and women in sundresses sat in the plastic chairs, sipping a variety of pretty drinks. He recognized a few of the people from his sailing excursion. By their hand motions, he knew they were talking about their diving experience. There was no need for words. The light in their eyes told the tale of personal adventure and discovery.

There were some patrons who looked like honeymooners. They snuggled together despite the heat. They had built a small cocoon around their world where they could share intimacy.

The intimate couple was in contrast to those at the bar. There was a line of men and women who seemed to *need* a drink. Though there were couples sitting next to each other, they seemed to find solace in their own space, rather than the shared space of two people in an intimate relationship.

161

George wondered if the drinking couple at the bar was the makeup of a couple who had sailed together for too long. On a sailboat, traveling across the big blue ocean, couples would have to put up with each other for long stretches of time. When a crisis hit, they only had each other. When they were at odds with each other, the boat became a very small space. It was its own world. That world could be paradise, purgatory, or hell, depending on how well the couple got along.

George read somewhere that the man on the ship was the "captain." He was in charge of every aspect of the vessel. The woman, however, was the admiral and had supreme authority to tell the captain where to go.

George scanned the room and wondered which among the crowd were divers, sailors, or both. He turned his attention beyond the people to the tropical paradise that enveloped the restaurant.

The sun was illuminating everything with a golden hue, painting the landscape with the brushstrokes of an antique postcard.

George stayed out in the sun a little too long this afternoon and had a pale rosy chest, legs, and back. He had that prickly feeling of skin that needed some moisturizing repair. He put on his white shirt, but felt this was not the right place to wear a suit. Instead he put on his khakis, which were a bit too wrinkled, but a step up from his shorts.

Having arrived before the Dalburths, the waitress seated George at a table that overlooked the slips behind the Marina-Del-Mar. He imagined the Tartan parked with the other boats. He could see in his mind's eye the mast towering over some of the power craft that clogged the slips. He could almost hear the sounds of the halyards gently ringing against the mast as the boat gently rocked. He pictured Alicia in shorts and a blouse emerging from below, smiling and waving.

162

George returned to reality when the waitress asked if he wanted something from the bar. He was nervous, but didn't want alcohol for fear it would erode his ability for quick thinking. He ordered an iced tea. Jim and Donna arrived as the waitress delivered his drink. Beads of moisture had already started forming on the glass as she set it on the table.

"You're not going soft on me now, are you George?" Jim asked. Motioning to the waitress, he commanded, "A round of beers for all of us."

The waitress nodded and headed to the bar.

"You look like you're getting the hang of this place, George. You fit in, what with the tan and all."

George knew he wasn't exactly tanned, but this was the chit-chat before the interview. George was on guard. He replied with a practiced formality. "I really like Key Largo. I'm sure Alicia would love it also." He took a second to look at Donna before she sat down. She was in an aqua designer sundress that had a lavish print. She had done her hair and put on makeup. She knew how to transform herself into a radiant goddess. Heads turned as she sat down at the small table. Jim put his brief case on the table, nearly knocking over the tea. George remembered Jim's briefcase from the *Industrial Spotlight* front page photograph.

"How was your business trip?" George asked.

"Making progress, making progress. Rome wasn't built in a day you know."

George shot a quick glance to Donna who was finishing the involuntary roll of the eyes.

Jim leaned back, folding his hands over his protruding belly. Mindlessly twiddling his thumbs, he said, "You did it. I'm proud of you. You're the first you know."

"Excuse me?" George looked at Jim with a quizzical look.

"You passed the first test. You came down here. That shows initiative. You took the SCUBA dive tour thing with Donna. That shows desire. And you're here now. That shows determination. I need those things for what I'm about to tell you. But first, I need you to sign something. He unzipped his briefcase and pulled out a piece of paper. "It is a non-disclosure statement. You can read all the legal mumbo-jumbo, or just sign and date the bottom. I gotta tell you, if you so much as tell your wife about this, I'll sue your socks off."

There was a pause. No one moved. Then Jim let out a belly laugh. "Aw hell George, lighten up! You look too uptight! I just don't want Disney or somebody stealing my plans. That's all. So let me clue you in."

As George signed the paper, Jim got out a thin laptop from the briefcase. He moved the case off the table and replaced it with the laptop. He raised the laptop lid and sat back, glancing over his shoulder, looking for the waitress and his beer.

"So, Donna didn't spill the beans, did she?"

George answered, "I tried to pry it out of her, but she kept her mouth shut."

Donna remained oddly quiet. George could tell that she was trying to paint a neutral face. She didn't want to be read. She offered no comment. Oddly, she seemed as nervous as George.

The waitress came with the beers and menus. The small table couldn't accommodate the laptop and the menus, so everyone propped the menus in their laps as they scanned the specials and standard fare.

After ordering, Jim turned his attention back to the laptop.

"Damn these things..." He tapped some keys and tried to move the cursor around using the small track pad below the keyboard. He was struggling to get something going, but had no success. Frustrated, he lowered the lid.

"George, if I can get this damn thing to work, I want to show you my latest project. Since you have come here, I've been showing you some things. First, what do you think of Largo?"

George didn't hesitate. "I love this place." This was no lie.

"Okay, but what did you *see?*"

"Of course most of my time was spent diving. It seems there is a big dive community here."

"Aha!" Jim pointed a stubby finger in George's direction. "You know, I have been here long enough to see the good, the bad, and the ugly. You saw that Key Largo is a pit stop on the way to Key West. Who comes here? Divers! So you know what my plan is?"

"You want to build a dive center?"

Jim paused as he took a long swig from his beer. He emptied it with the next gulp. George only had time for a taste. Donna's beer sat untouched, the glass bottle perspiring under the evening heat.

"Think bigger! There are already dive places littering this place. You know the reason that people are heading out of here for Key West? They have great places to eat. They have places to shop. They have entertainment. Largo is stuck. Look, if all this place offers is diving, then why am I here? I don't dive. Never will. But that doesn't mean that I'm not fascinated by the ocean. I could take a glass bottom boat and look down on the reef, but that doesn't do it either. It doesn't get me down there with the fish."

The waitress came with another beer for Jim. "When I was a kid, I saw the movie '20,000 Leagues Under the Sea' and wanted to be Captain Nemo. I'd forgotten about the movie until I came here. Once I saw all these divers, I knew there was an untapped market. It took me a couple of years to put it together, but I came up with an idea."

Jim opened the laptop again and tried fumbling with the machine.

"I have a damned PowerPoint slideshow here, but I can't.... goddamn." He wriggled up his face into a stern gaze as though the intimidation would cause something within the operating system to bend to his will.

George looked to Donna. She kept her face expressionless. He wondered how well practiced she was at maintaining this mask. It seemed like an ability acquired after their marriage started deteriorating.

George slid around closer to Jim. George saw the icon shortcut on the desktop and double clicked it. The slideshow opened up without a problem.

"Excellent. This is why I need you on the team. You have computer skills."

Double clicking an icon hardly seemed the test of "computer skills" but the act appeared to be beyond Jim's comprehension. The program loaded the file and Jim seemed to know what to do from this point forward. He set the slideshow in motion.

"The world is mostly submerged underwater." He started with a voice that sounded like on some bad radio narrator. "But we are stuck on land. A lucky few can dive beneath the waves." He changed the slideshow to a picture of his wife with a skimpy bikini, BCD, and tank. She was waving underwater. Though she wasn't looking at the computer screen, she instinctively knew which photo was being displayed. She covered her face in embarrassment and some other emotion George couldn't read.

"But the rest of us are relegated to land." The picture showed a purchased royalty free picture of crowded downtown New York City.

"But what if we could all go underwater? What if there was a place where we could all enjoy the underwater world, with all of the comforts of land?"

The image faded slowly to a computer image of a large domed structure underwater with what appeared to be submarines heading to, and docking at, this submerged structure of steel and glass. Jim paused for dramatic effect. "...Nemo Land."

A large, curved, metallic skeleton held oblong and spherical transparent bubbles. Transparent tubes connected areas in a complex array, which made the whole architectural design look like the beast from the deep that threatened Jules Verne's Nautilus.

George looked dumbfounded. The scale of the project was enormous. It could have been authored by the likes of Verne. The image showed small children looking out of the submarine windows with eyes wide and hands splayed across the large glass portal as it made its way to the docking areas. Through the curved structure, a hallway of people made their way to various locations around the main, domed, multi-level structure. Schools of fish surrounded the subs. Groups of people in SCUBA outfits swam around the exterior of the grand structure.

Another slide showed the cockpit of the submarine, with its crew resembling that of a jumbo jet. Computer readouts relayed approach vectors. A waitress was serving coffee to the communications officer. The scene could have been lifted from a science-fiction movie. The illustration was life-like and conveyed the scale of the operation.

Another slide highlighted the interior of the domed structure. The point of view came from someone standing on the second story of the domed structure looking up to the submarine overhead. Popular retail chains lined the walls. Schools of fish darted on the other side of the glass.

"Wow... incredible." George said automatically. Donna huffed.

Jim continued. "This is a big project. Jacques Cousteau created an underwater laboratory or something way back when. Every time somebody builds one of these things it is for 'scientific purposes.' Yeah – I know there are a few little underwater hotels with five or six rooms. But they are small and in remote places like Fiji. We need to build this structure right here. We have to become the only under water community with stores, hotels and restaurants. We are perfectly situated for something like this." George pushed his stubby index finger on the table. "Look - to the north we have Disney World and all those theme parks. To the south we have Key West. This is a natural spot for an attraction. But Largo's greatest asset is buried under fifty feet of water. I can't bring it to the people, so I'll bring the people to the attraction."

Jim changed slides again. There was a water park inside the dome. Pictures of little children going down a slide with the ocean overhead seemed to contradict logic. "What about this? An underwater - water park!"

He changed slides once more. People dressed casually were dining at a restaurant. "How about getting the freshest seafood you could ever imagine at the 'Coral Paradise Restaurant and Lounge?'" The non-bearing walls of the restaurant were made from clear acrylic. A variety of sea creatures swam within these transparent walls, eyeing the patrons seated at the table. Waiters carried seafood dishes as the living marine relatives from the aquatic walls looked on.

In the next slide, women clothes shopped. Fish overhead gazed down in wonder at the customers picking their way through racks of coral colored dresses.

Other women looked at purses with sea-shell clasps. The rendered images displayed products, each, in some way, tying back to "Nemo Land."

"This place has a line of shops and galleries with the best of the best." Jim smiled, knowing that George was taken by the project. The slides were professionally created and captured Jim's vision.

Jim pressed the arrow and a scene of a family, asleep on beds in their hotel suite faded up. The picture window looked out, not on a parking lot, but a coral outcrop.

"Eh? Eh? We put a hotel inside the dome! It will be a complete underwater getaway. People who want a grand view will have to pay the price tag for a large window. Those who might be a little more squeamish can have windows and terraces that look out on all the activity inside. We would have suites that extend out and provide both."

George couldn't help but feel drawn toward the idea. He, too, had seen the movie, read the book, and fantasized about being Captain Nemo. With his latest diving adventure, he could grasp the beauty of the aquatic landscape. He tried to put himself in that place. George imagined himself as a twelve-year-old boy taking a submarine ride with his mom and dad to this place. He would be holding his mother's hand, not looking where he was going because of the life teeming outside the clear walls. He pictured himself eating an icecream sundae as a shark swam by. He could see himself going through the translucent water slide as dad waited at the bottom with open arms. Though the engineering hurdles seemed insurmountable, George could understand the appeal.

"I see that look in your eyes, George." Jim leaned back and put his hands behind his head and stretched. "You have the vision, right? Damn – when I started

169

thinking about it, I had the same look. It is every boy's wet dream. We all wanted to be Captain Nemo at some point or another. Hell, you dove under the water George!"

Jim poked George in the shoulder with a stubby finger.

"You did it! You swam with the fish. I can see it in you. You have that look."

There were butterflies of excitement fluttering around George's belly. His nervousness was replaced by intense curiosity. After a pause George said half to Jim, half to himself, "It is an amazing venture, but the place…. It seems so huge."

"You're right. We don't have all the resources to do everything at once. So here is the plan."

Jim went to the next slide and showed how construction of this massive piece of architecture would evolve. The images were spawned from a 3D computer generated model created by an advanced architectural firm. Each piece of the building was lowered into place and the progressive images demonstrated how the leviathan would emerge.

"We start with a docking platform and restaurant. This technology exists, pretty much. There are some marine labs that are as large as the restaurant area. So we build this main structure first. This will give us the capability to transport the equipment and material in an orderly fashion."

Jim pointed to the first structure. Donna sat back, ignoring the two men. She looked out at the water which had turned bronze with the setting sun. Jim moved his finger to the next larger area on the computer screen, leaving a little greasy streak on it as he did so.

"Then we move on to the shopping area. We need to build the revenue stream… then this larger area where we can put the hotels, and then finally, the amusement center."

With the slideshow completed, Jim shut the lid to the laptop. The waitress brought their meals.

There was a pause between the presentation and eating where George tried to soak it all in. Jim sat back and watched George pondering. Things made sense. He now understood the tour of Largo. He knew why he was sent on a dive. Their trips to Ocean Divers, the bar, and the dive shop were not merely coincidental. The purpose of the extra days was brought into focus.

"So whaddya think, George?"

"I am a bit overwhelmed. I don't know where to begin. It's an incredibly large project." George's wheels were spinning. Both the creative and practical sides of his brain were firing off with the notion of such an incredible idea. He wanted to know where he fit into the equation, but he didn't want to seem too forward.

Putting his napkin in his lap, George asked, "How far along are you with this project?"

"We are still in the development phase. We need to raise enough capital to make this work before we break ground. I don't want to start the project unless I know I can finish it. So, right now, the damn lawyers and accountants have control. I'm just looking for the right people to put in place once I pull the trigger. That is where you come in."

"Me?" George was waiting for this for days. This was the culmination of his stay.

"Yeah, I need you to help with marketing this thing. We need backers. We need some sheik sitting in the middle of the fucking desert to open his checkbook and get this party started. I think you're the man."

George was stuck on the idea of a Verne centered attraction. "Doesn't Disney own the rights to 20,000 Leagues?"

Jim's eyes narrowed and imparted the next statement like a monk sharing some God-given secret. "That's the beauty of Nemo Land... I'm not saying '20,000 Leagues' or anything like that. This way we can get away with it."

"So you want me to help promote – Nemo Land?" George had a problem with the name. "Wasn't Captain Nemo's hideaway called 'Volcania?'"

"Yeah, I think it was," replied Jim as he shoveled shrimp and rice into his mouth." But who knows that? Who would want to go to a place called 'Volcania?' Hey, if you can think of a better name, then go for it. That is why you're a marketing guy and I'm the idea man. I mean, the way I look at it, I need a partner in this. You might just be the guy. Heck, I just offered you the job and you're already making changes." Jim shoveled more of his food into his mouth. A few grains of rice escaped from his lip to the floor. Donna wondered if Jim actually tasted anything.

George stumbled over the word "partner." Was that an offer to be a partner or some slip of the tongue? "Partner? You mean someone sharing in the project, or a legal partner of the company?"

"You demonstrated your loyalty to those idiots at Watsitumi. Wouldn't you rather have something that you can put your heart into? Think about what you saw on your dive the other day. What about all those people who can't see what you saw? Maybe they're handicapped or something. I dunno. Maybe they would never be able to see what you saw. Right?"

Donna quietly ate her food, methodically raising her fork to her mouth like some Japanese tea ceremony, where every movement is articulated with the greatest of care. George still didn't understand the implication of the word "partner." Jim seemed to be dancing around the idea, making this more of a sales pitch than a job interview.

"So you want me to do the marketing? Would that mean travel? What would my responsibilities be?"

"Good questions," Jim answered. Just then a catamaran was heading out for a snorkel/sunset tour. Bob Marley played over the loudspeakers.

"See that?" Jim pointed to the catamaran. "You need to get the word out to them."

"So I'm professor Arronax," said George making a reference back to the Verne novel.

"Who?" George wondered if Jim had read the novel. He wondered how long it had been since Jim had seen the movie.

"Professor Arronax, he was the professor who…." Jim was looking at him with his head slightly tilted. It reminded George of a dog who couldn't fathom the activities of his master. "… never mind."

Donna blurted out a single chortle, which she masked by pretending like a piece of food had gone down the wrong pipe. Jim looked at her with glaring, evil eyes. George felt a divided loyalty between the couple.

George tried to envision how he might use the presentation and other promotional materials to market this underwater playground. This opportunity was a far cry from selling *Run-Rite* motors. But it still would be an American-made product. He could feel pride in that. He could see the potential for joining the ranks of the mega-theme parks.

And, more practically, he needed the job that Jim was offering. He could build a lifetime career out of this endeavor. Donna had shown him the beauty of the coral reef. It made him feel that this was an opportunity to bring his newly discovered love of the undersea world to the masses. He could see how this might be used to educate the public about the ocean waters. This might be an opportunity to teach the next generation how to care for this fantastic aquatic world. Donna explained the fragility of this eco-system. If she hadn't taken the time, perhaps he would have been more ambivalent about the project as a whole. She was quite positive about the love of diving.

However, she warned him about Jim. George trusted her. He had seen a tender side of her. He had seen her strength. What was it that gave her such concern? George wished Donna just blurted out her concerns. Nothing Jim had said, beyond the grand scope of the project, seemed unreasonable. He looked to her to try to read her face and get some insight as to why he should be wary. But she was not the Donna he had encountered recently. Rather she was now a china doll merely mimicking the beautiful Donna. He wanted her to speak, but she seemed to be under a gag order. He wondered if Jim had threatened her before their meeting.

"So when do I get started?" George asked.

"Whenever you want!" Jim replied, slapping George on the back. "But I don't want you involved unless you're one-hundred percent committed. I want to hear what you think about the project."

"I think it is plausible, but very complex. I don't see anything happening for years and I'm worried about the capital necessary to get this underway. "George pondered for a second. He wanted to make sure he knew what he was getting into. "Oh – I liked the slideshow. Do you have a site picked out?"

"Yep, sure do." Jim put down his fork and rummaged in his briefcase. He pulled out a map and opened it over everyone's food, not caring if the map landed in the linguini or the fish. The map was a navigational chart used by boaters. It had depth soundings and markers of interest. Jim had a large black area marking the primary site. "Here... see? There is the line of coral and we are placing the facilities there. This is where the subs will be parked."

George looked carefully at the map. He studied it in silence as Jim and Donna looked on. George got his reading glasses out from his shirt pocket so he could look at the areas in more detail. He saw that the docking area for the subs was the space currently occupied by Ocean Divers. A line was drawn from that point to the site of the underground facility. He noticed a red line that bisected the area. He traced his finger along that line. "Jim.... Hold on a sec..." George wanted to be sure that he wasn't in error. "Isn't that piece inside the park reserve...? See? This is part of the John Pennekamp Coral Reef State Park. It extends out to here." George pointed at the red line inside Jims black lines.

"Details, details." Jim went for the map, but George kept it open by placing his hands on the corners.

"In fact..." George hesitated. He knew that he was heading for trouble, but he couldn't let it go. "That is Eagle Ray Alley.... I went diving there. You want to put the dome over this spot? Don't you think that the conservationists would put a stop to that? You would have to destroy part of the reef for the foundation footing."

Jim snatched the map off the table from under George's hands and started folding it up all the wrong way. He couldn't get it to collapse properly. The food had migrated from the back of the chart to the front as a result of his failed origami.

Jim explained in a flustered tone, "Okay, I need to put it somewhere so you can see something interesting. There is only one place – Eagle Ray Alley. Look – you can't put this thing in the middle of nowhere. You know what all of the real estate people say about property. Location, location, location."

"How are you going to get permission...?"

"Money talks," said Jim regaining his composure. "I have already talked to the people at Pennekamp about making a secondary submarine dock at the park. You saw the amount of parking that place had. We rent the space from them. But we get it back in ticket sales for the sub ride. One hand washes the other. Simple. It is all about money. The park has trouble making ends meet anyway. This would give them a revenue stream that would allow them to extend their park in new directions. They would lose some ground, but would be able to get it back somewhere else."

George thought about the sandy trench. He reflected on the schools of fish. He could see the purple fan coral waving in the aquatic current. He imagined the other divers, young and old. He imagined the consequences that such a large structure would have on the environment. The structure would likely destroy the fragile balance of life that is already stressed by much lesser forces. He couldn't reconcile this in his mind. Jim had a point. They might be able to encompass a larger reserve, but Eagle Ray Alley was where he had seen life revel in a glorious underwater dance. Would he be able to compromise?

"Couldn't we move the location?" George started.

Jim turned to Donna. "You took him *there*. Didn't you? You took him *there!*" Jim's face turned red. He looked like someone who fell asleep out in the sun all day without any sunscreen. "You bitch!"

Donna remained cool. "You put no restrictions on *where* I was to take your prospects. You simply said to educate them about the underwater world. That's what I did. I'm only following orders."

Jim tried to regain his composure but his neck had gone from red to purple. He motioned for the waitress. "Whiskey sour... more whiskey than sour....

Double... oh, no ice." He turned back to George. "Sorry you had to see that, but she has been undermining my authority on this project since its inception. You need to understand that I have a vision for the greater good and I want you in as a partner. Do you understand? I'm not just looking to you as some employee."

George's mind was reeling. He felt that he couldn't say 'no' to this offer. He had a millionaire offering him a partnership. His wife and son would be set. He knew it. "Partner?"

A smile crossed Jim's face. "Partner!" Jim knew this was the key word – the bait – upon which George would bite. Donna's eyes widened but she didn't interject. "I need someone who can work with me... not against me on this one." He shot a glance to Donna. "With a small buy-in you and I can get rich on this thing."

Those words stunned George. Up until now, everything went beyond his wildest expectations. The offer of a partnership was what he wanted with *Run-Rite*. Now he was getting it in the form of "Nemo Land." But those two words stopped him short..."Buy-in?"

Jim let out a sigh. Quickly and matter-of-factly he said, "Of course I need some indication of commitment on your part. You seem behind me on this vision, but I need some assurances."

"What kind of assurances are you talking about?" George was starting to get nervous. The same feeling he experienced at Watsitumi when he was let go started creeping into his bloodstream. Though it was warm outside, George felt a cold breeze across his forehead.

Jim acted surprised by this question. For Jim, there needed to be some kind of sacrifice in order to demonstrate allegiance to this cause. This reinforced George's notion that this was more of a sales pitch and less of a job interview.

"Most of the people I have contacted about this have bought into it right away. Why even Mr. Sakimoto? Ishr...? Oh honey what the hell is his name?"

"Ishiri?" Donna responded without looking at Jim.

"Yeah, that's the one. He's in for $300,000. I talked to him last month."

At the sound of the name Ishiri, George's blood went cold. The man at Watsitumi who had found joy in destroying George's world was somehow tied to this endeavor. The man who fired him from Watsitumi would be involved in his new employment. "He's a partner?"

Jim sensed the tension in George's voice. "Yeah! Though not like you. You would take an active role in things. He's helping to fund the purchase of the first submarine. I know your predicament. I would say $100,000 would be sufficient. You could take out an equity loan on your home and have it paid back in three years - guaranteed."

George wanted to run away at this news. The opportunity was a sham. He had wasted days and wanted to run back to Alicia and cry. Each day he had hoped that this would be – "it." He wanted the security of employment and wanted to believe that there was a prospect for a job that he could embrace. But this was not it. It was not even close. He could feel his temperature rise at the back of his neck. His skin, already prickly from sweat and sunburn, started to crawl. He was in the early stages of reliving the dread when he was fired.

Perhaps if he had not gone SCUBA diving, he would not be in this predicament. Perhaps if he had distanced himself from Donna, he would be able to remove himself from the dilemma. Somehow, the dream made sense, but its implementation was a nightmare. If

178

he said yes, he would be putting his home – his future – in jeopardy.

He knew he had to say "no."

Jim could feel George slipping. "Okay. You don't have to pay the $100,000 for the first year. I understand you're concerned about your finances." George could only hear the thumping of his heart and the blood coursing around his ears like a freight train. "It is the opportunity of a lifetime. You're not likely...." Jim went on and on. With each word George sank deeper into that abyss of failure and dejection. He forced back tears. He wanted the security of being home. He wanted his wife.

With all of the courage he could muster, he said in a crackling voice. "I'm sorry Jim. I can't."

George rose from the table and walked away. His eyes clouded over as he made his way down the stairs toward the pool. He couldn't see where he was going, his ears rang, and he didn't care. As he made his way to the small path leading to his room, he could hear Jim say, "You bitch! It's all your fault! You bitch... you bitch!"

George was devastated. He wanted to give up. He wanted to just forget everything that happened and return to his room. But as he heard Jim curse at Donna, George's feet began to feel like lead. Jim didn't stop berating his wife. The words echoed through the night, shattering any peace for the patrons at Coconuts. The word 'bitch' echoed across the small cobblestone walkway. It reverberated against the million dollar boats. The word resounded off the water.

George stopped walking. Donna was his friend. Jim was not stopping. He was drunken enough that something more might happen. George turned and headed back. His personal defeat was replaced with courageous resolve. Somewhere in the rubble of his personal life, he discovered something he thought long gone. He bounded back up the steps.

"Stop!" George yelled as he headed to the table.

Jim turned. "Who the hell are you?"

Jim was beet red. He was like a defiant bulldog.

"Stop yelling at Donna! She did everything you said! She did nothing wrong!"

"Shut up! You shit! You're a nothing but an unemployed bum! Get outta here!"

The people in the restaurant stopped with fork midway between plate and mouth. The bartender was heading toward the arguing trio.

George knew the futility of trying to engage Jim in a shouting match. Jim had already pulled out the ace, and it didn't work. There was nothing that George could say to this drunken piece of lard. Reasoning was out of the question. George took Donna by the hand. Her face was puffy from the tears that had fallen when George left. But, now that he had returned, her tears spoke a different story. Someone stood up for her. Beneath the crushing pain, she expressed wordless hope.

Ignoring Jim, George started to lead Donna toward the night. "Let's get out of here."

Jim grabbed George's shoulder. "Where do you think you're going with my... wife?" Jim hesitated saying the last word, as though he had to ponder the relationship before uttering the name. For the last few days Jim had been trying to reject that marital claim. Now he was using it as a weapon. He wielded it like a slave owner.

George looked him in the eye with courage that came from deep in his soul. "I am leaving with my *friend* and there is nothing — not one goddamn thing — you can do about it." George broke from Jim's hold. George and Donna walked away. Jim started after them, but the bartender stopped him.

"I am sorry, sir. But you're going to have to leave." The bartender pointed him in the opposite direction of George and Donna.

Jim took a deep breath. "I'm leaving, but I'm going that way. That man is leaving with my wife!"

Jim lost his composure and started to try to walk through the bartender. The bartender didn't budge. Jim bounced off of him. "That is my wife! Don't you understand?"

The bartender said, "If you do not leave now, I'll be forced to call the authorities. It's now time for you to go. If you do not go peacefully, you'll be forcibly removed from this place. Do you understand?" The bartender had dealt with far more dangerous, inebriated, and cock sure individuals. Most of them carried their dive knife strapped to their calf twenty-four/seven. Jim was soft.

Jim had no words. He couldn't control the two that were fading into the darkness. He was too drunk to think of ways to get back at them, but he knew he would when his mind cleared. He would not let them get away with embarrassing him. He would black-ball George. Jim would make sure George would never get a job. He would leave Donna in the lurch. He would hire the best lawyers. He would get the witnesses from this restaurant to prove her lack of fidelity toward him. He hated her. He would leave her with nothing. Jim picked up his laptop and put it in the case. He headed out of the restaurant, but not before tipping the table with all of their food. The plates shattered and the remnants of food spilled out along the floor, over the edge and down to the deck below.

Donna heard the crash of plates and drew closer to George. She was afraid that Jim would do something foolish. She imagined him drinking until he was irrational. He could get violent. The upending of the table was simply the first step in a night of escalating violence. George was as scared as Donna, but he tried to uphold his demeanor of courage. He squeezed her hand and she returned the gesture. Wordlessly they walked on, with no specific destination. They simply walked down the narrow brick lane, with the boats docked on one side and the hotel on the other. The lights of the dock reflected off the water, looking like a school of white snakes moving against the inky blackness.

"Are you going home tonight?" George asked.

"No, that would be stupid. I'm going someplace safe. There is a cot in the back of Ocean Divers. Jim has no access to the store. I'm just too tired to deal with anything tonight. I'll work it all out tomorrow. How about yourself?"

"I'm not sure. I think I need to walk around for a while and clear my head. I thought I had a future here. I hate the thought of going home empty handed. But, like you, I'm just too worn out to even think about it. I'll head back to the room, eventually. They have security there. Jim isn't that stupid."

George stopped walking and looked at Donna face-to-face. "I'm leaving tomorrow. But before I go, I want to say 'thank you.' You helped me see something extraordinary. You kept me from selling my soul. I hope everything works out for you."

"And I know that things will work out for you. Thank you for rescuing me over there."

"You were holding your own quite well."

The two hugged. Donna headed toward Ocean Divers and George headed back toward the road. George was going home, but he felt a fire stir within him born of the crisis. He had stood up for his principles, even though his world was falling apart. That part of him had not atrophied in the years of his cubicle life. He felt stronger now than he had in years. He took a deep breath and inhaled the night. The air was warm and had a slight overtone of the salty sea. He loved that smell. As he walked, he breathed deeply the warm moist night. A smile came across his face.

ல் ல் ல்

After his long walk, George returned to his room. He didn't bother to take off his clothes. He headed to bed and crashed. It wasn't a deep sleep. It was the kind of survival sleep that some people go into so they can think, but not think. It was the kind of sleep that animals go into so they can endure a harsh winter. It was the kind of sleep that allowed George the ability to create a framework of dialog for the phone call he would make to his wife.

He didn't know how she would respond. He left her alone during this stressful time and now he was returning home empty handed. He didn't want her to feel the anguish that he felt. He also didn't want her to try and be the stronger person over the phone. He got out of bed after an hour of this meditative state of grief. Though it was late, George knew she would be waiting up for his call. He punched in the number.

"So how did it go?" Alicia asked with anticipation. He heard her expectation of good news.

George couldn't hold back. He let loose with an explanation of the discussion and apologized repeatedly for saying "no." Each time he started to apologize Alicia said, "Look don't apologize. You did the right thing. You didn't sell your soul."

George was physically exhausted and emotionally drained. The day's events had taken their toll. Alicia was crying quietly on the phone. They both let their emotions flow and they lifted each other with their love.

"So when do I get to come down?" Alicia said, trying to lighten the mood.

"Hah, Jim will probably stick me with the hotel bill. We're screwed."

"No, I don't think so. Come home. Just come home and we'll talk about our future. You got a boat out of the deal, right?"

George had forgotten about that. "No, I never signed the paperwork. I'm done here. I just want to come home."

"Do you think you could leave tonight?" George could hear the hope in her voice.

"I don't think so. I'm just spent. There is no way I could trek all the way back. I am exhausted. I'll head out early tomorrow."

They continued to talk. George felt much better hearing Alicia's voice. They talked about their dreams from their past. They talked about their history, what went right, and what went wrong. They talked about living on a sailboat.

George realized that they were starting over. It was not just an attempt to return to what was comfortable. They were taking time to rethink their future. They were giving up complacency for adventure. They were giving up comfort for challenge. At this point it was all dreams. They had no net. The couple was not limiting themselves. They refused to give in to their age, education, and location.

Even through the pain, he felt young again. He felt the scales of banality in the routine of the everyday had been stripped. He felt that Alicia shared that new perspective.

"I love you – wife," said George. When he used that word, he thought of how Jim had snarled that word. For Jim it was a word of control. For George it was a word that expressed gratefulness, love and intimacy.

184

George reluctantly said good-bye. He felt infinitely better. He could sleep.

8

It was time to go home. He packed his clothes, realizing he had no mementos from his diving adventure. George lugged the bags to his car and headed to the lobby to see if he had been stiffed for the bill. He opened one of the glass doors and noticed Donna was there talking to the hotel clerk.

"Yep... he won't pay the bill," she said sardonically. "The bastard..." She walked away from the counter and sat in one of the chairs that surrounded the television. "Don't worry. I took care of it."

"You didn't need to do...." George started.

"Hey, you came all the way down here with the promise of employment and you got the shaft. It is not fair. "

George sat in the opposite chair. "Well... thank you. If anything came out of this, I found a friend in you and I appreciate that."

"Well, I hate to leave unfinished business, and I have an agenda today." She pulled paperwork out of her leather bag and handed it to him. She rummaged around and found a pen. "The 'Lady' is yours – as promised."

"You know I can't take your boat. That is just crazy."

She smiled. "You talked about friendship. Consider this something a little bigger than a friendship ring."

There was something inside him that prevented him from taking the boat. He couldn't put his finger on it, but it just seemed wrong. Alicia wasn't there to share in the dream. He felt he couldn't claim this gift without her by his side. By signing, he felt he would be taking advantage of a woman in distress. He put his hand up to decline the offer. "I can't – it is too much. You know that. I appreciate the offer, but..."

Donna interrupted. "Look, I have something important to do so I can't hang around. What can I do to get you to sign this?" She paused, not waiting for a reply. "Give me your phone. I need to call your wife."

"What?!" George was a little alarmed at Donna and Alicia speaking. It seemed like a collision of worlds. He wanted to divorce himself of this place and these events. By handing over the phone, George felt that there would be some ongoing connection. George just wanted to go home.

Donna held out her hand and twitched her fingers, waiting for him to hand over his cell phone. He thought of saying 'no' but couldn't. He pulled out the phone and handed it over. Donna figured out the number on her own by looking at the recent calls. She stood up and started walking out the door, toward the canal. George stood up to follow her. She put her hand over the phone and said, "You stay here. This is girl talk."

She walked out of the lobby. Not knowing what else to do, he got a cinnamon roll and started eating. He had trouble swallowing because his mouth was dry. He wondered what the two were discussing. George watched Donna pace up and down the sidewalk as she talked with both her mouth and a free hand. He got up and poured some coffee, hoping he would be able to read Donna's lips. He hovered by the sliding glass door, but he couldn't make out what was being said. He heard Donna laugh as he made his way back to the chair.

Donna came back into the lobby and handed the cell phone to George. She had a smirk that George had never seen before. With difficulty maneuvering the

187

coffee, cinnamon roll and phone, he managed to get the cell to his ear. "Hey – hello? You there?"

Alicia said, "I like her! But I have some bad news."

George could feel himself blush. He wondered what Donna said to Alicia. "You are not coming home today."

"What?" It was at this point that he felt he was in a strange 'woman's world' where they tell you to do things, or tell you to say things, or tell you to wear things, and it makes absolutely no sense. However, somehow, it's the right thing to do, say, or wear.

"Donna will explain everything, but she needs your help. Trust me. You'll like this one."

"Uh... okay. Am I in trouble?"

"What? Of course not. But we are not going to make things easy for your friend Jim."

Without a clue what these two concocted, he simply responded, "Okay – I love you."

Without hesitation, she replied, "Love ya, too. Take care. I'll see you soon."

He hung up the phone and Donna had an evil grin on her face.

"What have you two cooked up?"

"I need your help. We are taking the boat out on the water."

"The 'Lady?'"

"Nope... the other boat."

"I thought you said you would never set foot in the Catalina. You said that the 'Fickle Girl' was for Jim's girlfriend."

"Yep, but a woman can change her mind." Donna ushered George out of the lobby. She put her arm in his and spoke in the hushed tones of two spies, "We are taking that boat out and not telling Jim. That fat ass couldn't pilot a fart in the bathtub. It is not *technically*

188

stealing - community property and all that. I figure if he can find it, he can have it."

George looked alarmed. "You're not going to scuttle the...."

Donna laughed, her eyes widened in surprise. "Why George I'm amazed at you! Do you think I'm that evil?" She smiled with catlike charm. "Of course, I thought of that first, but then I would want both Jim and his blow job queen safely bound and gagged below deck. No, I'm demonic, but not quite that bad."

They headed out of the lobby and down the street. The morning was young and the clouds drifted quickly by. The wind was picking up. If they were going to sail, it would be an incredible day.

"My plan is a little less criminal. Remember when I told you I had a slip in Key West? Well, you up for a little voyage south? If he wants a divorce, I'm fighting for *everything*. That includes the 'Fickle Girl.' Our discussion made me realize that I had been rolling over for him. After he chewed me out last night, I knew I couldn't take it anymore. So if he wants it, he has to find it. I plan on getting the boats, my stuff, and everything else out of the house. Let him beg to get it back."

George smiled. Under other circumstances, he would have declined. He wanted to go home. But he had instructions from his wife. It wasn't that he always obeyed those instructions, but in this instance – a boat - sailing – Key West? This task was much better than going to the grocery store for tampons. He regained an inner strength after standing up to Jim. Now, he was getting a taste for adventure, which was bordering on the absurd.

Donna took his silence as a 'no.'

"I talked to your wife about it. She was in favor of a little payback. But I don't know this boat like I do the

'Lady.' So I would not want to single-hand it. Are you with me?"

George smiled. "One hundred percent." He clapped his hands together. For a moment, he imagined himself a pirate of the old sea. It was a moment of revenge and subterfuge and it felt good.

Donna hastily grabbed some things from the Tartan and threw them on the other boat. She instructed George where to stow the necessities: maps, binoculars, boat hooks and an array of tools and parts. She scrambled to find the key to get the motor started. Once it was started, she wasted no time casting off the lines and pointing the boat toward the Atlantic. George felt like he was of little help, but he had excited butterflies in his stomach. Donna kept looking back over her shoulder, wondering if Jim would notice the boat leaving the dock. It was early, and if he was even at the house, he was probably snoring off an evening of drunken bed spin.

Donna wondered if Jim would set 'Property of a Lady' adrift in retribution. She wondered how far Jim would go. Last night worried her. But she knew she could no longer submit. She had to be proactive. She would be hauling both boats to safe harbor, far away from the fat man.

George took the fenders and dock lines and stowed them as the boat entered the open channel. They headed toward the rising sun. It was hidden behind a layer of thin grey clouds. A golden haze radiated across the horizon. The breeze was brisk once they separated themselves from land. The swells had small whitecaps. 'Fickle Girl' seemed at home, playing and bouncing along the waves. George felt a little tentative accepting the offer to go sailing. He always imagined the soft tropical breeze, not unlike that evening when the two of them sailed the Tartan into the Gulf.

But this weather was set up for someone skilled. He went below to look for a windbreaker and found one of Jim's. It was too big and when he returned to the deck, it flapped in the breeze. Donna looked at him and smiled.

Donna had to raise her voice to be heard. "When I come into irons, I'm going to unfurl the main. I'll need you on the wheel."

He took the wheel, more sure since his evening sail with the Tartan. She went forward. Using the automatic winch, she pressed the button and the sail came out a brilliant white. George wondered if this sail had ever seen daylight before. It looked like a newly pressed shirt as it emerged from the mast. She hadn't gotten the sail halfway out when the boat started to turn to starboard. The boat listed about thirty degrees. The Catalina sped up immediately. White spray came up from the starboard side and splashed George. He hadn't anticipated this immediate reaction to the growing wind. He didn't know what to do. He leaned on the wheel, but the boat seemed to have a mind of its own. Because of the listing of the sailboat, Donna clung to the grab rails as the made her way back to the wheel. Once in position, she eased the boom. The boat righted and picked up even more speed. The arc of the mainsail funneled the wind across the deck.

Once underway, Donna tweaked some of the rigging. The shifting winds kept the two busy. Donna wanted to make good time, and the winds seemed to be working in their favor. The sky grew darker grey and the sea churned more than George had ever seen before. The wind ripped white foam off of the rising swells. Donna didn't seem concerned, but the weather prevented detailed discussion between the two of them. This was no training session. This was real sailing. George sensed when the jib needed to be relaxed or the traveler adjusted. Wordlessly they both kept 'Fickle Girl'

191

heading south at a good clip. Jim had evolved beyond the text book knowledge of sailing. He could feel and react without the necessity of intellectualizing.

Occasionally the boat would find the remnants of a wake from a craft now far out of sight. It would plunge its bow into the water, sending up a mist that embraced the bow of the boat. Donna had George take the wheel as she went below. George gripped the wheel tightly. Occasionally the wind would kick up and the boat reacted, leaning into the wind and surging ahead, trying to exceed its hull speed. Donna returned from below wearing a life jacket with a red harness around her waist. She held a duplicate set of gear in her left hand.

"Safety harness and life jacket. Put them on." He let go of the wheel as the boat kicked. He toppled into the seat above the lazarette. Since the storm slammed him to that spot, he decided not to fight the force of nature and donned the equipment there. He had to look at Donna to figure out how to get the straps set and buckles tightened. The crotch strap was uncomfortable, but the weather was not abating and George knew this was necessary. A ring with a tether ran from the harness at George's midriff. In the case of having to move forward, they could connect the tether to jack lines, which ran forward to the bow. Donna didn't want anyone toppling into the murky blue.

At one point, Donna tried to haul the main in a little, but whether by the force of the wind, or a jammed piece of rigging, the sail would not furl into the mast. They had too much canvas for the amount of breeze. They had been fighting the boat to make good time. George was not used to the physicality required to tend the sails. His shoulders ached from manually winching the lines.

To starboard, George could see one of the many spans that connected the Keys via the overseas highway.

Both kept an eye on the wind direction, wind speed, and depth. They didn't want to suffer the fate of other ships over the centuries that found the coral coastline in foul weather. However, they also didn't want to stray too far from the coastline. If things got dicey, they needed to be able to find a safe harbor. Under normal conditions, they would need to dodge fishing boats and other sailboats. With the storm strengthening, the smaller craft and pleasure cruisers found shelter in the docks and marinas that dotted the island chain.

The morning was warm when they left from Largo, but out here George started to shiver. Donna noticed that he was uncomfortable. She told him to go below and warm up. He didn't want to leave her while the weather grew more ominous, but he thought he would go down, only for a moment, to get out of the wind.

George sat at the table opposite the galley area. He stopped shivering, but was getting seasick. He had never felt this way before. He always thought that seasickness was something that came on gradually. But, now that he was below, he felt an instantaneous desire to retch. He thought about fighting it, but his body didn't obey. Though running to the galley only required a few steps, he almost missed the galley sink. Donna could hear the groaning from below and knew what was happening. George couldn't see the horizon while he was below deck. With the pitching of the sailboat, George's mind tried to compensate but kept having to readjust. The message from his eyes betrayed that of his sense of balance. The two competing strains of information couldn't be reconciled and George's body rebelled.

Donna yelled from behind the binnacle, "Get some crackers and come back up here. You'll feel better."

The wind was too strong and the message never made it to George's ear. Donna wanted him topside because things were getting uncertain. A crack of thunder made her look out to sea. A dark swirling mass was churning overhead. There was no distinction between sky and sea. Both seemed to be churning a cauldron of wind and water. Normally, Donna would have checked the Doppler radar for any incoming storms, but she hastily set out to perform her plan and overlooked that detail. She knew it was a big mistake.

"Should have sacrificed to the gods before we left," she muttered to herself. The swells were growing larger. Donna was able to keep the boat pointed fairly well, until now. A rogue wave slammed the port side knocking the boat ten degrees to starboard. "Shit!" Donna heard George bang into the nearby counter. He came up the stairs bracing as he made his way back to the deck. He rubbed the back of his head to make the sting dissipate.

"You okay?" he asked.

"Yeah, I heard you get knocked around downstairs. You alright?"

"I'll be a little black and blue tomorrow."

"We have to get that sail back in the mast. We have to reef it or else things could get difficult. I tried pulling it in using the automatic winch, but it didn't respond." Donna said. "Do you think you can go to the mast? There should be a lock switch. I'm thinking maybe it's in the locked position. That's why we can't furl the mast. Hook on to the jack lines first, though. Do you see the switch?"

She pointed to a spot just below the mast where the boom connected. George could barely see a metal lever just below the boom. He wasn't sure if that was the apparatus in question, but he prepared to head forward anyway. He snapped onto the protective line that ran to the bow and slowly made his way toward the lever. It was half crawl, half walk. He made sure he had one hand

194

on the boat at all times. "One hand for you, and one for the boat," he recalled reading in one of his many manuals that gathered dust in his unmoving, warm, and comfortable home. Lightning cracked and the rain followed instantly with a sweeping deluge. The pelting came at an angle, making everything wet and slippery. It only took a few seconds and George was thoroughly drenched. George pulled the hood of the windbreaker over his head as he arrived at the mast guarding himself to find a moment of relief from the combination of rain and sea spray. Through the sheets of rain he tried to get a good look at the mechanism which locked the main sail. The toggle was sitting in a three-quarter position. He couldn't easily read which way was locked and which way was unlocked, so he pulled the toggle switch to the right. It snapped in place. He tried to pull the line that would roll the mainsail back into the mast. It held firm.

Thinking that was the locked position, George jammed the toggle switch in the opposite direction. The result was immediate and dramatic. The wind pulled the sail out of the mast the rest of the way with a violent flurry– opposite of Donna's desired intention. This actually put more canvas to the wind and the boat leaned so far to starboard George thought it would capsize. George grasped for the mast to keep his footing. His fingers slipped off the wet aluminum. The boat rocked even further as more hull surface was now exposed to the windward side of the storm. George toppled backwards. His heel caught a handrail near a starboard side window. He had a split second to turn his head. The short walkway was completely submerged by a violent frothy green liquidy leviathan. His legs buckled as he toppled toward the churning water. His neck hit the lifeline as his tether to the jackline pulled taught, preventing him from being washed overboard. His entire upper body went into a whiplash motion, arcing over the final obstacle separating him from the watery world.

Donna looked on in horror, wondering if the jackline would hold. She witnessed George's body contort as his harness stopped him in mid-fall. Knowing George was not going overboard, she locked the wheel and moved forward, trying to ease the boom to reduce the stress on the groaning rigging. The boat had the possibility of "turtling." If it capsized, and George couldn't undo his jackline, he would drown. The wind was fierce and the rain felt like needles on Donna's skin. She clamped onto the life-saving line and leaped toward the line holding the boom in a close reef as the boat recoiled in the other direction and the wind took a pause. She let the boom out all the way and tried to pull the sail back into the mast. The boat had righted, but the tempest didn't let up its fury. The weather was winning. However, when George slipped from the mast, he had also reset the lever, so the sail could be furled back into the mast. With great effort Donna pulled on the line to retract the canvas that kept the boat on the edge of chaos. Each time she tried to haul in the sail a little, a gust would come and pull it back out. She was exhausted.

George, recovering his senses, made his way aft to give Donna a hand.

Donna yelled, "Pull!"

After putting their backs into it, she yelled "Hold!"

Regaining a handhold so they could repeat the maneuver, she continued, "Pull!"

With both of them on the furling line, they were able to reduce the canvas and the opposing forces of the boat were minimized. With the boat under control, Donna turned to George and said, "That's what I get for coming out here with ill intent. Poseidon is having his way with us."

George laughed. He imagined the poster he had on his wall at Watsitumi. The old man wouldn't be pointing his finger at the young throngs under his command. He would be hailing the coast guard on the emergency channel of the VHF radio. He didn't know if it was "pan-pan" or "pahn-pahn," which was an emergency non-life threatening distress call. He wanted to ask Donna, but now was not the time. He had never seen anything like this on any of the calendars in his cubicle at Watsitumi. He saw Donna, with a look of relief, head back to the wheel, and unlock it.

He hadn't been watching their direction. He couldn't see the shore. They may have been close, but the rain left limited visibility. He glanced at the Compass and they were still on course. He had no clue how long they had been at this, but the weather didn't abate. Waves crashed over the bow. He was feeling sick to his stomach. Looking at Donna, George saw intensity in her concentration as she analyzed the complexity of sea and sky. She was handling the boat like a pro, and it was even more remarkable since this was her first time sailing "Fickle Girl." George was spent. He had seen more physical activity in the last forty-eight hours than he had in years. His hands were cramping from grabbing and holding the furling line. Blisters had formed and broken. He was cut and bruised, but the crisis of the moment kept him from feeling their full effect.

"I'm sorry about this George," said Donna as she tried to shorten the jib. Her hands were red from working the lines. There was a cut on her forearm and the blood mingled into a small red stream that cascaded off of her arm with the rain. The droplets got bigger and lightning flashed around them like an army of paparazzi. Thunder rolled, banged and seemed disconnected from

197

the strobic light show. Both sky and sea seemed to be boiling. Not only were there waves crashing from all directions, but the sea created large rolling waves. 'Fickle Girl' toppled down the incline of one of the waves, only to crash into one moving in the opposite direction. Donna sailed to prevent getting trapped in the "V" – being at the base of two waves smacking into each other.

It was getting darker by the minute. George didn't know if this was because of a setting sun after a hard day on the water, or the increasingly violent storm. He thought they would have cleared the tempest, but it only seemed to intensify. Donna realized that they could no longer sail.

Donna was getting hoarse, but used what voice she had. Yelling at George with a rasp, "We gotta motor. I'll furl the sail. You take the wheel."

George looked at her with panic. He was a novice and in no way able to command the vessel under these circumstances. Yet, he had no choice and ran on instinct, feeling the waves as she pulled in the mainsail. They were running with the jib alone when Donna returned to the wheel. She pushed the button to start the motor. Lights came on for the engine. But, somewhere in the depths of the cabin, the motor only choked. It wouldn't start.

"Fuck!" she said as she tried to light the motor again. Not wanting to flood the engine, she had George take the wheel again as she went below. George was getting that sickly feeling again and wanted to hurl, but couldn't leave his post. He swallowed the little bit of puke that made its way up his throat. The acid sizzled his nostrils, but he wouldn't give up. He had trouble seeing beyond the jib. The darkness kept him from seeing the rogue waves that might send them toppling.

Donna's head poked out from the hatch. "Try it now."

George pushed the button and the engine sputtered, choked, but would not come to life.

"God dammit," she yelled as she disappeared below. A wave caught him on his port quarter and the boat was pitched. "Ow..." came a voice from below. The clamor of metal tools being dumped from their box sounded as if a marching band simultaneously tripped.

Donna's frustration was mounting. George could hear her below. "Goddam motor, you mother..."

George tried to calculate when and from which direction the next wave would come. But he also tried to maintain a south by south-west direction. The wind shifted and the jib started fluttering. Donna came running up. "You've put us in irons."

George knew the devastating consequences of putting the bow directly into the wind. With no power, they would lose speed and ability to steer. She took the wheel and started turning it while releasing the jib, hoping to back fill the sail and regain control.

"We gotta get the motor started. I think somehow we got sea water in the fuel line. I tried to open the filters, but they're stuck tight."

George felt the boat move in an unnatural way. It seemed to skirt sideways and then seemed pushed from behind. The stern of the boat smashed against the water and the dive platform was completely submerged. Donna expertly got the bow to turn away from the wind and the jib bounced from one side to the other.

"Tighten the jib," she yelled.

George almost went to the wrong line, but followed it with his eyes before releasing the line from the jam cleat. He used the winch to flatten the jib. He could feel the boat stop its idle pitching and knew Donna had regained control.

Returning to the wheel, he said, "Sorry, I didn't mean to do that."

She replied, "Actually it's okay. That's what boats do under these circumstances. They will head up into the wind when they don't have any choice. It's okay." She turned to him, out of breath. "You know anything about boat motors?"

George remembered his days with Craig and Jim in the small shop. He saw them engineer and assemble motors. He had helped them when their orders came rushing in. He had a working knowledge of them, but had only worked on motors in a workshop. He had never serviced a boat while it was rocking in the midst of a hellish storm. He mustered his courage and said, "I'll take a look."

"Be careful down there," she said, not looking at him, but staring off to some point in the distance.

George went below and saw that Donna had removed three wall plates that enclosed the engine. It looked brand new. He checked the engine odometer which listed the number of hours on the motor. It registered 2.5. This was a new motor. He looked at the two filters over the engine. He wasn't sure if they were two fuel filters, or if one was a filter for the closed system coolant.

He took off his lifejacket and harness so he could maneuver a little better in the cramped space where the engine was housed. Then he saw it. It took a moment to register. The world seemed a million miles away, but this brought him back home. The motor had a plate on the side with a single inscribed word – *Watsitumi*.

9

George let out a yell, more animal than human. He slammed his fist on the engine. The engine didn't budge. The pain went through his hand, up his arm, paused at his neck and rested in his temples. It was a searing pain, but George didn't mind. It was the kind of pain that brought clarity. It was the kind of pain that mingled with revenge and a "job well done" feeling. He hadn't started the motor, but he felt he had achieved a milestone. He paused, sat back and started to laugh. Tears rolled down his eyes. He had descended to hell and at its core was a red engine with the name *Watsitumi*.

He rubbed the tears from his eyes. For a moment he closed them. With his back against the wall, all of the anxiety that he had felt since he was fired left his body like a demon that had been successfully exorcised. In the midst of the raging pandemonium around him, he was at peace. Though it was but a moment, the freedom lifted years of oppressed tension from his soul.

He opened his eyes to the non-functioning red metal beast in its dark compartment. He didn't focus on anything in particular at first simply willing to look at the engine as a whole without trying to discern what might be wrong. Something caught his attention. In one of the plastic filters, George noticed a lighter clear fluid resting atop a darker yellow fluid. Perhaps one of the jarring waves caused water to enter the fuel line. He started topside to inform Donna of his observation.

He started to rise, but the boat pitched so violently that he was knocked completely to the floor.

His elbow broke his fall, sending that strange combination of searing pain and numbing as the nerve bundles shut down in an attempt to give the brain some mercy.

The boat felt as if it was caught in a swirling vortex. The wind came across the boat and down the hatch with a hooting sound. It had an eerie human quality to it, as if some great spirit was emerging from the netherworld with a haunting birth-cry. George shuddered at the sound.

Rubbing his elbow, George rose and made his second attempt toward the deck. He could see Donna spinning the wheel.

He pulled himself to the deck. "Hey, I think I found...."

"Watch out!"

George could see the alarm in Donna's face but didn't know why she was crying out. He turned and saw the boom coming at him with the speed of a baseball bat hitting a home run. He put his hands up to guard his face. There wasn't enough time to duck. The massive aluminum structure hit him, forcing his hands to his face. It kept driving him as he was propelled off of his feet. Instinctively, he tried to grab hold of the boom, but he had used his hands to protect himself and they were in the wrong position as he was hurtled backward. He hadn't put the harness and lifejacket back on after working on the engine. In that instant, he knew that mistake might cost him his life.

He felt the lifeline catch his ankle, only serving to put him into a back flip as he was propelled off the boat and into the dark churning water below. George couldn't tell up from down as he slammed into the cold salty violence that surrounded the boat. The impact forced the air from his lungs. He started to take a breath but stopped immediately, realizing his head was still

202

underwater. In fact, he was completely submerged. He wanted to breathe. Disoriented and feeling that burning desire that started from the fingers and toes, George felt the intensifying bands of pain. He forced himself to not breathe and remain conscious and still. Everything seemed to go red around him. There was a beam of light that seemed to move across the water like a living thing. It darted back and forth and gave George a moment to take advantage of this situation. Still flailing, he let out what little breath he had retained and watched the bubbles against that light.

He swam in the direction of the bubbles, trying to catch the last remnants of escaped air, but they surfaced too quickly. He was blacking out. There was now no light for him to follow. His last thought was Alicia.

10

The pot bellied security guard of the hotel had wanted to be a police officer. He enjoyed patrolling the short beach at night, not to fulfill his dream of becoming an officer of the law, but to see if any couples were "doing it" in the sand. He had only stumbled across a few while working as a rental cop, but took his time before approaching them and telling them to move on. As he ambled the perimeter of the private beach, he ruminated on those times when he found two naked bodies performing some sexually perverted act. That's why he enjoyed the sea breeze and cool evening walks along the beach. He rarely, even with his uniform and air of "trained rental police," had sex. He didn't get to "do it" with anyone. No one had been physically interested in him since he was a kid in high school and so he led a sad and lonely life. Most of the time, he just "took care of business himself." This, however, was getting increasingly more difficult as he got older. So when he was able to watch others "doing it," his personal task was made somehow easier.

Tonight there was a storm out to sea. He could see the lightning bolts. The waves came in much stronger and the tide was a little higher than normal. Perhaps the sound of the crashing waves would be the siren's call for a horny duo, and he could watch a lucky young stud getting some prime nookie.

He spotted something in the distance which might just make this night perfect. But as he approached, he realized that there was only one body, fully clothed, and it was not moving. Had a dead body washed ashore?

That was the second best thing to finding two people copulating. He would be working like a real cop. Who knows? Maybe he would get his picture in the paper. He hiked up his pants as far as possible, but physics and gravity returned them under the fold of his stomach fat. He felt like a police officer, but knew he would have to get rid of his rolls if he was going to join the force.

The body lay on its back, perfectly still.

The security guard pulled out his night stick from its loop holster and poked the lifeless form. It didn't move. There was a gash on its head but no blood came out. The guard felt the butterflies of giddy excitement try to overcome the cool, collected demeanor of a "wanna be" police officer. Before radioing the 911, he poked the body one more time.

This time, the body convulsed with a water-filled cough. The person was wearing an ill-fitting windbreaker and no shoes. The man rolled over, pulled himself up to his knees, and promptly wretched up a vile fluid that spattered on the security guard's recently polished black shoes.

Disgusted, the security guard pulled the man to his feet.

"Move along. This is a private beach. Do your puking somewhere else you dumb drunk – geez."

The man looked at him dazed, not comprehending what the security guard had uttered. He had only noticed the shoes. He knew he had fouled them. He hated black shiny shoes. He hated them with a passion.

"Go on. Get a move on. The Methodist church is four blocks down the street. Don't make me call the cops."

Instinctively George started walking. He didn't know where he was. He didn't know who he was. He just knew that a fat man told him to walk that way and he was going to walk that way. There was no higher brain function involved. There was no memory of being cast overboard. There was no discussion about almost dying. There was no talking to the fat man about being, miraculously, washed ashore. George's brain had shut down and was on autopilot. He was simply walking. George resembled a zombie from some Romero horror movie.

The security guard left for the hotel, feeling he had rid the establishment of another of the vermin that occasionally panhandled in his neighborhood. He made his way to the lobby bathroom to wash his hands and clean his shoes.

George was walking. The beach gave way to a sidewalk. He was only dimly aware of that fact because his feet seemed to go from warm to not so warm. The street lights told the story of a shower that had passed through earlier in the day. Like Key Largo, this island was so close to the water that large pools formed along the roadways with nowhere to go. It felt good on his feet when he stepped in the shallow pools of rainwater because, unlike the officer, he had no shoes.

He entered a small municipal park. This late at night, the place was abandoned. A warm moist breeze blew from the ocean making the swings gently move as if some invisible mother and child were finding recreation. George wondered if he had died and was invisible. He thought, if he was a ghost, maybe the dear departed would not be able to see people in the real world. The swings, as a surreal pendulum, creaked as they arced back and forth.

On the other side of the small park, George stumbled through a residential neighborhood. Blue lights flickered from the windows as television addicts got their latest fix of cop shows, hospital dramas and inane comedies. A dog barked from a backyard as he passed by, which sent a rooster high stepping into the road. He wondered what a rooster would be doing, roaming free. But, then, he wasn't really sure if any of this was real.

The suburban homes gave way to a few shops. This led to an area with restaurants and bars. It was much brighter, and the activity was disconcerting. Some onlookers stared and pointed at him. The lights made his head spin. The nausea returning, George doubled over and hurled a slimy green substance that foamed and bubbled when it hit the road. A long strand connected his mouth to the puddle he had created. People on the other side of the street watched this poor soul literally spill his guts. Once the entertainment was concluded, they simply walked on, ignoring him and murmuring to themselves. Weakness forced George to all fours. He tried to retch again, but only dry heaved.

George was trying to think, but his mind was still resetting. He saw palm trees, but they made no sense to him because he knew there were no palm trees where he lived. He wondered if somehow he had fallen into the July photo of his calendar at work. Maybe he was in someone else's calendar. They were looking at the palm tree George was now leaning against. It was a pretty picture, except for the guy about to puke again. One more time George expunged whatever he had consumed on his long dark journey across the river Styx.

He started crossing to the other side of the road, trying to articulate enough English to ask for help. As he stumbled across the crosswalk a black Mercedes, driving way too fast came up on George, blinding him with the blue-white headlights. He put his hands to his face as the car honked its horn. The blinding lights of the car made his mind scream in agony, though he never uttered a sound. He could feel the heat of the headlights as if they were a pair of large sun lamps, drying him in some posh hotel. He felt a cold perspiration form on his forehead and a single note start to resound. It was the trumpet heralding his coming unconsciousness. George put his hand on the hood of the car, hoping the trumpeter in his head would march on before that black cloud enveloped him.

"Get your hands off my car, you fuck!" The blaring obscenity came from the driver who rolled down the window, gesturing with his middle finger.

George couldn't move. He had no more strength. His breathing became labored. His heart was racing. The man got out of the car. He was dressed in a white shirt and black pants. He looked like some young thug who had prettied himself up to greet a mob boss. He smelled equally of cigarettes and cologne. The passenger side window rolled down and a gorgeous blond woman wearing a black evening dress, with her hair pulled back, looked on expressionless. If she had the ability to articulate an expression, it would have been one of mild amusement, as her boyfriend demonstrated his masculinity by dominating the vermin in the headlights.

"I said get your goddamn hands off my car." The man grabbed George by the windbreaker and threw him across the street. Following his Newtonian destiny, George flew to the curb. He didn't put his hands up to break the fall as he careened to the sidewalk. People sidestepped him as he rolled, bloody and smelly in their path. George started convulsing again, but there was nothing left. He could feel the blackness consuming him. He tasted something metallic when he swallowed.

The driver of the Mercedes didn't look at George, but instead pulled out a cloth handkerchief from his pocket and rubbed the handprints off of the hood of his, now perfectly shiny, black Mercedes. The woman, now satisfied the impediment was sufficiently removed, pushed the button which raised the tinted glass of the passenger side window. To put his final dominant exclamation mark on the situation, the driver peeled away, squealing his wheels as he rounded the corner.

George could only comprehend the sound of someone behind him yelling.

"Hey you dumb jerk!"

George didn't know if "dumb jerk" was directed at him, or at the disappearing red taillights. People looked down at him. They offered only a fleeting glance, fearing that if they gazed at him for any period of time, they would somehow have to become involved with this piece of human flotsam.

"Oh my God, are you alright? Are you okay?" The voice was still disembodied, but seemed closer.

George lay with his eyes closed. The questions were directed at him, but they seemed to float above him. He slowly comprehended the questions, and was working on a response, but he felt like his brain was four boxes of puzzle pieces all jumbled together. He opened one eye, and then the other. It took a while to focus. He tasted sand and blood in his mouth. The current bloody rash from the sidewalk encounter kept its individuality only for a moment until it ebbed into the tide of general pain that flooded George. Slowly he realized that two people were looking down at him. George wanted to say he was okay, but he knew he wasn't. He wanted to ask for help, but all that came out was a gurgling sound like a baby makes, only an octave lower.

George tried to articulate a plea for help, but this resulted in a cough and wheeze.

The general haze of the figures became clearer. George saw two women, with bouffant hairdos and pearls, looking at him. They seemed rather large, but kind of reminded him of the show *Family Affair*. He wasn't sure why that show entered his mind, because he really didn't know much about the show, having forgotten most of his childhood viewing details, but they seemed like they could have been in that series. Or perhaps they were two sisters who had managed their way onto the set of the *Newlywed Game*. However, these bits of actual thinking, though totally random and seemingly pointless, hurt more than the physical maladies which were hogging his nervous system's highway to the brain.

"We have to get him some help," one of the women said to the other. George could feel the larger of the two women pull him up. The woman showed incredible strength as she hoisted him to a standing position. He willed himself to maintain consciousness as the blood tried to leave his brain and head elsewhere. With an arm around each of these individuals, he was barely able to walk again. It was only a few steps, but to George it felt like a marathon. Hailing a cab, the two women sandwiched George between them.

The cabbie, though at the southern most portion of the continental United States, still retained his New York accent. The air conditioning inside the yellow cab brought sweet relief from the humidity. There was a stale cigarette smell, but a "no smoking" sign had apparently been recently installed on the passenger side visor. None of this mattered for George. Time seemed to move like the water from which he had emerged. It flowed in and out with asymmetrical rhythm and intensity.

He was being propelled forward in the cab at what felt like supersonic speeds. The view outside the window was a blur. He had become the passive recipient of a reality he didn't quite understand. Given his circumstances, however, he accepted the reality that was dealt him and quietly sat between the two women.

These sisters of mercy directed the cabbie to stop at the pharmacy. The larger of the two ran into the building. The fluorescent lights glowed through the glass doorway. George could see this strange woman run around the aisles filling a plastic basket she clutched in her left hand. The speed and urgency seemed to stall when the woman behind the counter took her time finding the elusive UPC symbols for her scan gun. The large woman didn't wait for the teller to bag the items. The woman threw some money on the table, grabbed a plastic bag and with a single arm sweep, loaded the contents.

Back in the cab, the two dressed his wounds. They offered him a few crackers and some ginger ale. He ate the cracker, which instantly became pasty glue. He sipped the ginger ale to dislodge the mass that was now stuck to the roof of his mouth. The beverage sent a wave of relief. Its effects were almost immediate. Because of his now burning thirst, he wanted to chug the bottle.

"Slowly, slowly. Just take a sip," said one of the ladies.

He only took small sips, thus avoiding the serious gastrointestinal consequences. Because of his moderation, he was able to keep the food down and felt a modicum of strength return.

"Thank you." George mustered, finally able to speak.

"Yea!" The two exclaimed, ecstatic that the man they had rescued hadn't delved into a coma – or worse. "You okay? What's your name? Do we need to take you to the hospital? How much have you had to drink? What drugs did you take?"

George's breathing was still labored. "I'm George... George Forder." He struggled to recall what happened. He knew he was on a sailboat, but couldn't remember with whom, or why he was there. He didn't know if he had been drinking, though he was pretty sure he hadn't done any drugs. "I... I was on a boat. I didn't... I don't... nothing. I haven't had anything to drink... no drugs."

The two women looked at each other, skeptically. It was then that George realized these were not women. "Oh..." George was still in that weird place where the surreal and reality mixed together on this canvas of the absurd. He didn't know where he was, and barely knew who he was. Had someone told him a week ago that he would be in a cab with two men wearing pink and purple dresses being fed crackers and soda after nearly drowning, he would have called them mad. Ever since he left his quiet, mundane life for Key Largo, he had entered a new plane of reality and entered some transcendent state of higher being which allowed him to see his, rather gruff, angels. He was grateful for these two "sisters" of mercy. They seemed to go in and out of focus. He could feel the waves throughout his body, though he was nowhere near the water. It felt like the sea had cast a spell and forever made his innards rise and swell with the complexity of the ocean. George remembered, if only in a dreamlike state like one looking down as a disembodied soul, the events which brought him to the two angels. After being beaten, all of the "normal" people had ignored him. These were all the people who never looked you in the eye when you passed them on the street. They were the people who ignored you in the line at Wal-Mart. The word that best described the moving mannequins who didn't bother to help a man bleeding on the sidewalk, George thought, was "throng."

However, it was these two cross-dressers who exhibited the best in humanity. With compassion, they took a stranger under their arm. George was the beaten man helped by the unloved Samaritan.

For a moment George reflected on the fact that he had very few friends. Perhaps he had been looking in the wrong places. Acquaintances seemed to want to talk sports and bragged about their children. George never wanted to do either. Perhaps he should have tried to expand his circle. Perhaps it should have included more cross-dressing caregivers.

Taking a deep breath, George once again echoed these words with as much sincerity as he could muster. "Thank you."

Realizing the two had no clue what put him in this state, he started to explain, having regained some of his senses.

"I was on a boat and a storm came and I fell overboard."

The larger of the two put her hand to her chest and the other uttered, "Oh my God."

"Who are you?" George asked.

"I'm Scott and this is Kelly."

"Thank you." George seemed limited in his vocabulary. He was weak and tired. He wanted to expound on the details of his day. The soda and crackers seemed to lift him from his physical distress, but he was overcome with exhaustion and could only make a vague sketch of events in his mind. They never congealed into a coherent thought and just seemed to spin like a marble in a coffee can rolling down a hill.

Sensing that George might be telling the truth, Scott, the one wearing the purple dress, said, "We need to contact the authorities. Were you the only one on the boat? Did it capsize?"

"Yes – no..." George could only handle one question at a time. He slid his finger into his mouth because he felt something odd. There was a cut along his cheek where he had bitten through the skin. This pain was trying to get the attention over all of the others he was experiencing.

Having successfully determined that he had his teeth intact, he withdrew his finger. He could still taste blood. He paused as a slice of logic landed in his brain.

"I was with…. Donna." His heartbeat and breath noticeably quickened as he relived the moment when he flew over the side of the boat. He let out an involuntary 'huh' as he imagined the impact of the boom. With his ability to utter the name, the flood of memories from the last few days tumbled back like a DVD put on high speed. The images flashed by rapidly, but in succession, so George could recall more of the events. He saw the Watsitumi motor and felt his blood pressure rise. Even in the dark, the two could see George's face blush.

"Are you ok? You don't look good."

"Yeah, just remembering things."

"Yes… I'm okay. I need to call my wife."

"Was she on the boat?"

"No."

"We need to call the Coast Guard. We need to call my wife and let her know…. We need to get in touch with Donna. The boat is the 'Fickle Girl'"

They were in the midst of a crisis, yet Scott felt it necessary to tread through a social landmine. He knew George was married but Scott still asked, "Is she…" Scott paused…. "your girlfriend?"

"No, just a friend. I hope she's alright. The storm…" George was getting fuzzy again. He leaned his head back. It was throbbing mercilessly, and the tribal drumming that echoed in his brain interrupted his thinking process. "We have to call them."

"You need to take care of yourself," said Kelly patting George above the knee like a mother consoling a sick child. George realized that his pat identified one spot on his body that *didn't* hurt.

"We're almost home. We'll make the calls. Don't you worry," Kelly spoke reassuringly.

The cab pulled up to a modest home outside of the downtown hustle and bustle of Key West. The house was a modest white Cape Cod style home. It sat on a decent sized lot. George figured that the house must have been built in the late fifties or early sixties. All of the surrounding homes looked similar. Each was well kept. The lawns had that coarse thick beach grass. Though it was late, the street lights illuminated the cozy neighborhood.

The place was immaculate. A corner cabinet had a collection of Hummel figurines, neatly arranged. Little ceramic boys played with fire trucks. Others huddled together under an umbrella. One shelf was dedicated to the little hand-painted musicians. A small quartet was accompanied by a cello player and a boy with an accordion. Antique marble-top tables held gas lamps, now modified for the electric age.

The hallway floor was dark wood. Straight ahead was the kitchen, and along the left wall was a small set of stairs leading to the second floor. Kelly headed for the kitchen. Scott led George up the stairs.

"We need to call...."

"Don't worry about that," Scott interrupted. "Kelly is calling the authorities now."

"But I need to let my wife..."

"Okay...okay... It's late. Give me your number and we will try and call. You need to rest. If we get in touch with her, we'll wake you and you can talk to her."

The fatigue and exhaustion of walking up the stairs made George concede to the motherly ways of Scott.

"Take off those things and leave them outside the door. There is a robe in the adjacent bathroom. Your clothes smell. There should be something about your

215

size in the chest along the far wall. Try and get some rest. We will make the calls for you. What is your home number?"

George gave Scott the number.

"I can't thank you two enough."

"Ahh, don't mention it. Are you sure you don't want to go to the hospital? We would be glad to take you."

"No," George replied. "I think I'll be okay."

"Try and rest."

Scott headed back downstairs quietly reciting the number so he wouldn't forget between the upstairs bedroom and kitchen.

George stepped into the bedroom. He flicked the switch. An old brass bed sat between two nightstands. The two reading lamps on either side of the bed were controlled by the light switch. A door to the left was open and a nightlight offered illuminated navigation to the bathroom. He took a whiff and noticed that he did, indeed, smell as Scott had mentioned. He wondered why these two would be so opened to helping a total stranger. It would have been far easier to simply dump him off at the police station, or simply give him cab fare. Instead, they dressed his wounds, fed him and offered their home. Such care was rare in modern society.

He opened the bathroom door a little further and noticed a fluffy white bathrobe on a brass hanger. He turned on the light. The medicine cabinet mirror reflected a man George barely recognized. He was cut and bruised. His hair was disheveled and his shirt hung off of him like a scarecrow. Matted blood along his right temple made his hair fan out in a way that resembled a broken bird wing. He filled the basin with warm water and started scrubbing himself clean. There was no shower or bath, so he used the bar of soap and washcloth to clean himself as well as he could. He had to drain the water from the sink because it had turned a dark pink-brown long before he was done. Refilling the basin again, he finished the job. He felt - and smelled - much better as he donned the robe. He opened the door to put his dirty clothes in the hallway as he was instructed. He could hear Kelly giving the details to the Coast Guard, over the phone.

He shut the door, knowing that he needed a moment to rest. He would go downstairs and check on them after a few minutes of shut-eye. He plopped down on the bed, not bothering to get under the covers. He could feel the rolling ocean move through his body while he lay perfectly still. The ebb and flow of the current had worked its way through the fibers of his being and was churning through his veins. He knew he was still in the midst of an emergency, but he felt like he had been given anesthesia before an operation. He was rapidly slipping away and the pain that reminded him of the last day made him lose focus as he began to drift in and out of consciousness. He chose not to fight the incoming tide of darkness because it seemed friendly.

It was the smell that drove him back from his slumber. For a moment he wondered how he had been transported, both in time and space, back to his grandmother's guest room. The light streaming through the window had baked the air with a scent that was both musty and antiquated. He forced his eyes open with difficulty. They had been crusted shut and he needed a few draws across the seam with his index finger to get them open. This did little to remove the vision of his grandmother's place. The doilies under the night lamps were exactly like hers. By the window an ivory colored pitcher and basin sat on a small table. A large shaft of light streamed through the bedroom window making the dust circus play in the beams which cascaded through the sheers. He rolled over to put his back to the intense brightness. The smell in the room changed to a mix of kitchen smells – all breakfast. He sat up, placing his elbows on his bed. He was disoriented. His brain tried to shut out the horrific events of yesterday. He had no frame of reference for explaining his presence in grandmother-land. He focused on the far wall full of pictures. He expected old family photos complete with camping vacations, reunions and the mix of old and young posing and smiling. Instead he saw Rod Stewart, Cher, Bette Midler, and others smiling as they hugged, put their arms around, or shook hands with the two "women" who saved George. He had apparently been saved by celebrities. The image of these "ladies" allowed a partial burning off of the fog that had engulfed his brain.

     His intention was to only sleep a few minutes, but George realized by the brightness of the sun that he had been out for hours. George looked down and noticed that he was in a pair of blue striped pajamas. He had no recollection of changing. The previous night was just a hallucination wrapped in a dream. His mouth tasted vile. Part of George's tongue was swollen where he had apparently bitten it. He felt like his body was the moon, pock-marked with isolated craters of pain. His head throbbed and he was hungry. Smelling the cooking, he rose out of the bed and did a self-check to make sure he had all of his parts. They were all there, but most of them hurt. When he stretched, some parts beckoned a return to the comfort of the bed.

     It took a moment to realize that he was still in the midst of crisis. George had been flung overboard. He didn't know what happened to Donna. George wondered if Alicia thought he was dead. There was a suppressed urgency mixed with a sense that he had fallen through the rabbit hole.

He opened the door and used his nose in GPS fashion, seeking the source of the meal that was being prepared. George found the two men in the kitchen, one with an apron covering his shorts and polo shirt, the other in dark blue shorts and a white button-down shirt. Surprised, they turned to him with smiles on their faces. The men looked familiar, but he couldn't quite place their faces. Then it dawned on him who they were.

"Oh, George, you look so much better!"

"Kelly, right?" George questioned.

"Why yes! And this is Scott."

Scott was pulling an egg casserole out of the oven. The spread looked like it would feed ten people. Fresh oranges were cut and arranged in a bowl with blueberries and quartered strawberries in the crevasses. A cherry was artfully placed in the center. Orange juice, milk, and coffee were on the table. The O.J. was in a clear glass pitcher, sitting like a yellow pillar on a foundation of crushed ice. The coffee was in an old percolator and from its mouth it exhaled the steam in spurts, like a child breathing while waiting for a bus on a chilly morning. Fresh biscuits poked their heads from under a tea towel.

"I'm George... George Forder. Thank you. I can't thank you enough. You saved my life." He put his hand out.

"We know. You introduced yourself last night. You were a mess." Scott put the casserole on a cooling rack, took off his hot mitt and shook George's hand. "When we saw you we thought you were one of the homeless people who live here. They get abused by assholes like that guy in the Mercedes. We thought you were going through withdrawal or the D.T.s and were going to take you to a hospital. But you said you went

219

overboard on a boat. We only half believed you, but the Coast Guard confirmed your story."

The crisis had come to a head and George couldn't contain the false pleasantries that came crumbling down. George welled up with tears and said, "Oh my God. Oh my God. Alicia...Donna...."

Kelly placed a hand on George's shoulder.

"Calm down... calm down. We called the Coast Guard. They got a distress call from your friend and were able to tow the boat last night. We let the Coast Guard know you were okay. She had radioed as soon as you went overboard. They were looking for you all night until we called."

George felt the crushing weight on his chest disappear. "Thank God."

The distress from the possibility of losing Donna was replaced with the angst of calling Alicia.

"We tried to call your home number last night, but there was no answer. We left messages on the answering machine. We left our number, but no one has called back."

"I need to use your phone. I have to call my wife."

"Of course," said Kelly. He grabbed the pink kitchen phone and handed it to George. George dialed the number too fast and fingered the buttons wrong. He started over, with more determination and skill. The phone rang. With each ring he could feel his blood pressure rise. He wondered if anyone notified her that he had fallen overboard and was now okay. The answering machine picked up and he could hear his own voice giving the standard "we're not here right now..."

George left a message that he was okay and gave the particulars. He hung up and tried to dial again, hoping that Alicia had been in the bathroom or something. After the third try, he decided to call her cell phone. The cell phone went straight to the answering machine. Frustrated, he hung up wondering where his wife had gone. He checked his watch and wondered if she had already left to volunteer at the elementary school. He wanted to be with her now more than ever. Though the day was clear, there was still a storm of emotions brewing inside him. He didn't know what to do next. He felt helpless. He wanted to do something – anything – to find his way back to normalcy. He tried to remember the number of the school, but it didn't come to mind. He wondered if it would be too much to call the police and have them track her down.

"Sit down and eat. You left the message. We whipped this up just for you. It's been a while since we last cooked a meal like this."

George sat down. The other two joined him. "You… guys… you were…"

They both smiled. Scott put his hand around Kelly's shoulder. "We're the 'Bitch Sisters'. You never heard of us?"

"No. Should I have?" George took a bite of the egg casserole. The taste radiated through his mouth and made him eager for the next bite. "Oh my…this is good… really good." George didn't want to seem like a hog, but he was starving. He served up some of the fruit which had just a hint of sugar sprinkled on the top. He drank a glass of orange juice. While he was inhaling his food, Kelly poured a steaming cup of coffee. He moved the cream and sugar closer to George.

George couldn't remember when he ate his last meal. He had expended an incredible amount of energy over the last twenty-four hours. The abuse took its toll on his body and needed the nourishment. George grabbed a biscuit, tore it in half and put some butter on it. The biscuit was still warm and the butter melted instantly. George tried being polite, but he was famished.

Kelly sat down and said, "We have been the Queens of the Fantasy Fest. That was years ago. We don't do that so much anymore, but occasionally we hear about a party and just can't refuse. Last night we were out and saw you nearly get run over by a car."

"I sort of remember that." George couldn't remember the particulars. His mind was not willing to relinquish the crisis points just yet.

"Yeah, we don't know what the world is coming to," Kelly started. "Key West ain't what it used to be. If there was somebody who needed help, everybody would pitch in and lend a hand. Today, we have the fancy hotels and nightclubs and the people don't give a damn about anything anymore. It's sad. I wish we could go back to the good old days."

The two looked at each other and entered a zone of hazy reminiscence. George asked, "So you were with all those stars in the pictures back in the bedroom?"

"Oh yes, honey, we were the cream of the crop! With a little more cream and a little less crop."

The three laughed at the remark.

"We used to run a bed and breakfast, but after the hurricane, we just got tired of keeping the place together. It was so much work, and you never knew who was going to come through the door." George wondered which hurricane he was talking about. George knew that hurricanes regularly raced across the small island at the end of the U.S. Perhaps there was one that was greater than the others.

"When Isabelle rolled through," Scott started, "we thought it would be like all the others. We had seen them come and go, but this one was different. It was relentless. Water came through the seams of closed windows. It howled all night long. We lost electricity."

Scott stopped. He swallowed. He had started reliving that moment and wanted to forget. He regained his composure after closing his eyes for a second.

Kelly continued, "We sold it when the market was good. So we are pretty well set. We might dress up and do our show at a club every now and then, but we used to be respected for what we did. Nowadays it just seems like people come to see us as if we were in a freak show." Kelly waved his hand in disgust. "We are thinking of moving somewhere else."

Scott said, "Maybe Belize. The people are nice there. The expats don't seem to have as much of an attitude. And the idiot tourists haven't found it yet." He paused in thought and then continued. "You can tell when the assholes arrive. The jet skis start buzzing around like wasps." In a sing-songy voice he said, "Anyway..."

"I appreciate your hospitality. You have been very generous."

"We're glad to see you on your feet. We need to get you back to reality, though. After we eat, we'll take you to the Marina. The Coast Guard told us where your friend is located. We should let her know you're okay. We'll also get you in touch with your wife. Don't worry. We'll bring our cell phones and we can just keep trying. I'm sure she is fine."

"I don't know how I can repay your ...."

"Hey, we are just the Bitch Sisters of mercy!"

Scott and Kelly called for a cab and they headed into town. They were transporting George, but it took on the makings of a tour. They rounded the airport along the coast line. A line of palm trees were being replaced, so the trees were supported with long two-by-fours until they could establish themselves. George vaguely remembered the hotel where he was beached as they rounded a corner and turned in toward the hustle and bustle that makes Key West famous. He saw the playground that was just a hazy moment he would never fully regain.

Heading down Truman Avenue they pointed out the bed and breakfast they once owned. It was a beautiful white house with rocking chairs on the porch. They showed no regrets as they moved on to the next sight. The traffic slowed to a near stop as they headed up Duval Street. The place was hopping with tourists.

"Hmm. Looks like the cruise ship has let off its cargo," said Scott.

"Monkeys are out of the cage," replied Kelly in a well rehearsed response. "Used to be this place was a ghost town until about lunchtime. Then everyone in the know was at Camille's." They pointed behind them to a small pinkish colored restaurant. They were heading away so George couldn't see the detail of the place. He craned his neck to see out of the rear window, but that sparked a pain in his head. He turned back and the internal objection subsided. George looked out his passenger window. A crowd of tourists gathered around a few stores. Some of them, with large colorful shopping bags, dared to enter. George tried to read the French names of the fine jewelry stores. Kelly noticed him looking in that direction. "Honey, those used to be a head shop, a wig emporium, and a liquor store run by a guy from Vietnam who didn't speak a word of English."

George nodded silently. A family was getting their picture taken in front of the Hard Rock Café. George knew this was not part of the "old Key West." Beneath the growing veneer of corporate vacation enterprise, there was still the beating heart of Key West. Through the T.V. land surface of tourist America beat the fading heart of a unique island that had its own special character. Under an awning, a thin, shirtless, well-tanned man was weaving palm leaves into hats and baskets. A band was playing on a street corner and lovers of various sexual combinations walked hand in hand. Freedom hadn't quite lost its battle along Duval Street, but the scars of sponsored fun ran deep. George tried to think back to the seventies when Key West was in its heyday, but because of his own isolated lifestyle, he could only think of some video he had seen of Freddie Mercury on stage with Queen.

George realized that Scott and Kelly were woven into the fabric of the disappearing "real" Key West. They did their part, like educators in a museum, to dress and live the life of a place quickly losing its particularity.

They turned off Duval and headed toward the marina. A group had gathered for an afternoon trip to the Dry Tortugas. The large transport ship was churning its propellers in idle mode and the smell of diesel permeated the whole block. The captain was entertaining the throng of passengers before boarding. George could only hear the punch line before the cab had past.

"The best time of the day for a pirate is happy arrrr."

They passed the larger boat and stopped at the marina parking lot.

"Here ya go," said the cabbie. The three men got out and Scott paid the driver. George didn't have his wallet, or he would have helped. His identification, money, and credit cards were now part of the big blue abyss.

Even though noon was a few hours away, waves of heat had already started baking the pavement. Many of the cars lined up in the marina lot had a thin layer of film on them. These cars were awaiting the return of those who had been sailing for weeks. This close to the marina, salt and sand started accumulating on the vehicles as soon as the sojourners got the last suitcase from the trunk. It would have been an easy mark for someone wanting to carjack one of these vehicles. But crime – at least in this parking lot – didn't seem to be an issue. Layers of heat distorted the white lines of the vacant spots. The three of them walked across the parking lot to a set of small shops along a wooden dock. Some of the boards had been replaced, so it had become a standard dull grey dock with a few tan lines, making the whole scene look like a set of teeth from a West Virginia hillbilly.

The stores along this watery strip were unlike those found along the main drag. They were geared toward the boating crowd. One was a bait and tackle shop. A small hardware store specialized in gudgeons, pintles, shackles, cleats, and a variety of hardware necessary for the sailing community. A number of charter and fishing mom-and-pop shops listed the fares for half and full day expeditions.

They stepped down a few steps onto the dock and spotted a woman sitting on a bar stool in front of one of the small shops. She looked like she had been on a boat all of her life. The creases and lines in her face looked like a thousand rivulets. She resembled an old dried potato before it starts to smell.

George approached the woman. She was wearing a white shirt, which had yellow stains under the armpits and a vest that had large flowers printed in a set of colors no art teacher would have combined.

"Excuse me ma'am." George hesitated saying "ma'am." After last night he didn't presuppose a specific gender based on apparel. Her visual response gave him the confidence that he'd guessed the correct gender. He felt he was okay to continue. "A boat came in here last night. It was a Catalina. It was a white boat – brand new. There was a woman with hair down to here," he said gesturing just below his shoulder.

George figured he could ask for the boat by model. The woman appeared to spend hours a day looking at hundreds of boats as they made their way up and down the channel.

There was a long pause as she thought. She played back events in her mind. Her eyes widened slightly as she recalled the Catalina. She coughed before she spoke. It was one of those coughs from someone who would have contributed to the profit of a number of cigarette companies. George wondered whether she could actually talk, or whether it was some kind of coughing Morse code. Finally she stopped.

"Came in on the storm last night. Solo skipper – a woman. "

"That's the one," said George, enthusiastically. He was sure this was 'Fickle Girl.'

She pointed and gave a pier number.

"Thank you." George wasn't sure if he should give her some money for her trouble. She didn't say another word, or even seem to acknowledge his presence. She reminded George of some witch or fortune teller travelling with gypsies.

Turning her head, she sat on the chair and stared out to the great water beyond. Perhaps she was once a young woman waiting for her man to return from the sea. Perhaps, this was the place where they would meet and then go to the church and wed. She seemed to be looking out to the water with an expectant look towards something arriving just beyond the horizon. Almost imperceptibly, her head would cock, like some bird, as she craned to see what was just beyond her line of sight. George decided to let her find her space again. Some might look upon her as just another piece of Key West that made it – well – Key West. She continued to seek out the divine mystery of the deep as George headed along the dock with renewed energy.

Scott and Kelly joined George as he hurriedly made his way along the narrow juts of wood. Boats of every size and condition shared row after row of slip space. Some of the derelicts seemed like they should have kissed the bottom a long time ago. Barnacles acted as putty holding the framework together. Others were polished daily so their sheen could be seen from high in Earth's orbit. Each pier jutting out had a gate with a rusty sign forbidding anyone entry unless they were permitted. The signs, though weathered, looked official and foreboding. However, the gates were all unlocked and no police, dog, or pot bellied security guard manned the area. Some sailors were performing the endless ritual of cleaning, inside and out. George found the location the woman had indicated. He opened the gate and headed to the slip. The white Catalina, 'Fickle Girl,' sat bobbing unharmed in the quickly warming day. It looked as new as the day he first saw her. Though she had been through a trial, she was no worse for wear. George couldn't make that same claim. As he neared her, he started to smile, looking forward to reuniting with the familiar. He was anxious to meet Donna and let her know that he was okay.

George boarded the craft and started poking around. He called for Donna but there was no response. The hatch was latched shut. The boat was abandoned. He stepped aft and checked to make sure he was on the correct boat. The large dark blue letters 'Fickle Girl' were there. The watery plasma lightshow danced across the lettering. George paused. He looked at the two men on the dock. He put his hand over his brow to block the glare, looking for Donna up and down the marina. She was nowhere to be found.

He didn't know if he should try to call Donna at home. He feared getting Jim on the other end of the phone. He banged on the bow floor, thinking that Donna

228

had headed to the master cabin for a nap. He put his hand over his eyes and tried peering into one of the portside windows. No one was inside. George threw up his hands in the international "I don't know" gesture to Scott and Kelly. They looked at each other with mild concern.

"I don't know where she could have gotten to." George's voice seemed to have dropped a few notes and both of the Bitch Sisters could tell George was entering into a state of depression, having lost touch with the world he understood. Everybody else was playing poker and he was playing tic-tac-toe. He felt that he was in permanent exile of this land of the lost. He jumped off 'Fickle Girl.'

"What is going on?" he said, more to himself than to Scott and Kelly.

"Maybe she stepped out for a minute. We'll walk around or something and come back in a few minutes, okay?" Kelly looked into his eyes with genuine concern.

"Can I try to see if my wife is at home?" George asked.

"Sure. No problem."

Borrowing Scott's cell, George tried calling his home again, but again only got the answering machine. He redialed and started pacing. Despondent, he strode back on toward the marina parking lot and shrugged his shoulders. He didn't know what to do. His wallet and identification were somewhere in the Atlantic. His cell phone was gone as well. He was feeling increasingly isolated and confused. He wondered if he had been hit harder and suffered a concussion which only now was interfering with his ability to reason. He had already taken up too much of Scott and Kelly's time. The other two opened their hands in a gesture of "oh well."

George felt awkward, taking advantage of these two. They had been incredibly hospitable.

Scott spoke up. "Hey, let's get a drink and we'll come back. Maybe she headed out for groceries or something. George could feel his depression deepening. He wanted to hear his wife's voice. He longed for the banality of his former self. But, he had slipped too far through the strange events which brought him to this moment of exile. He wondered if he would ever return to "normal" life. He remembered looking at himself in the mirror before he slept. There were cuts and bruises, but he saw something different. Only now, as he reflected on the image that gazed back at him, did he realize how much he had changed. This place and these circumstances had altered him. He had been transformed and nearly broken in the process. But he felt no fear. At Watsitumi, he was always afraid – afraid he wasn't doing a good enough job, afraid of not hitting the day's quota, afraid of...nothing. In moments when he should now be filled with fear, he was only filled with a longing for a reconnection to his world, but not to go back in time. He would never return to the way he was.

The three headed to Sloppy Joe's bar. He vaguely remembered Alicia talking about this place. She was a fan of Hemingway and he struggled to remember a story about the bar moving, and something about a urinal. He couldn't put the pieces together. The moment faded as he thought of Alicia. He would love to bring her here for a drink and some fries. It was open and airy. There were black and white photos of the place lining the wall. A couple was singing James Taylor and Carole King tunes that George recognized. The musical duo sounded incredibly like the originals, though these performers were much younger.

Tourists came in, grabbed a T-shirt, headed to the cashier, and darted right back out. Perhaps they had a timeline before they had to get back on the cruise ship for their magic show or something. They spent money feverishly. Instead of being "in" the place they were visiting, they chose to hit up as many stores collecting evidence of their travel. Back in their small rooms they would pull out their shopping bags and, based on the T-shirts, could claim that – "Oh yeah – Sloppy Joe's – I was there – see?" George, however, was very much "in" the place – its lazy ceiling fans doing nothing to cool the heat. That would be left to the drinks from the bar.

Scott and Kelly ordered fries for everyone. The Bitch Sisters – incognito - each ordered a rum and coke. George ordered a beer. As they sipped their drinks, the Bitch Sisters spoke of the day that Key West rebelled against the U.S.A. and attempted, in some small partying maneuver, to become an independent nation – the Conch Republic. Of course the media was covering the event with the seriousness of a drunken brawl.

"We were part of the revolution! I'll never forget 1982. Sure there were drugs down here. Everybody knew it. There had been drugs for years," Scott began. "Then some Nazi in the U.S. government sent a border patrol down here. They had been set up along the overseas highway trying to stop drug smuggling. The single artery to the mainland was cordoned off."

"You can imagine how we felt. We didn't want the government suits invading our freedom. Their presence incited the already boisterous and fiercely independent residents of Key West, like ourselves."

Kelly chimed in. "The Keys were cut off from the rest of the United States. The mayor of Key West declared the keys an independent nation. This was cause for celebration throughout Key West and the Bitch Sisters were caught up in the revelry."

Scott picked up the thread of the story. "So what were two girls like us to do? The residents got their boats and started a blockade. It was madness. The party rolled out onto the streets. There were cries for independence. It was a revolution!"

The two looked at each other and smiled. Scott continued. "So, we donned our best Egyptian outfits and headed out on the bow of one of the boats. I am still not sure why we picked the Egyptian theme. Oh well..."

"We stepped aboard one of the many yachts. Someone on board gave us a sign – 'Give us Freedom or give us a spliff."

George didn't interrupt their story, but only had a vague notion of what a spliff was.

"As we paraded with the other boats, celebrating our independence, a Frenchman came along side our craft and tossed us a bong and a bag of reefer."

With this additional reference, George was now able to confirm the spliff reference in his mind. Those days of open drug use seemed years away, though George, having grown up in rural Pennsylvania, never encountered much of that culture. The most deviant part of his youth was spent reading dirty magazines supplied by his friend Ronnie, who had no trouble obtaining them from his father. During George's teen years, his neighborhood was going through a radical transition as an ever increasing flux of "outsiders" moved into these new housing areas called "developments."

As Scott and Kelly related their story, George pondered where these two men had come from originally, and how they found Key West. Were they originally from some small, rural area, like himself? How did they end up in Key West? He wondered if there was some kind of gay "siren song" for those who had ears to hear.

The two continued to reminisce about the "good ol' days." George listened with half an ear. He was still focused on getting home. Someone, in the far corner of the long bar along the far wall, fired up a cigar. There didn't seem to be a 'no smoking' policy in the place. However, most of the smokers were not lighting up cigarettes. A blue haze began to dance around the two performers like some wizard's invisible hand.

The smell of the cigar was like a Key West version of Roman Catholic incense. It made George's head swim in the detached purgatory he now faced. He wondered if the singers would enter into a Latin version of 'Fire and Rain.' Perhaps the fries and beer staring at George was the communion of Key West. Hemingway's image was the pope, staring down with a pontificating scowl.

After finishing their drinks, they headed back out into the daylight. The fresh air cleared George's head. The sun felt good. He rationalized that the boat was there, so Donna was somewhere nearby. Alicia, though not answering the phone, would eventually pick up.

The Bitch Sisters thought it would be a good idea to give it a little time before returning to the boat. They wanted to get George walking. Though still somewhat a stranger, they had seen him going into a funk and thought the sights of a few blocks would quell his downtrodden attitude.

The three walked Duval Street for a while and saw the sights. There was a costume shop which required proof of being over eighteen. The treasure museum was a gathering place for many of the "cruisers." George realized that you could go to a Cuban restaurant, or visit a chic gourmet palace. They were both side by side. Every now and then, you could see a gallery showcasing one or more pricey pieces of Wyland's artwork. Dotting the streets were a number of knick-knack shops all selling the same coconut shell carvings or tumblers with cute saying - all imported from China.

233

Under other circumstances, George would love to take in all that this great city had to offer, but for now, his mind was elsewhere. He couldn't get into the rhythm of being a sightseer when his world was in such turmoil. His guts were in a knot from the stress of the unknown. His two new companions were doing the best they could to try and placate a man who had been through a great ordeal, but there was a distance between him and them now. His world was no longer theirs, and he wanted to return from his exile.

Outside Kelly's restaurant George stopped. He had seen numerous tour buses come and go. Some of the vehicles looked like a train, some were closed air-conditioned buses. George noticed a smaller, open bus slowing down as it tried to get through a crowd of people. The bus had the sign "Buffett Tours." A woman with dark hair was talking to the tourists on the bus as they looked on, maps in hand. It wasn't the bus that caught George's attention, but the woman tour guide. He changed direction and started in a slow trot to the tour bus before the crowd parted. Scott and Kelly looked on with questioned looks wondering if George had somehow become possessed as he wandered off like a lost child.

"Rachael? Rachael is that you?"

The woman stopped her banter and looked out into the crowd. She heard her name, but in the throngs was unable to identify the source. George lifted his hand and waved it over his head.

"It's George.... George Forder! From Watsitumi! I was in the cubicle two up from yours."

Rachael squinted. Then her eyes went wide. "George!" She motioned him to get on the bus as it stopped in front of the treasure museum. He hopped up. In the bizarre whirlwind that was George's new life, this figure from his distant past had somehow managed to cross his path. What the gods had in mind for this particular encounter, George didn't know.

"Wow - this is so strange. Who would have thought that I would see you here? Last I saw, you were fired for putting up those Jimmy Buffett pictures in your cubicle at Watsitumi! And look at you now – you're giving tours in Key West on a Buffett tour bus!"

"Yeah, well I gotta go where it's warm."

"I hear ya!" George responded.

She stopped and looked at him. George felt a little uncomfortable. Perhaps she didn't recognize him, but pretended to go along with this strange man. She appeared to be focusing on his face, as if trying to place it in the context of her former life. Then he realized that he had been bruised and banged up and she was looking at his wounds.

"Oh yeah, I got a little banged up last night."

"Key West has a way of doing that to people," Rachael replied. She looked tan from being in the sun, but her smile and hair were the same.

"Well, that is a story unto itself. Isn't it strange that we don't see each other for years, and then suddenly we run into each other thousands of miles away?" George could feel his spirits rise at the site of this connection with his former world. He felt like a kid, returning from a journey, and recognizing some landmark that meant 'home.'

"You look good. You know I was fired from Watsitumi. I got screwed just like you. So much has happened since then. But it looks like you landed on your feet. You look good!"

"I got the same old walk, the same old talk." Rachael smiled. "I'm lucky. I'm doing what I want to do, where I want to do it. I'm on the Buffett bus. I wouldn't want to be anywhere else."

Talking to her, he couldn't help but feel like he was encountering some kind of Zen master. Things took on an esoteric quality. People seemed to glow. He wondered if he was entering some post-traumatic hallucination.

George, dumbfounded by the coincidence said, "I didn't know I would end up here. You see – last night I was thrown overboard in a storm."

Rachael's mouth dropped. "Yeah, I saw it last night. The seas were high."

"Yeah, the storm was incredible. Luckily, I came out the other end okay. I don't want to hold you up, but when I saw you, I had to run over and say 'hey'... you should get back to work."

Rachel handed him a card with her tour bus logo, name and number on it. "It is good seeing you George. What a surprise! Sounds like you're on an incredible journey. Just keep looking forward!"

"You too," he responded. George thought her goodbye a tad strange, but these were strange days. George hopped off the bus. Rachael rang the bell on the bus as she started to make her way through the crowd crossing the street.

As George rejoined his two new friends, he couldn't help but wonder whether some large force was controlling these strange events. The probability that he would encounter Rachael seemed too far-fetched. Perhaps she was a sign, though he was not sure what it meant. Since he had met the water and befriended it, his world moved laterally from before.

Scott asked, "What do you think the odds are that you would be here, and run into someone you know? I think it is a sign. It has to be some kind of good omen."

Kelly put his arm around George's shoulder. "It has to be. You see, the gods are telling you something. Neptune is working on land today!"

George laughed. These two were working hard, giving up their day, to take care of this stranger with a most extraordinary tale.

The three of them continued their walk around Key Largo, returning to the marina as they made repeated visits to the 'Fickle Girl.' Each time they were met with an empty sailboat. With each return, George fell deeper into despair.

The day was wearing on and George was retracing his steps along Duvall Street. The crowd thinned as the cruise liner bellowed its loud trumpet for the tourists to return. The town was in that afternoon transition between the shopping crowd and the dining crowd.

They made their way back to the marina with the same result. George hopped back down off 'Fickle Girl.' The three headed along the pier repeating the ritual which was becoming aggravating. Once again George contemplated calling Jim. He was about to dial when he heard a familiar voice.

"Look at what the sea gave up! I thought you died out there!"

Donna was walking down the pier. She was in capri pants and a white bikini top. George turned and ran to her. They both hugged. There was a pent up well of tears which broke free. George and Donna began to weep. Both had lost what was good and comfortable. The crisis had broken both of them. Both started saying the same thing, "I'm sorry." They were crying, but their tears fell for different reasons. Donna was shedding tears of guilt and George was shedding tears of relief.

They parted the embrace. Donna said, through a hyperventilating panting breath.

"I thought.... I thought you died. I thought..." She could barely get the words out. "I thought I killed you. I couldn't live with myself. Everything... it was all so wrong. I was so scared."

"I am okay... a couple of cuts and scratches, that's all." George felt much worse than that but was not going to let on to her the details of his pain.

"I let the sail out to regain control of the ship. When you came topside, I...." She started to explain. She wanted to give him a reason to understand that she needed to regain control of the craft. She had to open the sail. She had loosened the boom vang because of the incredible tension from the wind just as George emerged from below.

George stopped her. He raised a hand and said, "Shhh.... It's over. I'm fine. You're okay. It's over."

Donna looked at the cut on George's forehead and ran a soft finger over it. They both embraced again, this time for the same reason. They cried because they had found each other alive and safe. It was a moment when each could drain the emotions that they had harbored the last twenty-four hours.

"Don't worry about it. I'm safe and sound. I have these two to thank for saving my life. Seems I was in more danger on dry land after the sea spit me out." George pointed to Scott and Kelly who were watching from a distance. Both were wiping tears from their eyes. They had their arms around each other watching the moment like an afternoon soap opera.

Donna waved and they returned the gesture in exactly the same way. George introduced the two to Donna. Their tears were soon replaced with smiles.

Scott said, "I thought he was some drunk or junkie about to go into a coma. You should have seen him hurl. It was nasty." Kelly held his nose in a gesture of disgust.

George started the story which he, only now, remembered in full. "I washed up on the beach and there was this officer that...."

With a surprise rush of energy, Donna smiled at George and interrupted, "I have a surprise for you!" Just moments ago, Donna was crying and now she seemed downright giddy. George had never seen this side of her. Until now, she had either been the eloquent queen, or the intense and knowledgeable dive instructor. Now she seemed like a child at Christmas.

"I don't want any more surprises!" George replied. "You almost got me killed with your last surprise!" George wondered whether he should have used that phrase, but there was a bridge of forgiveness that both had crossed together and now the past was the past.

"Trust me!" She pulled him by his hands and the four of them headed off with Donna at the lead trotting down the pier. George was being led like a small dog pulled by a little girl who was going way too fast. When George slowed because of his bruises, she would tug on his arm and he was jerked forward.

The Bitch Sisters could barely keep up as they headed up some stairs and across a pier jutting out perpendicular to a small café. She was not heading toward 'Fickle Girl' as George had assumed. A row of various sized and shaped sailboats pointed their masts toward the sun shining past its zenith. The sound of halyards hitting the mast resembled muted wind chimes as the crafts rocked, gently amplifying the movement of the water with the "tink tink" as the lines slapped metal.

George blinked in disbelief. He stopped and looked at the end of the pier. It seemed like a mirage at first, the light playing against a sailboat that looked amazingly similar to one he had seen before. The Tartan 4100 was tied at the end of the pier. 'Property of a Lady' was parked in Key West, standing out among the other boats.

When he first embarked on the mission to move 'Fickle Girl,' he had last seen the royal blue hull of 'Property of a Lady' securely docked in Key Largo. Donna must have not slept and brought the second boat down. He remembered Donna talking about getting the boats away from Jim. After last night, this seemed like an impossible feat. How could anyone have muscled the 'Fickle Girl' into port with that storm and then gone back for seconds? George didn't know. Donna had both strength and reserve rivaling any man George had met. Scott and Kelly looked on quizzically.

The beautiful blue hulled craft sat at the end of the pier, not in a slip with all of the others. It was alone at the head of the class. It was like a queen sitting at the end of a banquet table. All of the other sailboat subjects were lined on either side of the table, jostling to get as close to the royal queen as possible.

George expected Donna's surge of girlhood giddiness was because she could now sign over the sailboat to him. His confusion was replaced with the embarrassment of having to, once again, refuse her generous offer. He still had not reconciled that in his mind. He couldn't put his finger on it, but something was not right. Indeed, he had forgotten the offer all together until the 'Property of a Lady' showed up with the lines of small wavelets sparkling off her bow as she perched at the end of the pier. He wanted to leave. He wanted to go home. He wanted to part on good terms and find a way to continue his friendship with her. He didn't want the sailboat to come between them. They slowed and walked toward the boat. George could feel his face flush. He was about to explain why, once again he would decline the offer.

But as he was about to speak, someone came up from below. He wondered if he was dreaming. She didn't see him at first, but standing on deck was his wife Alicia. She was in shorts and a white short-sleeve top. She seemed radiant in the sunlight. It was as if God had somehow answered his prayer. It made no sense that she would be emerging from the depths of 'Property of a Lady,' but her presence demonstrated otherwise. He had been in some strange altered state since entering Florida. What seemed like years ago, but was in reality a little over a day, Alicia was at home. They were speaking over the phone talking of his return. Now she was in the middle of a tropical paradise on the ship of his dreams. For a second he wondered if he had indeed passed away and this was a version of heaven no church could have described.

Alicia had always been there for him as he embarked on this zany journey. Now she appeared from the depths of his dream boat making his transition to this strange, bizarre yet beautiful new world complete. She was carrying a coiled line and put it on the deck. Only then did she look up and see her husband, teary-eyed and standing in awe.

"George!" she screamed and leapt from the boat to the pier with the agility of someone far younger. She was already crying as she ran toward him with her arms outstretched. He grabbed her and lifted her off her feet. He could smell her and the embrace was the best thing he had experienced in a week. She cried and couldn't get any words out. He thought he had used up his tears on the dock with Donna, but he had plenty in reserve for his dear wife. Minutes passed without a word being spoken. They kissed. They kissed more. They kissed and the saltiness of their tears mingled with the sweet taste of each other's lips. They cried together and their tears mingled on their cheeks as they held each other as though the world would end and they were facing their last moments together.

When they finally found language, the first words were "I love you." They passed the "Love you, too..." back and forth, both realizing that the words were but pale symbols of the deep feelings they both had for each other. For both of them, this marked something new in their relationship. They had been closed up in their shell. The love had been there, but it had been masked and marred by the banality of everyday life. It took this crisis to reveal the inner light of love that now poured out of each of them and spilled onto the dock.

Nothing had changed. George was still out of a job. Alicia had only promises of work. Donna was still getting a divorce, and the Bitch Sisters were – well - the Bitch Sisters. But in that moment each knew that they had been transformed into something greater – something better than they were days ago. They all realized that what mattered most was not finding the security of their past, but relishing the adventures of the future. They appreciated not what they owned, but what they had. Everyone had gained and regained relationships, self-reliance, and a kinship born of adverse circumstances. However, like a hammer molding steel, they had been pounded into something more useful than when they had started.

A tour bus went by and tooted its horn. No one turned around.

Alicia looked up into George's eyes with a rekindled love. George saw her more beautiful than ever.

With a smirk, Alicia said to George, "What do you think of my boat?"

"What? Your boat?" He looked at the Tartan 4100.

"When I got the call from the Coast Guard that you had fallen overboard, I didn't know what to do. The

Coast Guard was dispatched from Key West. The first thing I did was book a red-eye to Florida. Along the way I got a call from Donna. I was devastated. I don't know what I would do without you." Alicia started to get teary, but pulled herself together. "Donna got the news that you were okay. She actually radioed the news to the pilot as I was en route. She said she would meet me here. We knew you were here, but couldn't find you."

George could feel the tension in Alicia's throat. She paused and tried to control her breathing, taking longer breaths to stem the well of emotion that was erupting. They hugged again as though both had no short-term memory of the embrace just seconds before. Alicia pulled back to continue her story.

"She had gone back and gotten her other boat in fear that Jim would do something to it. I met her here. She said you never gave her the five dollars. You never signed the paperwork."

George looked at Donna and smiled. Donna smiled back, her arms around Scott and Kelly.

"So she offered the boat to me. We'd talked on the phone and while we were waiting for you, we covered a lot of territory and became fast friends. She figured if you didn't want the boat, maybe I would. So...of course she made an addendum that we would be co-owners. So all you have to do is sign your name below mine."

She pointed to the Tartan 4100 with its royal blue hull and crisp lines.

"After all," Alicia continued, "it is the 'Property of a Lady.'" Alicia batted her eyes and hugged George again.

George had never felt so alive. He no longer held the fear of the future. He no longer wanted the security that had held him captive. It had drained his soul. It had diminished him to nothingness. Now he could feel. As if awakened from a deep sleep he was alive and refreshed.

He could live again. He could love with a depth he had thought had been lost forever. Alicia looked as though she had been drained and refilled with the same vitality that possessed his soul. Where they had banality – they now had opportunity. There was no security for their future but then, George realized, there never had been. The cage had never been locked, but he had never considered just walking away. The strange ride had led him to his dream. It was not the boat, but his love for Alicia and the realization that both of them had a chance to *live* their dream that was the real quest. The metamophosis was complete as Alicia emerged from the boat and Alicia joined George in this new reality.

The five of them boarded the Tartan 4100. George and Alicia took the boat out as the sun turned from silver to gold. George pointed to a spot where they could anchor. Alicia was behind him close to his shoulder. The other three helped trim the sails as small white foam parted on either side of the bow.

Epilogue

It took a while, but George and Alicia sold their house. They knew they were safe for a while since the slip was paid for. They now live on the Tartan 4100. George got in touch with Craig, the other partner with *Run-Rite* motors. He had been busy and was unable to get back to George immediately. After a lengthy phone conversation, George learned that Craig was getting back into the motor business. He had signed paperwork when he sold *Run-Rite* and the terms of his non-compete were now fulfilled. He knew that the Watsitumi Company had cut corners. He also knew how to improve on the engine he had initially created.

Unlike his partner, Craig didn't succumb to the same forces that brought Jim's moral demise. Though age had made him a great deal heftier, the pictures of the two of them with drinks with funny little umbrellas were nothing more than photo-ops. Craig lived on Tortola and sailed. He enjoyed racing boats and took a keen interest in the myriad of stories about boat construction, engine problems, and maintenance headaches. Through the intervening years of his non-disclosure and non-compete clause he kept a notebook of ideas and innovations.

Jim continues to struggle to get his "Nemo Land" off of the design table and into reality. However, he has met an army of people who have set up roadblocks along the way. They call themselves "Eagle Rays." It is a non-profit corporation spearheaded by his ex-wife Donna. His girlfriend Trish left him for the lead singer of the "Taliban Monkey Elite," Mr. David Blade.

Mr. Ishiri was fired from Watsitumi when it was discovered he was colluding with Jim. He was given no notice. He was handed a box and told to only put his personal items in the box and a security guard would inspect its contents before he was escorted from the building.

Donna continues to work at Ocean Divers. She has had many offers of marriage but chooses to remain unattached. As part of the custody battle she was granted possession of 'Fickle Girl' and now lives on this boat docked in Islamorada.

George now works as a sales person and mechanic for Craig's newly formed company, *West-Rite*. George repairs boats using the new parts designed by his former boss, Craig. He has become so popular that there is a waiting list for boat owners wanting to repair and upgrade their Watsitumi engines. On weekends he sometimes works with a company called 'Danger Tours' as a deck hand. He sets out on the sunset tours with an open white shirt and deck shoes. Half of the time he spends trimming the sails, and the other half he spends pouring wine to anxious tourists looking for a piece of the life that George now fully realizes.

Because of her tie to Key West's tourism industry, Rachael, the Jimmy Buffett aficionado, found a job for Alicia. Alicia works part-time as a tour guide at the Hemingway house. She loves being able to draw on her love of American literature. The rest of her days are spent at the school, volunteering for students with reading disabilities.

Alicia and George's future plans include making some modifications to the holding tanks of the Tartan so they can go on a tour of the Caribbean. They both received their SCUBA "Advanced Open Water Certification" from Donna and have a new found passion for the underwater part of the world. They have already taken the 'Property of a Lady' to many of the islands where the breeze is refreshing and the fish are plenty.

They plan on buying a house in Cayman Brac but the two are in no hurry.

Author's Note

Cubicle World

I am indebted to my wife for living in that space and imparting the horrors of corporate life. I have skirted this world. Part of the inspiration for this book is to be the knight in shining armor and rescue her from the clutches of the evil empire.

Tartan 4100

This boat has been in my dreams. I own a small boat, but nothing compared to this one. I do not know all of the technical issues that make one boat better than another. I have a rudimentary knowledge of sailing and own a Macgregor twenty-two footer. However, when I set foot on the Tartans at the boat shows, I get goose bumps. I wanted to impart my thoughts about how a boat gains personality.

Catalina 445

I treated the Tartan and Catalina as characters in this book. Both are beautiful boats. I like the Catalina's innovations, particularly the work area accessible from the deck. This is a masterpiece of design. As there is no *Watsitumi* company that builds boat engines, Catalina would never consider putting such a motor in its boat. For that, I apologize.

If you own either of these fine sailboats, I would love to hear your opinions on my description as I have never had the pleasure of sailing either craft (hint hint).

Key Largo

After going through an excellent training program with *Brass Anchor SCUBA Center* in Frederick, Maryland, I had the distinct privilege of doing my first "recreational" dive off the back of an *Ocean Divers* boat. I commend that group on taking care of me and making my first diving experience the marker upon which I base all my other dives. The reserve of Pennekamp State Park is a dive mecca and should not be missed by those in the SCUBA community.

I stayed in the complex of Coconuts, Marina Del Mar, and Ocean Divers. It was a great experience and much of what you have read is more autobiographical than fiction. I highly recommend these places. The food at Coconuts is excellent and shouldn't be missed.

The restaurant at marker 88 is spectacular. My wife and I celebrated our anniversary there, and it sticks in my mind as an incredibly romantic moment. For those who witnessed the stalled motor boat chaos from this novel, I hope you saw what I saw.

The nearby pizza place, Boardwalk Pizza, is also fantastic. It was there the news flashed the story of the Taliban Monkey Elite. My wife and I never laughed so hard.

Key West

The Bitch Sisters are not fictional characters. As winners of Fantasy Fest, they were elevated to stars in a community that truly knows how to celebrate life. I met the two "sisters" when they owned a bed and breakfast. Unfortunately I was one of their last patrons as they sold their place. I have tried to get in touch with them, but to date, have had no luck.

I am saddened by the transition that is occurring in Key West. The younger crowd is losing a heritage of America found in this island town. Progress is grinding out the wonderful aura and madness perched at the edge of land.

Cayman Brac

You only got a parting nod at Cayman Brac in the epilogue of the story. But its memory haunts me. I stayed there with a dear friend and explored its nooks and crannies.

If you love palm trees and getaways, I encourage you to ditch the planned trips, cruise ships, and travel packages. Find a spot on the map that is obscure, get there and find its heart.

Cayman Brac taught me this lesson. I didn't SCUBA, but put my face in the water there and emerged as if from a baptism. The heaven's opened up and said, "This is my island, which I am well pleased."

Sincerely

M. T. Harber